THE WOMAN WHO TURNED HER LIFE AROUND

FIONA GIBSON

First published in Great Britain in 2026 by Boldwood Books Ltd.

Cover Design by JD Smith Design Ltd.

Cover Images: Shutterstock

A CIP catalogue record for this book is available from the British Library.

Paperback ISBN 978-1-83617-235-2

Large Print ISBN 978-1-83617-236-9

Hardback ISBN 978-1-83617-234-5

Trade Paperback ISBN 978-1-80656-351-7

Ebook ISBN 978-1-83617-237-6

Kindle ISBN 978-1-83617-238-3

Audio CD ISBN 978-1-83617-229-1

MP3 CD ISBN 978-1-83617-230-7

Digital audio download ISBN 978-1-83617-231-4

This book is printed on certified sustainable paper. Boldwood Books is dedicated to putting sustainability at the heart of our business. For more information please visit https://www.boldwoodbooks.com/about-us/sustainability/

Boldwood Books Ltd, 23 Bowerdean Street, London, SW6 3TN

www.boldwoodbooks.com

For Beverly

PROLOGUE

You know all that Tupperware you have with the lost lids? My mouth's like that – gaping open – when I spot him.

Shane Calvert. My heart stops and I almost drop the samosa I was about to bite into.

So he's here – all grown up and sipping a beer out there in the Kapoors' back garden. Frozen at their kitchen window, I try to wrestle my faculties together.

It's been thirty-seven years since we last saw each other. Of course he's grown up! Time hasn't stopped – although it feels as if it has. I lurch away from the window and gaze down at my food, realising I can't eat any of it. Pam's cooking is amazing but right now, I might as well be clutching a plate of stones.

Panicking, I mentally race through my options. Shane knows I planned to come to the party today (Pam was adamant that it *would* be a party – a joyous celebration for Ravi – and not a wake). But I don't have to go out there and talk to him. Instead, I could do another quick round of the Kapoors' family and friends, all chattering loudly in the living room, then quietly slip away.

I looked for you but didn't see you. Already, I'm formulating my message to him. *So many people there. So busy. Sorry we missed each other!*

Still alone in the kitchen, I creep back to the window to spy on him a bit more. He's standing a little apart from the group of men who've gathered beneath the blossom-laden cherry tree. It was a tiny, spindly thing last time I was here. Now it's almost the height of the house.

The early evening light is fading fast. I watch as Shane wanders down to the bottom of the garden, parks himself on the ancient wooden bench and looks around expectantly. He's still handsome, dammit. Age suits him. He still has a twinkle about him: a kind, open face, a full head of dark, wavy hair, peppered with only a little silver, and that full, sensuous mouth that I loved to kiss—*Stop it!* My heart is thumping now, my mind flooding with all the stuff that happened between us so long ago.

I'm aware that he could easily see me – a staring maniac at the window, nice! – but now I can't tear myself away. He's so near, I have to at least go out and say hello.

Just get it over with, I tell myself. Like when I was pregnant with Cora and one of my teeth rotted – one of the big buggers at the back – and my dentist explained, without one iota of sympathy, that he'd have to extract it (with pliers, basically) without anaesthetic. *Do it then! Pull the fucker out!*

My chest is tight, my mouth sandpaper-dry. I take a swig of white wine for fortification. Gripping my glass and laden plate, I stride purposefully to the back door. *Molar! Pliers!* I remind myself. *Just get it over with!*

I step outside and inhale deeply. In contrast to the Kapoors' overheated house, the evening is still and cool. Affecting a casual demeanour, as if I have just popped out for a breath of air, I gaze in rapt attention at the cherry tree.

How beautiful it is, this immense pink confetti cloud!

Without even looking over, I can sense Shane sitting up, paying attention. Shit, I'm not ready yet. Onwards I glide, towards the wooden bird table I remember Ravi's dad, Kamal, constructing with immense care when we were teenagers. When I loved Shane madly. Oh God. He's standing up now. I can see him in the periphery of my vision as I examine the bird table forensically. It's a little mossy and the roof looks as if it's been nibbled. By squirrels, maybe? But look how well it was made, to have weathered all these years—

'Josie?'

I swing round and he's right there in front of me. 'Shane! Hi! My God!' We laugh in a bewildered, *is-this-really-happening?* way and hug awkwardly.

'So good to see you,' he exclaims, smiling.

'You too.' I grin stiffly and sense the thermostat connected to my cheeks turning up to maximum heat. 'I mean, I wish it wasn't because of *this*,' I add quickly.

'Yes, same here.' He nods.

A small silence hangs and I scramble to fill it. 'So, how was your journey?'

'Oh, good, thanks. Great. How was yours?'

'Really good. No trouble at all.'

'You weren't on the 7.30, were you?' he asks.

'You mean the train?' *What d'you think he means, idiot – the hovercraft?*

'Er, yeah—'

'No. I, um...' I start.

'I did arrive a bit early,' he says with a small grimace, perhaps to highlight his ineptitude at journey planning.

'Better than being in a panic.' As I am now, as I sense what will be his next question.

'Did you drive up?' he asks.

'No, I decided to, er...'

'Quite right. It can be a nightmare, the motorway around Birmingham...'

'Absolutely,' I agree, wondering when we might tear ourselves away from our respective modes of transport and move on to the reason we're here, back in our West Yorkshire home town. Because our friend Ravi – Pam and Kamal's beloved daughter – died.

'So, which train did you get?' Shane asks.

'Oh, I actually got the bus,' I say brightly.

'From *London*?'

'Yes.' I smile to demonstrate how great it was. 'I actually prefer it,' I add.

'Right. Yeah.' He nods uncertainly and sips his beer, his green eyes catching the late evening light. 'Buses can be, erm... really pleasant.'

'And they're so comfy these days!' Now I'm a resurrected Victorian lady entranced by the Megabus. *They have engines now! They're not drawn by horses!* 'And we stopped at Donington Park services,' I babble on, 'which was great as I hadn't brought any food or drink with me. Nothing at all. Stupid, huh? It's an awfully long way to survive on your own saliva' – Shane's eyes widen – 'and I hadn't realised we'd stop, that we'd get a proper leg stretch...' *Shut up, you loon!*

'At the, erm... service station?' Looking wary now, Shane has taken a step back.

'Yes,' I enthuse.

'Oh, yeah. They're better than they used to be, aren't they?'

'*Definitely*...'

'Much more choice now.'

I nod, not quite understanding.

'Of food places,' he clarifies. 'There's Burger King, Costa...'

'The Cornish Pasty Company,' I chime in. 'It's a dilemma!' Nearly four decades since we last saw each other and we're discussing motorway food options. And never mind *saw*. It's not as if I merely glimpsed him in passing that last time. We were nakedly entwined in a lumpy little single bed, having just had sex.

Don't even think about it! I tell myself. *It's a spent conviction, wiped from your record. It no longer counts.* My entire body tenses as I try to stop the image flooding my brain. But it bursts through anyway and now it's all I can see. And somehow this causes my hand to spasm and my plate tips forward, and as I try to grab the tumbling pakoras and samosas, my glass flips towards me and empties all over my chest.

'Christ!' I cry.

'Oh no.' Shane looks aghast. 'Let me get you something to dry off with.'

'No, no, I'm fine,' I insist. 'Thank God it was white.'

'Yes, lucky, that—'

'Terrible waste of wine, though!'

Shane laughs uncertainly and his gaze flickers around the garden. He could be admiring the cherry blossom, but I suspect he's willing someone to come and take me away. *Help me!* is the message beaming out from his panic-stricken eyes. *Get me away from this crazy woman—*

Then his attention is snagged, and a small miracle happens. Pam has appeared at the back door, dinging a glass with a teaspoon. 'Everyone?' she calls out. 'Would you mind stepping inside now, please? We're having a little bit of a speech.'

1

FOUR WEEKS EARLIER

Josie

I can't believe it when the news first breaks. It's one of those random social media posts when you think: hang on, is this true? You hope almost immediately that another post will appear: *Reports of my death are grossly exaggerated!*

Soon, though, tributes start to appear on Facebook.

Remember seeing Ravi's band at The Ferret. Sticky carpets, dripping ceilings – happy days! What a terrible shame.

I'd heard she was ill. So very sorry to hear this.

Didn't they do a tour once? I'm sure I saw them in Pontefract. Such a talented person gone too soon!

She moved to Australia, didn't she? Sounds like she was living her best life out there. RIP Ravi Kapoor.

Lloyd arrives at my flat to find me huddled over my laptop. 'Aw, babe,' he says, hugging me. 'Was she a close friend?'

'Yes, she was,' I reply. 'When we were young, I mean. Teenagers. We were super close back then.'

'Aw, that's sad.' He plants a quick kiss on my cheek and then, after a respectful pause, adds, 'C'mon, let's get started while it's hot.' He sets out the array of takeaway cartons he's brought for us and I try my best to tuck in. 'It's a new takeaway on Bethnal Green Road,' he goes on, already stoking his face. 'Gave me the rice for free. Full of chat, the woman was. She might have some work for me.' Lloyd is a self-employed kitchen fitter and never seems to have a shortage of work. He appears to have forgotten about Ravi already.

As I finish my noodles, I remind myself that Lloyd is a good, kind man. We met on an app, and he was so refreshingly straightforward and funny – and, yes, strikingly handsome – that our first date flashed by in a blink. I'd tumbled into my second-floor flat a little drunk and dizzy from his kisses, assuming it would be a one-off. At fifty-seven, I'm ten years older than he is and couldn't imagine he'd want to get involved with me. Yet seemingly, he did – and things took off quickly. We've fallen into a pattern of seeing each other around three times a week and it's lovely. At least, it *mostly* is. Lloyd just doesn't know my history, that's all. He's not interested – perhaps because it's as unimaginable to him as the Tudors. Yet in the year-and-a-bit that we've been together, I've endured countless hours of Lloyd's tales of growing up in Essex; of wild nights out clubbing, and of course I should be fascinated to hear of someone called Hairy Mick puking on Caspers' dance floor in 1996.

'Remember I told you about that band I was in?' I prompt him as I clear away our takeaway cartons.

'Oh, yeah. What kind of music was it again?'

I smile, wondering how best to put it to someone whose musical taste is pretty much limited to techno. 'If you can imagine a chaotic Bananarama, but with two girls and a boy and guitars and drums and—'

'*Huh*?' He looks baffled.

'Never mind,' I say, but he's fazed off anyway as he switches on my TV. A trailer comes on for a World War II documentary. Tearful parents are waving off children with neatly combed hair and heartbreaking little suitcases.

Lloyd turns to me. 'Were you evacuated?'

I stare at him. Fucking hell, he thinks I was born in 1932.

'What?' he asks, frowning.

'Lloyd, how old d'you think I actually am?'

'I *know* how old you are, babe...'

I choke out a laugh. 'So don't you think it's pretty unlikely, seeing as I was born—' I quickly calculate '—twenty-three years after the war ended?'

'Oh, right. Sorry.' Chuckling, he cracks open a beer. 'I'm terrible with historical dates.' The football starts and he stretches out to his full, athletic six-foot length on my sofa, ready to watch.

Historical dates? Prickling now, I carry the cartons, plus my laptop, to the kitchen. What does he think when we're in bed together? 'She's not bad for... ninety-three?' Just as well he's always preferred older women! We're 'solid', apparently. 'No nonsense', 'grounded', 'self-assured.' Like an intimidating head nurse. Should I get myself the outfit? Give him a vigorous examination next time we're in bed? Our sex life has been flagging a little lately – down to me, not him, I have to say. Perhaps that would pep it up.

At my wonky fold-out kitchen table I open my laptop and carry on reading about Ravi, trying to find out what happened. I wish I'd known she was ill, and feel terrible that I didn't – but it's been decades since we've spoken or even been in touch. Thirty-seven years since I last saw her, I figure out. It's been an evening of calculating dates.

Lloyd stays over and, as ever, is up for it. Until a couple of months ago, I was too. But lately – since my GP prescribed me a low dosage of 'head pills', as I call them – orgasms have eluded me. It's not that I was depressed. Just generally out-of-sorts, I suppose, and my friends reckoned he should have offered me HRT. I tried to tell Dr Clearly-Uninterested-in-Women's-Hormonal-Chaos that it seemed to be all wrapped up in menopausal symptoms. That it had started soon after my periods had petered out (wasn't that a clue right there?). But he wasn't interested in any of that. 'Been googling, have you?' he crowed. Well, yes! 'Just try the medication. I think it'll help,' he insisted, virtually shoving me out of the door.

I didn't have it in me to argue or beg. The upshot is that part of me – the sexual part – has shut down like a faulty boiler component. *She never had it serviced. It finally gave up the ghost.*

Nowadays, not even my go-to fantasy gets me there. The one that's always been there for me, as undemandingly reliable as my Rimmel lipstick in a shade named Asia. It's my Brat Pack fantasy, featuring the adorable cast of those eighties John Hughes movies – in which neither they, nor I, have aged one jot. Perhaps that's the appeal. Because in my salacious mind it's never assumed that I experienced air raids or ration books. Instead, it's forever St Elmo's Fire in my loins (in a good way, not a raging thrush way), and one of The Pack – variously Andrew McCarthy/Judd Nelson/Emilio Estevez/Rob Lowe, whoever's available and trouserless at that precise moment – is going at me up against my fridge.

That's it. Works every time. At least it did before the pills. Now, I can get *close* to orgasm – tantalisingly close, like when you accidentally drop a sweet wrapper and chase it along the street. There it is, literally within your grasp. But as you go to grab it the wind whips it away, and it's gone.

That's what happens tonight. Lloyd doesn't comment; in fact, I wonder if he even notices now. It certainly doesn't seem to worry him as post-takeaway/football/beer/sex, he is perfectly satisfied, and within minutes he is sound asleep.

2

Next morning, after Lloyd has headed off to a job, I spot another tribute to Ravi on Facebook.

> Thinking of dear Pam and Kamal at this sad time.

So Ravi's parents are still alive. Their house, Cherry Cottage, was virtually my second home throughout my teens. I've no idea if they still live there. However, on my lunch break, I pop into the big Waterstones on Piccadilly for a sympathy card. With a little time to spare, I also nip up to the kids' floor in search of something for Poppy, my baby granddaughter.

At just two months she's probably a bit young for books. I also know that these precious years flash by so fast, and before you know it that little baby is a teenager, repulsed by the way you breathe or move through a room. Then they're a young adult who curls a lip at your multi-coloured plastic chandelier and vast collection of fridge magnets, and asks, 'Wouldn't you prefer *clean lines*, Mum?' And then she's moving out, and has fallen in love with an IT specialist called Zack with a brick-shaped jaw and that changes everything.

It's ridiculous, I know, to miss those cosy winter afternoons of just Cora and me, eating buttered crumpets and playing Buckaroo at our kitchen table. However, as I spot a book she once loved, I'm hit by a rush of nostalgia. With a small thrill, I buy the elaborately illustrated *Noah's Ark* for Poppy, and then pick up my boss's customary smoked salmon bagel from the ferociously expensive deli on Piccadilly.

Back at work – at Rupert Featherstone Fine Art Books – I attend to a bunch of online orders and queries, then devour the packed lunch I've been thinking about since 10.15 a.m. These activities happen not in the gleaming wood-panelled elegance of our actual shop, but in the small, windowless back room.

I *am* allowed out of here. I look after our window display – it's my favourite part of the job – and keep a tight rein on the shop's general appearance. I could do so much more, I feel – rearranging things, making the shop seem more welcoming and less intimidating. But Rupert – a florid, well-fed man in his sixties – is permanently stationed at his desk by the front door, and it feels as if that's his territory and this is mine. I often hear him, booming away to his regular customers and friends who've dropped by. And if I happen to emerge from the cave, it's all, 'Oh! Hello, Josie!' as if I'm his scruffy little dog who's broken out of confinement. A terrier whom he's quite fond of really, but she's a bit stinky and prone to jumping up at guests.

Today it's Charles, an old friend from Rupert's boarding-school days, who's breezed in. 'What would you do without this girl?' he chortles as I bring them coffees. 'Given her a pay rise yet?' There's a bit of jovial banter, then I retreat to the back room where I package up a customer's hefty photography book before switching my attention to the sympathy card.

Dear Pam, Kamal and family,

I'm so sorry to hear that you have lost dear Ravi.

Sending all my love and thoughts to you all.

Josie xx

Will they even remember me? It doesn't matter, I decide. They have far bigger things to deal with. But then it occurs to me that perhaps, at some point, Pam or Kamal might like to drop me a line. So I add my email address in tiny – almost apologetic – writing at the bottom and post the card on my way home from work.

Three days later, I receive an email from Pam.

Dear Josie,

Thank you so much for your thoughtful card. We know how much you meant to our Ravi. Yes, it's been a horribly tough time, and our hearts are broken. Ravi was a real fighter – but you'll remember that.

I'm not sure where you're living now or if you're still in touch with Shane. But as a family we'd love to invite you both to our celebration of Ravi's life. You know how passionate she was about her music and the band, and you and Shane were a huge part of that.

I'm not sure if you know that Ravi spent much of her adult life in Australia where she was very happy. She came back home to Yorkshire when she was ill, so we had those last few months with her close to us again. We're very grateful for that.

I should also tell you that Ravi left something for you and Shane. I'm under strict instructions to hand it over to you in person. To both of you, I mean – together. I know it seems strange, but she was very definite about this. You know how definite she was about everything in life!

We miss her so much, Josie, I can't even begin to describe the pain. Right up to the end she was our beautiful ray of light. It would make us so happy to see you and Shane after all these years, and for you to share your precious memories at our special day for Ravi.

Full details below.

Lots of love,

Pam and Kamal xx

I stare at it, letting the message settle. Ravi left something for me and Shane? That doesn't make any sense. I re-read it, more slowly this time to make sure I haven't misunderstood it. I feel terrible for Pam, Kamal and Dev, Ravi's older brother. But I can't go. Not if there's any possibility of Shane being there too.

It's an awfully long time since I've even thought about him. Actually, no. That's a lie. He pops into my mind far too often for someone I haven't laid eyes on since I was twenty. It occurs to me, as I get up and knock myself some dinner together, that I could concoct a tiny lie. *Sorry, but I lost touch with Shane a long time ago and I haven't been able to track him down.* But that's not tiny – it's pretty substantial – and I can't bring myself to spout *any* size of lie to Ravi's bereaved mum and dad.

Through my parents, I had heard that Ravi had moved to Australia. The fact that she hadn't told me directly seemed to signal that she hadn't wanted any further contact with me. I could have 'reached out' – a phrase frequently flung around by Zack, my daughter's partner ('Cora, could you *reach out* to the neighbours about that hedge situation? It nearly had my eye out on my run!'). But what would I have done? Apologised and begged for forgiveness? Or just wished her well? As nothing seemed right, I just left it. But the guilt still lingers and so, with a growing sense of dread, I try to build myself up to contacting Shane.

In fact, there's no 'tracking down' needed as I know where he is. At least I know he's on Instagram, although he's hardly an active user. There are several Shane Calverts but that's definitely his profile picture. Not that I've studied his account closely; my gaze might have *briefly* skimmed it, that's all. Just enough to confirm that these days he's a father of two, and he still has that adorable, slightly off-kilter smile, and those mesmerising green eyes with little amber flecks – not that I've zoomed in – fringed with long, dark lashes. Well of course he has the same eyes! Doesn't everyone? The once-dark hair that Ravi insisted on gelling before a gig – 'Stop it, Rav! For fuck's sake!' – is slightly salt-and-pepper now and is almost certainly product-free. He was boyishly fresh-faced back then, but his stubble looks good. I hope to God he hasn't seen my pics. Not that I care – I mean, why the hell would I?

I fork down a bowl of pasta and, bolstered by a couple of glasses of wine, start to type out a message at the kitchen table.

> Hi Shane, do hope you're well. Sorry to land this on you out of the blue but have you heard the terribly sad news about Ravi? She passed away earlier this month. It seems she'd been ill for quite a while. Pam and Kamal are having a celebration of her life at their place – they're still at Cherry Cottage, and they'd like us both to go.

The 'us' part triggers an involuntary shudder, but I plough on.

> Ravi left something for us, Pam says. Something she stipulated – is 'stipulated' a weirdly formal word? Something that has to be given to us in person, apparently. I don't know any more than that. I'm sorry to tell you all of this and hope it doesn't come as a shock.
>
> Best wishes, Josie

Relax, I tell myself. *It's just a quick DM.* So I only re-read it about thirty-five times, deleting bits and rewriting other bits, as if it's going to be graded. Now I'm worried that 'Best wishes' sounds as if I'm following up a job interview: *Thank you for taking the time to see me, Best wishes, etc.* Would 'Warmest wishes' be better? A stark 'Best', or a more familiar 'Love'? No, not love! Indifference, then? *Nonchalantly yours, Josie.*

Still too chicken to send it, I mooch through to the living room with my laptop, hoping a change of setting will offer a crumb of inspiration. Here I fall back onto my shabby corduroy sofa and stare up at my lopsided chandelier, as if it might spell out to me, in a code of dusty plastic droplets, what to say. Already, I feel as if I've panic-written a dissertation. Not that I have ever written a dissertation; I never went on to further education. But Cora did, and I can still picture her wild, blood-shot eyes after every caffeinated, essay-bashing all-nighter.

I gather myself up and have another stab at it. 'With thanks', like a colleague? A brisk 'Cheers'? No, no – Ravi has died. It's not and never will be a 'cheers' situation. I'm not sure a DM even needs a sign-off – it's never been an issue for me before – and I know I'm overthinking it as I consult ChatGPT.

Take it easy, it suggests. *Love and light. Stay golden.*

And they say AI is the future? Possibly, yes, if you want to sound faintly creepy. I type out further options in my fingerjabby Gen X way, rather than the speedy double-thumb method of the young. Cora keeps nagging me to change, saying, 'Mum, you always make things harder than they need to be.' *Story of my life*. However, my make-up – which I'm deeply attached to – is, by her reckoning, not complicated enough. 'No one uses powder any more, Mum!' she announced recently, as if it were dust I'd swept up from the road. Nowadays it's all illuminators and glazing sprays and a Korean twelve-step 'glass skin' routine. Twelve steps – and she's a new mum! When Cora was a baby, I barely had time to wash myself.

I refuse to be bossed around by a twenty-eight-year-old and will carry on texting and *powdering my complexion* however I like. I'm not getting into Botox and fillers and having my face yanked up (not that I can afford or have the nerve for any of that). Hair-wise I'm letting the grey come through, albeit muddled with chemical blonde. What I'm doing, I tell myself frequently, is embracing this marvellous life stage of anxiety and head pills and non-listening doctors! However, remembering him now – that cocky GP who was barely old enough to rent a car – triggers The Rage in me, which causes me to stab furiously at my phone. And this has the unfortunate effect of sending my message prematurely with the sign-off: *Best golden love Josie.*

My heart bangs. Oh God, I did *not* send that. No – I did! Fuck!

Don't panic, I tell myself. As we don't follow each other, my DM will have plopped into Shane's requests folder. If his is anything like mine, it's all bots and pervs – and who ever bothers to look at those?

Back in the kitchen, I grab the wine from the fridge and pour myself the last dregs, marvelling as I always do how an entire bottle can hold so little (is it the concave bottom?). Then another thought hits me. The unsend option! Does Instagram have that?

I rush back through to check and snatch at my phone, feeling quite sick as I stare at it.

Shane has already replied.

3

SHANE

Josie, hi! Lovely to hear from you even in these horribly sad circumstances. Yes, I had heard about Ravi. Tragic news. I'm so sorry. When is the celebration?

I stare at it, telling myself not to freak out. He's just being polite and wants to know when it is. It doesn't mean he's *going.* Better not respond right away or he'll think I have nothing better to do on an uneventful Tuesday evening than sit and wait for messages from him.

I pace around my living room, briefly examining my shrivelled spider plant, and reply:

JOSIE

Saturday May 3, 6-10 p.m.

Then, to suggest that everyone will understand if he can't make it, I add:

Awfully soon, I know.

SHANE

Right, thanks.

Well, that gives nothing away. Is he going or not? I don't even know where he lives, and my fleeting glances at social media have revealed nothing. How do I ask without sounding as if I'm remotely interested?

Another message appears:

SHANE

Where are you living these days?

So that's his game. He's sussing out the situation, and whether it's feasible for *me* to go.

JOSIE

London. How about you?

Please say, 'A remote Pacific island.' Please add that, regrettably, there is no means of getting off it.

SHANE

I'm in London too. Whereabouts are you?

My chest tightens. So he is in the same city as me. A city of nine million people, granted – but here all the same, and now he wants to know my precise location. In case he's local and I'll be living on my nerves every time I pop out for milk/wine, I ignore this and copy and paste Pam's email to him instead. A few minutes pass.

SHANE

Wow. Sounds like she really wants us both to be there.

JOSIE

It does. Think you can make it?

SHANE

I'd really like to. How about you?

With my stomach swilling biliously already:

JOSIE

I'm not sure. Have a lot going on at the moment unfortunately.

Well, that's nice – coming across as a cold, heartless cow when our friend has died. In fact, I'm fully planning to go because Pam and Kamal were always incredibly lovely to me, and my heart is breaking for them. What I'm trying to do is present *not* going as a viable option for Shane.

I wait, my gaze spearing the screen, for further communications. He finally replies:

SHANE

What about this thing Ravi left for us? And Pam saying we have to collect it in person. What d'you think it is?

Rather than answering immediately, I go and check on the wine situation. There is no second bottle and, actually, that's great! Because even though I've downed roughly two thirds of the recommended weekly units in one sitting tonight, I am now weirdly, shimmeringly sober and starting on a second bottle might alter that. However, mixed in with my pride at being so mature and sensible is no small degree of fury as there is no more fucking wine!

JOSIE

Honestly, I have no idea.

He responds immediately.

SHANE

I think we should go.

Then, clearly on a roll:

Just checking train times that day. How about we travel up together?

Hey, hold on a sec! If we're going to be thrown back together, I'll be ensuring that our face-to-face time is kept to an absolute minimum. My focus will be Pam and Kamal and Dev and the wider family, because that's what this is about. A celebration of Ravi, our old friend, who came up with the mad idea of 'Let's start a band!' and made us believe we could make it happen.

Ravi was fearless, brimming with confidence and strikingly beautiful. I'd observed her admiringly from a distance since we'd started secondary school. As her house was a little way out of town, and not on the estate where Shane and I lived, I didn't see her out and about that much. But then our extremely generous music teacher set up a little room for pupils to use, with a record player. And the three of us drifted together in there. Found each other, really. Secretly, I was thrilled that Ravi wanted to be my friend, and I'd nurtured a bit of crush on Shane since I'd started to have those kinds of feelings.

Soon we were hanging out after school and at weekends, mucking about around town and playing records at Ravi's. She lifted us out of the shabby ordinariness of our lives and made our home town, with its long-abandoned mills and scruffy park with the broken fountain, seem like the most thrilling place on earth. Once we'd started the band, there was no messing about. We had to practise, practise, practise until we were good enough to play live. Our first gig, in a pub veering towards dereliction, was a mess. But we got better – Ravi saw to that – and by the time we left school we'd established a bit of a local following.

Even that wasn't enough. We needed to branch out, Ravi decided, and do a short tour of northern towns, i.e. play for strangers who'd surely jeer and spray lager at us! Attack us, even, for our lack of musical prowess. We'd heard of far more successful bands being bottled off stage and I pictured the three of us fleeing for safety in a hail of glass. But Ravi wouldn't take no for an answer. Together, she assured us, we could do anything.

Now, as I study Shane's messages, I'm not feeling so brave. So I quickly type:

JOSIE

My plans are a bit up in the air at the moment. I'll see you there.

No reply comes. I wait and wait, repeatedly checking my phone, simultaneously freaking out at being back in contact with Shane, yet desperately wanting him to reply. Did my message sound curt? Oh God, it did. *Who does she think she is with her 'up in the air' plans!*

I re-read the whole thread, picking over it forensically. In just one evening I seem to have regressed to being that deranged teenager who once loved him madly. But then, I loved lots of things back then. Pints of snakebite! Spudulike! Fluorescent hair colour from an aerosol can! It doesn't mean I want them now.

Curt is fine, I decide. At least, it's preferable to *best golden love.* And maybe Shane has forgotten everything that happened between us. After all, it was a lifetime ago. It's not that I'm wishing cognitive decline on him, but I very much hope he remembers *nothing* before 1988.

4

ELEVEN DAYS LATER: A CELEBRATION FOR RAVI

Shane

As his train pulls into the station, Shane is already telling himself to *just get through this*. It'll all be over soon enough, and first thing tomorrow he'll be heading home, satisfied that at least he did the right thing. He'll have shown his face. Never mind the weirdness of seeing Josie after all these years. This is about Ravi and her family and nothing else matters.

As Shane crosses town he makes a conscious effort to unclench his jaw. His earbuds are plugged in, all the better for insulating him from the surrounding sights and sounds. It's been two years since he's been back in his home town, and normally he wouldn't venture into its beleaguered centre at all. He would actively avoid it. Instead, he'd drive up from London and drop in on his mum. Then – duty done – he'd head straight back home at the first opportunity. However, Fletch – his partner in their musical instrument shop – needed his car to pick up a consignment of guitars for sale in Cornwall. Figuring that a train journey would give him the chance to get his head together, Shane was happy with that.

As he plods along the main shopping street, he notices that the much-loved café where he'd hung out with Josie and Ravi is all boarded up. The signage now reads Mary's Milk Ba, the final 'r' seemingly long gone. But he shakes off the rush of nostalgia because things change, don't they? Life moves on and that's fine! He regrets losing touch with Ravi after the band – and everything else, really – had imploded. But that's what happened back then. No mobile phones, no social media; once you moved away, the thread was broken, friendships pretty much lost.

Shane cranks up his music to push away feelings of shame and regret. Shane *loves* music. It's his life, really – apart from his family, obviously: the kids he and Paula never thought they'd be able to have. It had taken several rounds of IVF. Now Ryan and Liv, sixteen and eighteen respectively, are spending the May bank holiday in Copenhagen with their mother and her partner, Tony Rich. Among Shane and his friends, he is referred to as Rich Tony, which was funny up to the point at which Shane realised that his equivalent would be Poor Shane. Or at least, Keeping-Things-Hanging-By-A-Thread Shane. 'We're keeping on *keeping on*,' Fletch always says with a shrug. And they are, Shane supposes. Their shop, tucked away down an alley in an unnoteworthy area of south London is, against all odds, just about staying afloat.

In contrast, Rich Tony is listed on LinkedIn as both a 'Mindset Engineer' and a 'Success Architect'. Although Shane has deduced that this is nothing to do with engineering and architecture as he understands them, he cannot begin to fathom what these terms actually mean. However, when he was woken at 2.47 a.m. by his housemate Elaine tumbling in, banging cupboard doors and setting about frying up a feast in his kitchen, he wondered briefly how a mindset engineer might have dealt with that.

Shane once asked his daughter what Tony actually does. 'I think he's like a motivational coach,' she explained, with a note of uncertainty. Shane suspects that he should be *motivationally coaching* Elaine not to start frying onions at all hours, filling his flat with acrid fumes and incinerating his pans. Still, he holds himself accountable for the awkward situation he's found himself in.

During a particularly tricky patch, Shane had taken on some evening shifts at a local pub where he and Elaine – a fellow bartender in her mid-forties – had formed a larky friendship. Among the sea of smooth-faced Gen Zs, he'd found it refreshing to work alongside someone who didn't make him feel quite so ancient, and who'd been around the block a bit. Long after he'd ditched the pub job, they'd run into each other in a supermarket. 'I'm being evicted,' Elaine lamented, 'just for complaining about mould in the bedroom!' Well, Shane had a spare room, didn't he? It had twin beds, set up for Ryan and Liv, but they never stayed over any more.

He'd imagined it would be a temporary arrangement until she got back on her feet. It's been six months now – Elaine's room and a good proportion of his hallway are crammed with boxes of her stuff – and he's at a loss as to how to suggest she move on. Or at least switch to an alternative method of cooking. Surely, he keeps telling himself, she'll tire of the single bed and lack of space pretty soon? And him! Why isn't she sick of *him*? Long divorced and apparently happily single, Elaine seems to have an extremely active social life. Surely this involves friends? Friends who'd be delighted to have her move in with them? Shane has been tempted to hack into her phone in its fluffy orange case and contact some of them himself. Even set up some flat viewings, if that would speed things up. He has a car – a shabby old Volvo, acquired for its capricious boot space – and would happily move her stuff. Anything to help!

Now Shane is frowning at his phone, having resorted to the maps app to locate his hotel. His mum and stepdad still live on the sprawling council estate on the edge of town, in the same house he grew up in. This time he hasn't told them he's here. His last visit was just as awful as all the others – and didn't someone once say that the definition of insanity is to repeat a terrible experience over and over, and expect a different result? Einstein, he thinks it was. And Shane has no desire to do that – to make this short trip even more of a headfuck than it is already. *Keep it simple,* he'd decided.

He stops again and checks his phone for messages. Nothing more from Josie. Not that he was expecting updates on her journey progress, but he can't help wondering if she's arrived yet, if she's close by.

He goes back to the map. It seems bizarre, having to follow directions in the town in which he lived for the first twenty-one years of his life. Every corner, every bench and bit of wall to sit on was once as familiar to him as his own hands. But the intervening years – and *life* – have faded the mental images, and also things have changed a lot around here.

The mill, he notices with a wave of some feeling he can't quite identify, is all spruced up, its crumbling facade rebuilt. It's now a Synergy Complex, whatever that is. The park, which he crosses briskly, is tidier than he remembers: the broken fountain replaced by a stark black windowless 'information hub'. Shane remembers him and Josie and Ravi lying out here one long, hot summer's afternoon. He'd been stupid, and declared that he didn't need sunscreen, that he never burnt in the sun. What followed sizzles brightly in his mind now, and he quickly shuts it down. How can these memories be so vivid when so much has happened since then? (Marriage, fatherhood and divorce, for starters.) He shakes them off, impatient with himself for even allowing them into his brain.

Out the other side of the park, Shane passes the stout stone building that used to be The Regal Hotel. There was nothing *regal* about The Regal. Its cellar club, with its red glossy walls permanently wet, as if sweating, was how Shane imagined the interior of a large intestine. Rank and smelly, yet also *fantastic* – a universe away from home.

It was amazing that their ramshackle band had managed to get any bookings at all. Musically, they were all over the place: an indie trio with a dash of Bananarama flung in. The girls back-combed their hair into wild thickets, wore a mishmash of charity shop clothes and bellowed out their vocals, roughly in unison. At least, no attempts at harmonies were made. As the drummer, Shane tried in vain to keep them in time. Sometimes he'd attempt to call order, like a teacher trying to control a rowdy class on a school trip to Blackpool. They'd just laugh him off, or Ravi would scoff, 'Shut up, Dad!' She was ambitious for the band, in a way that he and Josie weren't really. To Ravi it was all about *energy,* but to Shane it often felt as if their shaky performance was one note away from falling apart. Yet somehow, people liked them. Remembering it all now causes something like an ache in Shane's chest.

The Regal has shut down and the ground floor is now a solicitor's office: BEST CRIMINAL DEFENCE IN TOWN! NO WIN NO FEE! a sign screams. Just as well, Shane reflects, or he might have been tempted to nip in for a nerve-steadying pint.

He rounds the corner and spots his hotel looming in the distance. It's hardly salubrious – a gloomy grey concrete cube tucked behind a frozen foods cash & carry. Yet he's relieved to check in and let himself into his small, plainly furnished room, as it's one step towards all of this being over.

A single teabag and milk sachet have been placed thoughtfully next to the kettle. A packet of two digestives bears an illustration of a grinning old lady with her hair in a bun: presumably Nana Pickles of Nana Pickles's Yorkshire Biscuits. Shane pulls off his backpack, tugs out his phone from his jeans pocket and perches on the edge of the bed. Without even thinking, he's navigated to Liv's Instagram. He studies the photo of his daughter and son and their mother, all positioned around a table laden with platters of miniature open sandwiches, excessively garnished with brightly coloured dots and squiggles – like a picnic for Playmobil figurines.

Shane's heart twangs. Why is he even looking at this? Irritably, he tosses his phone aside.

In the shower, he sluices himself down with blue gel from the big plastic dispenser that's bolted to the wall. Although he already showered first thing, he wants to ensure that no lingering whiff of fried onion from Elaine's cooking has followed him all the way up from London. He worries about this sometimes: that he carries it with him to the shop, the swimming pool, and on those occasional nights out with his mates.

Plus, he is trying to blast off any residual bitterness he's harbouring towards Rich Tony. It's not that he dislikes the man (actually, no – all cordiality aside, he does!). And of course he's happy to see Ryan and Liv having a brilliant time. Paula too. He holds no resentment towards her. It's just a little tricky to accept that this is their life now – a life of lavish trips and holidays – as it's one that he was never able to offer his family.

As he pulls on clean black chinos and a smart shirt, Shane tries to mentally prepare himself for seeing Josie again. All day he's tried not to think about her, and how it will be to be flung back together again for the first time since—well, he doesn't even want to go there. Not today. Giving his appearance a final check, he spots that eyebrow hair: the freak one that shoots out, over a centimetre longer than all the others. This has been happening sporadically for the last couple of years. He tugs at it ineffectually until, in the absence of a pair of scissors, the only option is to hack at it with his disposable razor.

Calm down, he tells himself as he sets off on foot to the Kapoors'. How did Josie sign off that first message again? *Best golden love*. Sounds like she's a yoga/meditation type these days. Chia puddings and green juices, like Liv is into. It's obviously suiting Josie very well.

Over the years, he's had the occasional glance at her Instagram, to see what she's up to – the way you do with friends from your distant past. Just casually, out of curiosity, nothing more than that. He's seen the handsome, tousle-haired partner who seems to wear a vest in all seasons, all the better for displaying his enviably toned physique. Then there's the grown-up daughter, blonde and looking quite sophisticated – the way young people seem to be these days. As if they were *born* more groomed, more together and conscious of their microbiomes and protein intake. Josie's daughter has a baby, Shane discovered. So Josie is a grandmother. It hardly seems possible.

Maybe, he muses, that's why she looks so relaxed and happy and, he has to say, beautifully radiant in the photos he's seen. But then, to Shane, Josie always radiated joy. She was always laughing and messing about. Clearly, she is enjoying a full and vibrant life, and he's certain that she won't be in a stew about this event today, like he is.

She'll be *fine*, he's sure of it. And Shane will be fine too. He'll just express his condolences to Pam and Kamal and the rest of the family and not get into any conversations about his own life.

No need to go into the fact that his ex-wife and children are currently on a Danish riverboat with a success architect.

Having left the town behind, he marches briskly through his old estate and follows the country lane towards the Kapoors'. As Cherry Cottage comes into view, he makes a firm vow not to mention Paula, Rich Tony *or* Onion Elaine, or anything about the state of his life.

5

JOSIE

Hugs, tears and reminiscences. It's been dizzying, seeing Pam and Kamal and the extended Kapoor family again. So many faces, all at once – and Shane, of course. I'm still shuddering as we make our way across the garden and follow Pam back into the house.

What was I thinking, raving to him about bus travel and service stations? Like an old man from 1975! Somehow, I've done it all wrong and haven't turned out the way a grown-up woman is supposed to be. By this point, I should have acquired:

A car (my terrible Fiat died years ago) or at least the means to afford a train ticket.

The ability to 'do' my hair.

A manicure habit.

Decent, non-embarrassing pillows.

Signature dishes to cook for friends.

A signature fragrance.

A signature *anything.*

Illuminator!

Pension plans and financial matters all sorted. As it is, I'm perpetually overdrawn – although Lloyd has come up with a solution to that. We'll sell pictures of my feet on a fetish site. Easy money, he reckons: 'Yours are exactly the kind of shape that punters love.' And what shape might that be? 'Toes of a similar length. See how your feet are kinda... *blocky*?' Why, thank you kindly, sir. 'It's called the peasant foot,' he explained. And I wonder why I can no longer orgasm with this man.

As we all gather around Pam in the living room, I push such unseemly thoughts from my mind. Guests are still chatting, not quite settled down. Pam beams around at us, poised and stylish in a flowing blue maxi dress, her once long, bouncy dark hair turned silver now, scooped up elegantly into a sort of bun. The Kapoors were young parents – at least, younger than mine – but she and Kamal must be well into their eighties now. This house was our teenage gathering place, and how *glamorous* it seemed with its thick shagpile carpets and leather pouffes. Kamal drove a gleaming silver car – a 'saloon' – rather than the old bangers that everyone else seemed to rattle around in, if they had a car at all. They threw lavish parties and barbecues and always seemed to be adding some incredibly covetable feature to their home: a breakfast bar, a jacuzzi bath, a special bum-washing machine called a *bidet*.

My little terraced council house seemed so plain in comparison. Shane's too, which was just down the road from mine – although we only went there when his mum and stepdad were out. On top of all the glamour, the fluffy rugs and cocktail shakers and delicious home cooking, Pam and Kamal were happy for us to take over their rickety old wooden garage as our band's rehearsal space. 'Of course you can use it,' Pam insisted. 'You won't be bothering anyone out here!'

She dings her wine glass again and a respectful hush descends. I glance over at Shane and our eyes meet briefly. Pam clears her throat and hoists a smile. 'I'd just like to thank you all for coming here today,' she announces, 'to our celebration for Ravi.' She bites her bottom lip and her hands tremble. Kamal steps closer, his gaze radiating kindness, and touches her arm. 'And this *is* a celebration,' she continues, seeming to gather herself, 'to honour our wonderful daughter and all she achieved in life. A party, really!' Her brown eyes sparkle. 'I'm so glad we decided to do this, because a party is exactly what Ravi would want us to have.' As she takes another moment to steady herself, I marvel at her ability to even deliver a speech at all. If anything were to happen to Cora, I doubt that I'd be capable of standing upright in front of a room full of people, let alone of speaking coherently.

'We're delighted that so many of you could make it,' Pam continues, 'from all over the country, some of you! From as far away as London' – she catches my eye and I muster a smile – 'and we're so grateful for that...' She turns to Kamal, and as he tops up her wine glass she smiles gratefully.

I eye the bottle as he places it back on the table. After my performance in the garden ('The Cornish Pasty Company!') I could cosh myself on the head with it. I catch Shane again, looking the picture of composure over there. Very smart, too, in his dark blue shirt and black chinos, with his hair nicely cut. He's made an effort but there's no air of vanity about him. What I'd give to have that easy confidence, to be happy in my own skin.

I'd panic-bought my own Ravi-celebration outfit on Vinted. *Please don't wear funeral clothes,* Pam had stated in her last email. *It's a celebration, not a wake!* In the bleak budget hotel where I'm staying tonight, the simple shift dress looked dowdier than I'd hoped. But maybe that was just my state of mind? I was still feeling rattled after my walk through town – my first visit since Mum and Dad moved away, fifteen years ago now, to a bungalow on the Northumbrian coast.

I noticed that Mary's Milk Bar is all boarded up now, The Regal Hotel a solicitor's office, and the mill converted into some kind of business premises. We'd clambered into it, Shane and I, drunk and giggling among the startled pigeons and wrecked manufacturing equipment. The memory of what happened next hits me squarely between the eyes, triggering an entire-body sweat. I notice Dev, Ravi's brother, murmuring something to Shane who's standing next to him. Shane smiles warmly and nods. Why can't I be like this, acting normally at a gathering?

With his dapper silver beard as immaculately trimmed as ever, Kamal steps forward and claps his hands together. 'So, everyone,' he starts, 'we'd love you to take a bit of time to look through our photos and to write your memories of Ravi in our book.' He indicates the large leather photograph album, and a journal with a lavishly embroidered cover on the table to his side.

There's been no mention yet of whatever it is that Ravi left for me and Shane. I'm still amazed that she'd even thought of us at all. After all the terrible stuff happened, and everything fell apart – the band, our friendships – I'd moved to London, and she'd relocated to the other side of the world. I can only assume that Shane got on with his own life too.

Why hadn't I at least dropped Ravi a note? She could have ignored it, if she'd wanted to. But at least I'd have tried. As shame wells up in me, I make pleasantries with the other guests as if nothing untoward has ever happened. As if we'd still been friends. And gradually, I edge towards the table until it's my turn to browse through the album.

I open the cover, and my gaze drops to the first photo. It's of

Ravi as a beautiful, plump-cheeked baby with huge brown eyes. Something seems to clamp itself around my heart as I stare at it, then quickly turn the page. Here's Ravi in an elaborate tangerine dress at a family celebration. Ravi in school uniform holding her mum's hand. Someone is looking over my shoulder now; an older woman wearing a heady floral perfume. 'Oh, look at that,' she says, and I nod. There are more pictures, loosely in chronological order. Ravi as a teenager, her dark hair sleek and glossy and then the backcombing comes in, and the pink streaks.

And then come the band photos: a jumble of those small rectangular prints that everyone used to have done at Boots, and a few faded Polaroids. Ravi in ripped jeans and a crocheted top, a red spotty scarf knotted at the front of her bird's nest hair. Me with my bleached blonde crop, wearing a ratty old black silk dress I'd found in Oxfam, with my beloved oxblood DMs.

'Oh!' the woman exclaims. 'I remember Ravi's band. Weren't they good? So confident and full of energy!'

'They were,' I concur, relieved that she hasn't recognised me from the photos. 'Who's that again?' She pokes a glossy pink nail at the skinny boy grinning sheepishly from behind a cheap drum kit.

'That's Shane,' I tell her. 'Shane Calvert.'

'Oh, yes. Of course it is. Is he here?'

'Erm, I think so,' I say, focussing hard on the photo. We are on a small wooden stage that looks as if someone's dad built it. The local Scout hall, I remember now.

'Look at the three of you,' Pam announces, having arrived at my side.

'Is that you?' the other woman gasps.

I swallow hard. 'Yes, it is.'

'She hasn't changed a bit!' Pam says fondly, squeezing my

hand. Her eyes fill with tears and a lone droplet spills down her cheek.

'Oh, Pam,' I exclaim. 'I'm so sorry…'

'No, *I'm* sorry, love. God, look at the state of me. I told myself not to do this today…' Without thinking I've pulled her close and she lets out a muffled sob. I rest a hand gently on the soft silver pillow of her hair.

'I just miss her, Josie. I miss my girl so much.'

'I know,' I murmur.

'It's so unfair, love.'

I nod wordlessly, and we stand there, glued together for a few moments. 'I'm so sorry we lost touch,' I start.

We pull apart. 'Oh, these things happen,' Pam says firmly. 'And she *was* living on the other side of the world.' *Yes, but it wasn't just that,* I want to tell her. Pam steps back and smiles stoically. 'Ravi had a great life out there. A brilliant career. She trained as an art teacher, did you know that? And she set up courses for adults at an arts centre.'

'Yes, I heard.' Through more online tributes I'd learnt that, apparently happily single and child-free, her life in Australia was filled with friends and her love of art and teaching. Numerous posts from her pupils from all eras have flooded the Facebook memories page.

Pam looks around the room. My chest tightens as she calls out, 'Shane, come over here!' Dutifully, he heads towards us. 'I'm so sorry,' she announces, ushering us away from the table and through to the kitchen. 'I'd forgotten about the thing.'

'The thing?' Shane looks quizzical.

Pam opens a wall cupboard and lifts out a small rope-handled gift bag. 'The thing Ravi left for the two of you. The present…' She looks at each of us in turn, as if unsure of who to give it to, and then hands it to me.

I glance briefly at Shane, my heart thudding as I take in the soft green of his eyes. 'What is it, Pam?' I ask.

Smiling, she pushes away a twirl of silver hair from her cheek. 'Have a look, love. I think it's going to be quite a surprise.'

6

I peek into the gift bag. There's a chunky parcel wrapped in plain brown paper, and a crisp white envelope nestling beside it.

'Read that first,' Pam tells me. 'It'll make more sense that way.'

Obediently, I hand the bag to Shane and open the envelope, pulling out what looks to be a letter.

Dear Josie and Shane,

it starts, in Ravi's large, loopy handwriting that was once as familiar to me as my own. The sheet of paper is shaking. This, I realise, is because my hands are shaking. Pam has stepped back as if to allow me a little space to read it. However, Shane is standing so close, he must be able to hear my heart thumping.

Well, this is something, isn't it? Me writing to you after all these years. I hope life has been good to you both. It hasn't been so great to me lately, but I'm trying to sort things out and organise everything as best I can. Haven't changed much, have I! Wanting everything my way.

I glance briefly at Shane. We are reading it together, excruciatingly. Standing together like two ill-matched schoolkids being forced to share a script for the school play.

I hope you'll forgive me, because I'm making a load of assumptions here. I'm assuming, for one thing, that Mum and Dad will want to have a big fuck-off party for me. I know what they're like! It'll be all 'do NOT wear black – this is a celebration, not a wake!' I also know Mum will be cooking for days and bossing Dad into making the flower borders look amazing, as if it's one of those open garden days and people will be inspecting every— well, I was going to mention a flower by name, particularly one that flowers in the late spring. Which is when I think I will be 'passing'.

Don't you hate that word? Just say it like it is. Dying. Anyway, I've never bothered to learn any flower names haha. Too late now. Also too late to get through that big bottle of Jo Malone Mimosa & Cardamom that cost me £120!

Imagine if by some miracle I manage to hang on until September and mentioned a spring-flowering flower instead of an autumn-flowering one? The SHAME. Anyway, enough about that. My other assumption is that, if this party goes ahead, then you will not only get to hear about it but also COME. And if all that happens… well!

Here I am, taking charge of things for one last time. Please do this one thing for me, the two of you.

I stop, willing my blurry vision to clear. *Don't cry*, I tell myself. *Don't start plopping tears onto the paper!* I turn to Shane, and his mouth twists and I see that his eyes are moist too. 'You okay?' I ask, and he nods grimly. 'Yeah.' He clears his throat and I read on:

Remember how things had started to take off for us? Neither of you really wanted to do the tour but I pushed you into it. Why? Because I knew we could do great things. You wanted that too. Remember how we talked about all that, endlessly? How we hated our crappy jobs and wanted more?

In fact, Ravi's 'crappy job' was just an aside. At twenty – after a few misfires, college-wise – she was doing a foundation course and hoped to go on to art college in Leeds. But Shane and I were flailing, working variously in cafés and pubs.

That photo of the three of us, on stage at the Scout hall, burns brightly in my mind. We had dreams back then that somehow, the three of us would miraculously end up living together, in a house in London because that's where everything happened. Not around here.

To do that we had to move forward. And that meant doing the tour. Remember how I'd been bombarding record company people with letters and cassettes? I'd persuaded that guy to come, some A&R guy – I can't remember his name now. But we never did it. We didn't play that last gig and he never got to see us.

You might think this is mad, the two of you. But I can't help thinking, what if?

What if we'd finished the tour? How would our lives have turned out?

I know there's no answer to that. But right now, with everything turned to shit, I can't stop thinking about it. That we should have played all five dates. That we should never have let all the stuff that happened ruin it all.

It did ruin it, didn't it? Forever. I'm so sad about that. So I'm asking you, Josie and Shane, to do the tour together. Not to play, I don't mean that (unless you have a burning desire to!). I just mean to retrace our route and stay a night in all of the towns we played in. And in the one we didn't. The one right at the end.

On the back of this letter, you'll find our original itinerary. I've also left something to help you document every step of your journey. So no wriggling out of it! Mum and Dad will be expecting photographic evidence – of the venues, ideally, if they're still standing. I imagine they'll be making some kind of memory book for me so the photos can go in there. To finish our story, if you like.

This sounds mad, I know. I am *mad these days. Mad at everything my family is going through and also fucking furious about that Jo Malone perfume! Note to self: should have gone for the 30ml.*

Anyway, my dear friends, I do hope you're here together, getting drunkenly stuck into Mum's fantastic party buffet, and that you'll do this one last thing for me.

All my love, Ravi xx

7

I look up from the letter. People are wandering into the kitchen, chatting and loading their plates with more of Pam's party food. It's as if the volume has suddenly been cranked back up. As Pam drifts away, Shane lifts the parcel from the bag and looks at me. 'You open it,' I say. He hesitates, frowning, before unwrapping it carefully.

'Wow,' he says, cradling the Polaroid camera as if it were made from the thinnest glass. 'Haven't seen one of these for years.'

'Me neither.' I blink at it, not knowing what else to say.

'So Ravi wanted us to...' He tails off.

'Document our journey,' I murmur.

'There's film too,' he says, delving into the bag. 'She really thought this through, didn't she?'

I nod, hardly able to focus as I turn the letter over. Here, a smaller piece of paper has been glued to the bigger sheet. It's yellowed and looks as if it was badly crumpled, and Ravi had tried to iron it out.

It's our original itinerary, I realise. A relic from 1988:

July 4 – Laughing Haddock, Grimsby
July 5 – Marine Hotel, Bridlington
July 6 – Cockles, Scarborough
July 7 – Black Bull, Pontefract
July 8 – REST DAY
July 9 – Mucky Duck, Huddersfield ROB JESSOP COALFISH RECORDS!!!

So this is it. This is the route she wanted us to 'retrace.' Not exactly 'Hello Wembley!' – but back then, it had seemed better than that. Because, whereas Wembley Stadium was unimaginable to us, these were the towns of family days out and visits to aunties; places we understood.

'But where will we stay?' I'd asked her. 'And how can we afford to do this?' Ravi assured us that we'd be paid for some of the gigs. However, as this would be barely enough to buy us a Sherbet Fountain, we'd mainly be kipping in the spare rooms and on the floors of relatives and friends of friends, supplemented by a couple of nights in cheap guest houses, which her parents – being the only ones with money – would pay for.

Most excitingly was this Rob Jessop from an actual record company. A small one, granted, but to the three of us, he might as well have been God.

I fold Ravi's letter carefully and look at Shane. 'What d'you think about all of this?'

He blows out air and shakes his head. 'I don't know. I can't quite get my head around it…'

'No, neither can I.' Obviously, though, we can't do it. I'm sure he knows this too but, like me, doesn't want to be the one to say it.

The party is starting to wind up and all around us, there are hugs and vows to get together again soon. Shane slides the camera back into the gift bag, and I fold up the letter and slip it in too. As he places it on a shelf, someone calls him over to join a conversation. Seeming relieved, he excuses himself and beetles off.

Feeling a little stranded now, I help to gather up glasses and plates. Pam has snapped into practical mode and hasn't mentioned her daughter's letter, or the camera, again. It's as if, once satisfied that she had handed it over, that was that – job done.

'So where are you staying tonight, Josie?' Dev asks.

'The Craven Hotel,' I reply, glancing at the ornate brass wall clock above the sideboard. Not yet nine o'clock but I'm hit with a wave of exhaustion.

'Nice,' he says with a wry smile, and I laugh.

'It'll do the job.'

'Dad'll give you a lift if you like?'

'Oh no, I'm fine to walk,' I exclaim.

Now Kamal has appeared, with Shane at his side. 'Shane's at The Craven too,' Kamal announces.

'Oh, you're not staying with your mum?' Dev asks him.

'Erm, no. Not this time—'

'Aw, mate. I get it,' Dev says quickly, and he and his father seem to exchange a look. And now Kamal is jingling his keys, insisting that he'll drive us and reprimanding us for 'wasting good money on rooms – you could've stayed with us!' Then there are hugs – so many hugs – and Shane and Kamal and I step out into the cool, still night.

It's reassuring somehow to see that Kamal still drives a big, solid, dad-type saloon, immaculate inside and out. Having jumped into the back, I breathe in the aroma of citrus and leather as Kamal chatters away. 'So, how's life in London, Josie? I haven't had a chance to ask!'

'It's great,' I tell him.

'You've got a daughter, right?' He catches my gaze in the rear-view mirror.

'Yes, Cora. She's twenty-eight. Just had a baby.'

'You're a granny! Unbelievable! How's that then?'

'Wonderful,' I reply.

'Do they live near you?'

'Yes, just a couple of miles away—'

'We'd have loved grandkids, but it never happened with either of ours. You're very lucky,' he says wistfully.

'I know, Kamal. I really am.' With all that he and Pam have been through, it seems terribly self-pitying to feel hurt by Cora and Zack's determination to keep me at bay. The first time I held Poppy – this impossibly tiny, beautiful thing – Zack loomed over us, glowering, as if I might be about to bolt out and toss her into the back of a van. And last week I messaged Cora: *Okay if I nip over tomorrow? I have the day off. I thought I could take Poppy out, do a big park walk. Give you both a break.*

Weekend after next would be better, she'd replied. *Say Sunday between two and three?*

Such is the strictness of Border Control. By then, hopefully, my visa application will have been approved. I wouldn't want to try and enter my daughter's home *illegally.*

'And how's life with you, Shane?' Kamal glances to the left. 'How's Paula?'

I catch a beat's pause before he replies, 'Erm, we're not together these days. But it's fine, it's totally amicable…'

'Oh, it's good when you can work things out like that,' Kamal says. 'Especially when there are kids. You have two, Pam was saying?'

'That's right,' Shane says. 'Ryan and Liv, sixteen and eighteen.'

'Ah, one of each, like us.' *But not any more*, the brief silence seems to say. Kamal coughs dryly and the lull stretches until we pull up at the hotel. Shane and I thank him profusely, and in the hotel foyer we stop and look at each other.

'Well…' I start uncertainly.

Shane exhales. 'That was some day, wasn't it?'

'It was. So, this thing that Ravi wants us to do—'

'It's bizarre, isn't it?' He pushes back his wavy hair and looks around the featureless foyer. It feels wrong now to head straight for our rooms. I need to decompress a bit and try to make sense of Ravi's request; how she's set up this *project* for us. Is it a test, a challenge, or what? We make our way towards the lift. There's not another soul in sight; no one on reception, even. However, there *is* a bar. It looked pretty dismal when I glanced in earlier, but I'd hazard a guess that there's wine – and right now I'd kill for a nightcap.

However, I'm detecting a distinct lack of *I'm desperate to spend more time with Josie* vibes. More like, *Thank God that's over.* I steal a quick look at his handsome face – the soft green eyes, the full, expressive mouth – and a sharp pain seems to needle my heart.

'Well,' I start again, 'it's getting late…' Not yet nine thirty. Virtually a child's bedtime.

'It is, yeah,' he agrees.

I jab the button for the lift. An awkward pause settles, and we wait for so long that I start to wonder if the damn thing's working. There are faint rattles and creaks from a universe light years above us. Shane stuffs his hands into his trouser pockets and looks around as if suddenly captivated by the decor: scuffed white walls, a blue checked carpet, a lone office-type chair with a stained grey seat. My mind whirs as I try to dredge up a conversation starter. Something innocuously space-filling and *not* about the fabulousness of service stations, with their thrilling facilities. But nothing comes.

Finally, the lift arrives and we step inside. 'Which floor?' I ask as if he were a stranger. As if we'd never kissed passionately – and that kiss hadn't led to so much more – in the derelict mill.

'Three, please,' I say.

'Oh, I'm on three too.' And this is the part, I muse as we travel upwards, where we discover that we are in adjoining rooms. And at some point during the night, both of us will realise that we can't stand it. We can't bear lying in bed, wide awake, and so I blunder out of my room, just as he does, and we meet in the corridor and—

'Here we are!' he announces unnecessarily, stepping back to allow me to spring out first.

'I'm this way,' I announce.

'Oh, I'm along here.'

I force a tight smile, realising that this is probably the last time I'll ever see him. I feel hollow inside and yearn to throw my arms around him and tell him how sorry I am – about everything. 'It's been great seeing you,' I say.

'You too!' he enthuses, with what seems like a sudden wave of relief. The way you become louder and more animated when you sense a job interview drawing to a close. *Lovely to meet you! Thank you for seeing me, and now can I get the hell out of here, please!*

We hug stiffly and I turn and stroll away casually, waiting for him to call me back: *Josie, wait!* And when that doesn't happen, I pluck my key card from my purse, and the door clicks open, and I tumble in and virtually collapse onto the bed.

Instantly, my phone rings in my bag.

My heart jolts. Shane. He wants to talk, after all! I grab at it and glare at the name displayed. My boss, Rupert, is calling me – on a Saturday night.

Decline.

Checking my messages now, I see a whole stack from him.

Josie, something's happened, need to talk.

I know you're away but there's a problem.

JOSIE, CALL ME ASAP!!

8

SHANE

Shane stands motionless in the middle of his boxy little room. His eyes are squeezed shut, and as if an additional protective shield were needed, he has flattened an outstretched hand across his face.

What an idiot. What a total, bloody, patronising fool. *'Buses can be really pleasant!'* His inane comment ricochets around his head. Thirty-seven years since he last saw Josie and he's been so stiff and weird, and right now he'd do anything to be time-travelled back to the Kapoors' garden and do it all differently.

What must she think of him? The way he prattled on about service stations – dear God. Slowly, he removes his hand from his face and opens his eyes and stares at the blank wall. He feels like banging his head against it.

On top of all that, he's still trying to make sense of Ravi's letter, the tour schedule and camera. Obviously, they can't do as she's asked. Josie could hardly have made it any clearer that she finds his presence unbearable: the awkwardness of waiting for the lift just then, the stiff hug, and the way she seemed so keen to get back to her room. If it's anything like his, it's pretty dismal:

one step up from a police interrogation room. But maybe it's not? Maybe she has a suite, and wanted to retire early to do her yoga or meditation or whatever it is that she's into?

He is desperate to know about her life, and how it's all panned out for her since the *thing* happened – the thing he's banned himself from even thinking about today – after which she'd hotfooted it to London with Dale Watson and he never saw her again. Yet Shane knows virtually nothing about her life now, because he didn't get it together to ask. Too busy banging on about the motorway around Birmingham. Look at Kamal, quizzing her about being a grandmother and all that, during the ten-minute drive into town. Why was that? he wonders. Because Kamal is a smart, fully functioning man and Shane is an idiot.

He exhales slowly and drifts around the room, pausing to glare at Nana Pickles, Our Lady of the Biscuits. Feeling thoroughly deflated now, he sits heavily on the edge of his bed and fishes out his phone. As if to further crank up his wretchedness, he navigates straight to his daughter's Instagram.

In the first picture, he sees that they are all out, at night, in a street of tall, elegant houses, all painted in different pastel colours. Paula and the kids are huddled close together and grinning. Behind them, Rich Tony is standing, also beaming and a good head taller even than Ryan, who's already five foot ten. His arms are outstretched around the three of them, as if he were gathering them up. They must have asked a passer-by to take the picture.

Shane studies it, aware that the photo isn't doing anything to lift him out of the awfulness of today. Because it *was* awful, despite Pam and Kamal's gargantuan efforts to be jolly and hospitable, and he hates himself for thinking this.

It was awful because everyone had only gathered at Cherry Cottage because Ravi is dead. And on top of that, despite his uncertainty of how it would be, a tiny part of him had looked forward to seeing Josie again. Sunny Josie, with the beautiful smile and clear blue eyes that always reminded him of forget-me-nots (every summer, the Kapoors' garden was full of them).

At least there was that, he'd been telling himself as the day had drawn closer. At least they would be able to talk and maybe straighten things out a bit. He certainly needed to apologise for his part in it. It had shocked him, how deeply he had hoped it would turn out that way – that somehow, Ravi's celebration might go a little way towards putting things right.

Giving Rich Tony's smug face a final glare, Shane tosses his phone aside, gets up to switch the kettle on and rips open the biscuits. Biting into one, he glares at the packet. *Baking your favourites since 1897.* Tastes like it, he decides.

He doesn't really want a biscuit. Nor does he want a cup of tea made with the sole bag sitting there. A proper drink is what he wants, more than anything – at this precise moment, even more than world peace. Wine and beers were flowing at the Kapoors', and Dev and his mates were definitely tipsy towards the end. Which was fine – no judgement coming from Shane – but he was determined to hold it together and not make an arse of himself and obviously he did a *fantastic* job there.

He circuits the room again, looking for a discreet cupboard that might have escaped his attention earlier and will miraculously turn out to be a well-stocked mini-bar. Of course there isn't such an amenity. No one came in to obligingly install one while he was at the Kapoors'.

He groans audibly and then he thinks, *sod it*. It's 10.13 on a gloomy evening in his home town and there's a bar downstairs. He doesn't have high hopes for its ambience, but they'll serve alcohol, and that's what matters.

Three minutes later, telling himself that the night is still young – why not live a little! – Shane is striding towards the lift. This time, it doesn't take a hundred years to arrive. It opens instantly, causing him to jump – as if it were waiting for him. Already, as he travels down, he starts to feel marginally better. Rich Tony and Paula are probably enjoying cocktails now, but so what? Shane is about to chug down a pint in a hotel bar that looked, as he passed it earlier, as alluring as a broom cupboard, and it'll be fucking *great*.

The lift doors open and he bounds out like a dog released from the boot of a car. He swerves to the right and, quickening his pace, he steps into what is optimistically named The Cocktail Club. It's plainly furnished with too few tables, spaced too far apart, and a couple of seemingly unyielding blue sofas.

A fed-up-looking woman behind the bar is checking her phone. There are only four other people in here: a gaunt young man picking at crisps from a packet torn open and laid flat on the table, and an earnest-looking couple huddled over a laptop.

And there in the corner, a lone blonde woman is lifting a large glass of white wine to her lips, while simultaneously engaged in what seems to be a furious phone conversation.

It's Josie.

9

JOSIE

'Hang on, Rupert,' I exclaim. 'You're not making any sense. What's happened exactly?'

Oh God. Here comes Shane. I do a silly little wave and grimace apologetically. He makes a glass-raising motion – *want a drink?* – and I shake my head quickly as he heads for the bar. 'You know the value of these books,' Rupert announces. 'We can't afford this to happen.'

'Can't afford *what* to happen?'

Of course I know their value. The bulk of our business is online sales – all handled by me. Rupert isn't interested in the tiresome business of taking payments, packaging up our valuable tomes and ensuring they reach their buyers promptly. His role is to occupy the front desk, bantering with friends and unwittingly intimidating potential customers.

'Remember that numbered limited edition on Picasso ceramics?' he snaps.

'Yes, of course—'

'The customer's been in touch. The book turned up in an *appalling* condition—'

'What?' I exclaim. 'It can't have! You know how careful I am. If it's been damaged in transit, we're covered for that. We just need to—'

'I don't *think* this happened in transit!'

I flinch and glance over at Shane, who's sipping his beer at the bar. *Won't be a minute,* I mouth at him.

'Rupert, can we please deal with this on Monday?' I say, but he carries on talking regardless. He knows I'm away, that an old friend has died, and that I'm back in my home town to pay my respects. 'Good luck up there!' he'd said with an alarmed expression, as if a trip to Yorkshire were on a par with traversing the Arctic.

'What happened exactly?' I ask.

'I've already told you.'

'Yes, but I didn't catch it.' I can't possibly have heard him right. 'Something about cheese?'

'I said, someone put a cheese slice between the pages of that book. I don't think that happened in transit, do you?'

I gaze around the soulless bar, trying to take this in. '*Processed* cheese,' he adds hotly.

'You mean... like a Dairylea slice?'

'I s'pose so, yes!'

'Put in between the pages? Like a bookmark or something—'

'I'm not finding this funny, Josie.'

'Neither am I! So are you...' My heart is rattling and I'm finding it hard to form the right words. 'You mean you're actually accusing me of doing this?'

'*You* packaged the order,' Rupert announces. 'No one else touched it—'

'Why on earth d'you think I'd do something like that?'

'I have no idea!'

Without warning, tears flood my eyes. 'You think – you

mean, you *really* think—' My voice wobbles and I break off, aware that my tears are about to spill over. Furiously, I will my body to suck them back in.

'I can't talk about this now,' I mutter. 'I'll see you on Monday.' With that, I finish the call and beckon Shane to come over and join me.

He takes a seat and gives me a concerned look. 'Everything okay?'

'Just a work thing.' I place my phone face down on the table. 'My boss can be an idiot sometimes.'

I'm aware of him scanning my face, as if trying to figure out whether I want to talk about it. 'It's nothing,' I say firmly. 'Anyway, I, erm... I realised I wasn't remotely tired any more and wouldn't be able to sleep, so—'

'Me too.' He smiles, looking sheepish, as if acknowledging that we've caught each other out. 'I need this, to be honest,' he says, lifting his glass.

'Same.' I smile and sip my wine, which is bland and acidic – a step down, if that were possible, from the cheap stuff I usually drink at home, but somehow weirdly delicious.

'I'm sorry,' Shane starts, 'but I haven't even asked what you do.'

'My job?' I bite my lip, conscious of my heartbeat returning to something like normal. 'I work in a bookshop just off Piccadilly. A little independent place specialising in art books.'

'Oh, lovely!'

I make a spluttery noise and he looks at me quizzically. And then – because he suggests another drink, and I can't think of a reason not to – I splurge it all out: about Rupert, the cheese, his accusation. 'You're kidding!' Shane exclaims. 'As if you'd do something like that.' And somehow this breaks the ice and conversation starts to flow. He asks about other jobs I've had –

temping, bar work, whatever I could fit around Cora's school hours – and tells me about his shop.

'Musical instruments?' I marvel. 'Wow. That's brilliant.'

I look across the table at him, at the clearly sorted man he's become. The kind of man who's 'totally amicable' with his ex. It wasn't like that with Dale – Cora's dad – and me. I'd tumbled into a relationship with him off the back of the whole Shane/Ravi/band debacle. Here was something I could throw myself into, I'd thought. With no real prospects, I'd jumped at the chance to move to London together because, well, wouldn't that be fun?

London had everything, we reckoned. Endless opportunities for adventure and larks. Dale knew of a room going in a house share in Camden, so we moved into that. This could have been written off as a youthful error but somehow, punctuated by many break-ups and reconciliations, at twenty-nine, I had our baby. The pregnancy hadn't been planned but it surprised me how delighted I was. However, within six months of Cora being born, I could no longer handle Dale and his stoner mates getting off their heads around her – and we were over for good. Reluctantly, he moved in with a friend, and for weeks afterwards, he'd turn up drunk, trying to barge his way into the flat. Crazed letters were pushed through my letterbox and once, two enormous Hawaiian pizzas were sent round by him, which I took as his way of trying to 'help'.

Shane sips his beer and looks thoughtful. 'I feel really bad about losing touch,' he says.

'With Ravi?' I ask. 'Yes, me too. It's awful, really. It shouldn't have happened.'

He sighs, nodding. 'Why d'you think she wanted us to do this?'

'The tour?' I shrug. 'Honestly, I've no idea. But maybe she felt it was... kind of unfinished?'

'Because we never did that last gig? The Huddersfield one?'

I cringe inwardly. 'Exactly, yes. But I still can't understand why that would have mattered to her, after all this time.'

'I guess it really did though, didn't it?' he suggests.

'Seems like it, yes.' A small silence hovers.

'But obviously,' he starts, 'it'd be really difficult for us to do it...'

'Yes, of course,' I say quickly. 'I mean, you have your shop, right?'

'Yeah, that's right.'

'And Rupert always insists that I book time off way in advance...'

'And there's your family too,' he adds. 'Your granddaughter—'

'Oh, yes.' The family who leans on me so heavily!

'Although,' Shane says thoughtfully, scratching at an eyebrow, 'it would only be a few days.'

'A few days up *here*,' I remind him. 'And how on earth would we get around?' Because obviously, travelling from one entirely well-connected town to the next would be logistically impossible! 'And where would we stay?' I go on. 'Five nights in hotels, that'd cost—' I break off, not wanting to admit what a mess my life actually is.

That I barely make my mortgage every month.

And the fact that my boyfriend's solution is to sell pictures of my alluring peasant feet.

That staying in hotels – even cheap hotels – is beyond my means right now. Hence the bus travel and this ill-fitting Vinted dress and the mainly charity shop books I keep buying for Poppy because I want to give her things. Things we can enjoy together.

'We're a bit overloaded with books at the moment,' Zack had announced last time. 'But this is lovely of you. We'll keep it for when she can read!'

Shane seems to be studying me, and I meet his gaze. 'There is a way, though,' he starts. 'I mean, one way we could do it without having to book hotels. That is, *if* we were going to do it...'

'Which we're not,' I remind him.

'Nope. Absolutely not!'

Curiosity is bubbling up in me now. 'But... if we were?' I prompt him. 'What were you thinking?'

He pauses, smiles and drains his glass. 'Well, I know a man with a van...'

'A van?' I repeat.

'Yeah.' He chuckles. 'A campervan, I mean. This guy Boris owns it. He's been popping into the shop for years, mainly to chat and hang about. Buys the occasional plectrum. A set of strings once a decade...'

I nod, willing him to get to the point. 'What's this campervan like?'

'No idea – I've never seen it. But I do know he's very fond of it. Of *her*, rather. Calls her Doris—'

'Boris and Doris?' I grin.

'That's right. Travels all over, apparently. I think it makes him feel like he's still a man of the road.' He laughs fondly, and I smile. Just for an instant, I wish it hadn't turned out like this. I wish we'd stayed friends – or *something* at least. That somehow, out of the wreckage of everything, we'd remained in each other's lives, even tentatively. But too much had happened, and if I allow myself to even remember any of it, I can hardly look at his face. 'He's always saying I can borrow it,' Shane adds.

'Well, it's a nice idea but...' I pause, shaking my head. 'What am I saying? It's a *terrible* idea!'

'I guess you're right.' He laughs, and as we finish our drinks and travel back up to the third floor together, it's a little less awkward this time. 'Night then,' he says with a smile. 'Hope it all works out for you.'

I blink at him.

'With the cheese business.'

'Oh, yes! Of course. Thank you.' We hug again and I muster a stoical smile. And this time, for some unfathomable reason, I feel a little lighter as I stride towards my room.

10

Don't panic, I tell myself as I emerge from Piccadilly Circus Tube station. On this cool, bright Monday morning I have nothing to fear. Certainly not Rupert because, as I remind myself now, he is just a man. An extremely wealthy man who, I suspect, doesn't really need to run a bookshop – or work at all. But still: he is not the police.

I'm not going to be flung into jail for the alleged misuse of processed cheese, and surely he can't sack me. I've done nothing wrong, and he *has* to believe me. Even if he doesn't, angry Rupert isn't actually that scary. That time I spilt my coffee on the shop floor? 'Oh, for fuck's sake, Josie!' But it was like the King swearing – faintly ridiculous. I couldn't take it seriously at all.

Reassured that all of this will blow over, I turn into the arcade and stride towards the shop. All curved glass windows and gleaming brass, this is a rarified corner of London of bespoke suits and cufflinks and those proper hankies that poke neatly out of a breast pocket. 'A pocket square,' Rupert corrected me once, with a note of bemusement. *Silly Josie has no idea about these things!*

I pass the eye-wateringly expensive leather goods shop. From the cashmere store, one of the sales assistants sees me through the spotless window and waves. I wave back and smile, then step into the bookshop. We're not open yet but, as usual, Rupert is already occupying the huge antique desk that dominates the shop.

'Hi, Rupert!' I say cheerily.

He looks up. 'Morning, Josie.' Bit of the steely-teacher vibe today. *That homework you handed in was disappointing.*

'Like a coffee?' At least he hasn't launched straight into the Dairylea incident. Hopefully it's been laid to rest.

'If you're making one,' he mutters.

Fine, I think as I head to the back room. As well as being my workspace, it also functions as what we grandly term the 'kitchen', consisting of an ancient mini fridge and a flimsy cupboard housing our motley selection of mugs. All are chunky and ugly apart from the delicate bone china cup with my initial on it, which Rupert gave me last Christmas. On the shelf below sits a catering tin of his beloved Nescafé granules. Three years I've worked here, and we're still on the same tin. From what I've gathered, Rupert's family owns roughly 70 per cent of Berkshire, yet our new shop kettle cost £12.50 (he insisted on the cheapest option I could find).

I put it on to boil, then switch on the printer on my desk. There's the ominous hum that happens intermittently, and within minutes its plastic casing is worryingly hot to the touch. The hum becomes an urgent whine, as if it's straining on the toilet, and as I set it to work it chews up the paper and shuts down abruptly. I glare at it, then carry Rupert's coffee through to the shop, prepared to share my diagnosis.

'You know how the printer's been a bit erratic?' I say. 'I think I know what it is.' He stares at me levelly. 'Its moods are all over the place,' I continue, 'and now it's hot all of a sudden.' I smile, trying to lighten the atmosphere. 'It must be menopausal! Should we see if there are HRT patches for printers, or maybe a gel—'

'Josie, could you please sit down for a moment?' Rupert cuts in, indicating the curvaceous wooden chair tucked in at the other side of his desk.

I frown and pull it out and bob down onto it. 'What is it?'

'About this book.'

I bite my upper lip, conscious of my racing heart, and glance around the shop. There are hundreds of books in here, neatly displayed on open shelves and in highly polished glass cabinets. But of course I'm fully aware of the book he's talking about. 'Rupert,' I start, 'I'm sorry it happened but honestly, I have no idea how—'

'Was it some kind of prank?' he snaps.

'A prank?' I exclaim. 'You honestly think I'd prank you?' I stare at him.

A clump of silvery hair springs forward and bounces against his brow, and he shoves it back distractedly. 'How else could it have got there?'

'I don't know!'

He leans forward, looking thunderous, hands clasped together. When I landed this job, I felt so lucky; here was this kindly toff who was prepared to entrust me with his online business. And he *did* trust me – or so I thought.

'Our customers are important,' Rupert announces.

'Yes, I know!'

'Excellent service is what we're all about. That way, they keep coming back—'

'Yes, but I didn't—'

'And that kind of cheese?' he crows. 'It's the kind *you* have.'

I look down at his desk, taking a moment to absorb his remark. He's right in that I bring in packed lunches because the prices around here are outrageous. 'Have you been inspecting my sandwiches?' I ask.

'Of course not. I'm just saying—'

'That's quite a leap, isn't it?' Anger is simmering up in me now, over being judged by my lunch choices and that he thinks I'd do something so pathetic. What motive could I possibly have?

'Not that much of a leap,' he says, and that's when I snap. I don't know if it's about Ravi and the Kapoors, or seeing Shane, or worrying about how to tell Pam and Kamal that we can't do what their daughter so desperately wanted us to do. I'm up on my feet now, glaring down at Rupert, my heart banging in my chest. 'I thought you trusted me!' I cry.

'I do. I *did.* But lately, your mind hasn't been on the job.'

'That's not fair!' I protest. 'In what way?'

'You've seemed vague. Distracted…'

'Well, yes, my oldest friend has died.'

He has the decency to flush deeply. 'I'm sorry about that,' he mutters. 'But I have to say, I've been getting the feeling that you don't love being here, Josie.'

'I do! Of course I do…' It's true. I genuinely enjoy my job, working methodically and helping our customers, despite the malfunctioning printer and the crappy tape dispenser that savaged my finger, which Rupert refuses to replace, despite his wealth. I saw a 'pocket square' just like his in a shop window in Jermyn Street – 'a welcome splash of colour to your summer outfitting', the display card said – for £95. Nearly a hundred quid for something to blow your nose on!

'And there was my umbrella,' he announces, having recovered his bluster.

Oh, so we're dragging that up? Two weeks ago, that was. 'I didn't want to *take* your umbrella,' I remind him.

'It was pouring with rain.'

'Yes, but I told you, I hate them—'

'That's like saying you hate coats!'

'Coats don't blow inside out.'

Rupert groans and shakes his head. 'Anyway, you left it in Tesco.'

Well, yes. I'd known, as he'd thrust it at me, that it wouldn't end well. With a rubbishy telescopic brolly – the kind that collapses to pieces on its first outing – I'd have been fine. But I was so nervous about being in temporary charge of Rupert's treasured maple-handed accessory – bought at great expense from a specialist shop that sells only umbrellas and walking canes and 'shooting sticks', whatever they are – that I'd lost it somewhere in the shop. I'd rushed back like a berserk mother who'd left her baby parked in its pram by the meal deal cabinet. But nothing had been handed in.

'I said I was sorry,' I murmur, 'and that you could deduct it from my wages.'

He presses his lips together and regards me stonily. What am I supposed to do now? Get on with our orders, I suppose. Utilise the – I have to say – slick system that I implemented, because when I arrived it was all conducted from a ratty old ledger book, stained with coffee rings.

I turn away, about to head for the back room, when I realise I can't do it. I can't get on with my work as if nothing's happened, as if he hasn't accused me of something I didn't do. I spin back round and glare at my boss, no longer angry but fuelled by a surge of something else. *Strength* – that's what it is. I think of Pam and Kamal and Dev, and how strong they were, despite being hit by tragedy. That's what I need; even the tiniest smidge of their bravery.

Ravi's letter flashes into my mind. Never mind not having the time nor the money. Five days, we're talking. Five days away from Rupert's big, florid face, not in a far-flung land but in the North of England. It won't kill me and Shane to carry out Ravi's last wish. Well, it *might*, but at least we'll have tried.

'Erm, Rupert,' I start, 'there's something I wanted to ask you.'

'Oh? What's that?' he asks archly.

'I'm going to need a bit of time off.'

'That might have to wait,' he growls.

'Just a few days,' I continue, aware of an eerie calmness settling over me. 'This thing's come up. Another trip up north...' He winces at that. Rupert fears 'The North'; he believes we eat bread and dripping, and set about one another with clubs.

'As I said,' he announces, 'it might have to—'

'No, I tell you what,' I cut in sharply. 'This actually *can't* wait.'

'Fine! Go then. Just go—'

'*What?*' I stare at him. Is he sacking me? 'You mean... you want me to go?' The words seem to float out of my mouth.

'Yes, I do.' He picks up his treasured fountain pen with the gold nib. What is he planning to write, I wonder? A letter terminating my contract but requesting instructions for how to get on the printer's good side?

He can't do this! I need my job. Trying to quell the rising panic, I replay Lloyd's consolatory words to me last night: *Tell him to stick his job up his arse. We'll have your other income stream pretty soon.* Foot porn, he meant. *It's not porn, babe. It's just feet!*

I take a deep, slow breath and briefly consider fetching my posh china cup from the cupboard. But instead, I study Rupert for a moment, captain of that vast mahogany desk, and I turn and walk out of the shop.

11

SHANE

Shane and Fletch have to be jacks-of-all trades in order to keep things afloat. While Shane is adept at drum and guitar repairs, his friend and business partner (not a term either of them would ever use) takes care of woodwind and brass. When Fletch disassembles a saxophone and lovingly pieces it back together again, it's as astounding to Shane as if he'd operated successfully on a human heart. Yet there are aspects which Fletch is, frankly, crap at – like managing their extensive online string business and the colossal amounts of admin involved in running a specialist shop.

Shane regards all of this with the same bleary acceptance of scrubbing out the charred remains left by Elaine in his frying pans. However, he is also rather good at it. That, and actually making sales as, for some unfathomable reason, takings are up whenever Shane mans the shop. He suspects that Fletch might be a tad overzealous, which can come across as pressurising. Shane is certainly more patient with people who wander in and proceed to 'try out' every guitar in the shop – it's all 'Nice action, man! Yeah, I'll think about it' – with no intention of buying.

One of these people is Boris: a permanently denim-clad man

in his sixties, his mop of grizzly grey curls poking out from a faded baseball cap. Shane hands him a coffee and they catch up on each other's news. 'It was all right, you know?' he says when his friend enquires about the Yorkshire trip. 'Sad, of course.'

'Yeah, tragic, mate.' Boris scratches at his beard. 'Those things are hard.'

Yet not completely, Shane muses – because it *had* got him back in touch with Josie. Thank God he'd gone down to the hotel bar because that had made things feel less awkward between them. He'd looked for her again at breakfast and assumed she'd decided to skip it. As he'd chewed gamely on an anaemic sausage, he couldn't say he blamed her.

He doesn't know if he'll ever see her again, but at least things were cordial – to the point where he'd messaged her last night to check she'd got home safely, and she'd replied that she had.

Coffee finished, Boris wanders over to a Fender Telecaster and caresses it reverentially. He likes it to be known that he's played guitar 'for everyone' (although he is vague about actual names). Apparently, he even recorded a solo instrumental album, although Shane has never found any evidence of this. In all the years Boris has been coming in, their friendship has never progressed beyond music talk, and tales of his travels. As a long-time singleton, Boris undertakes these campervan trips alone, apparently content in his solitude.

'I've told you,' he announces now, 'you can borrow Doris any time you like. 'Cause you look knackered, mate,' he adds, not unkindly. 'Take some time off from this place! Have a holiday!' Frankly, Shane's idea of a holiday is somewhere sunny and hot, with his kids, even though it's been a couple of years since they've gone away together. He's asked them, of course, but they have busy schedules, and in the two years that Tony's been in their lives, they've all gone to Florida, Mexico and skiing in the

Alps. On top of that, there are so many weekend breaks – Copenhagen being the latest – that Shane feels lucky if he is able to see his kids at all.

As the day goes on, the image of Boris's van buzzes away in Shane's brain. He's picturing a classic VW camper, lovingly restored – chrome fittings gleaming, a pot of tea on the stove, bacon sizzling in a pan. Admittedly, it's appealing. Boris was right in that he's spending an awful lot of time in the shop these days.

It's become his habit to stay on a bit later, long after the shop has closed, to give the place a thorough clean. By the time he's finished tonight, the floor is almost as shiny and gleaming as the trumpets and French horns. Even Fletch has commented on his efforts: 'Place is looking good, mate! Are we getting inspected or something?' In fact, the reason for Shane's recent vigour on the housekeeping front is to delay the business of going home.

His place isn't particularly smart. It's a post-war flat in a three-storey block, bordered by patches of straggly undergrowth and accessed by means of a rickety walkway. But it was a place of his own, which he was grateful to find after he and Paula broke up six years ago. He'd always felt comfortable there – until Elaine moved in. For a small woman, she takes up an awful lot of space.

Shane lets himself into his fuggy-smelling hallway. 'Hiya!' Elaine appears, beaming, in the kitchen doorway.

'Hi, Elaine.'

'Good day?'

'Not bad, yeah. How're you?'

'Good!' She plants her hands on her hips and does a little shimmy. 'What d'you think?'

Shane realises he is expected to comment on her outfit. The tiny porridge-coloured dress, in some kind of stretchy, bobbly material, brings to mind sofa upholstery. Usually, her crinkly reddish hair is pulled back and secured with a glittery scrunchie. But today it appears to have been flattened somehow. Ironed, presumably.

'You look great!' he manages.

'Thanks!' She grins.

'Going out?' he asks, unnecessarily.

'Yeah.' She continues to hover, clearly waiting for him to ask about her plans. All Shane is concerned with is opening every window to dissipate the sealed-canister atmosphere in here. She has been frying again – when is she *not* frying? – and the place has the fuggy air of a greasy spoon café. Yet even when he does this, the odour still hangs. It must be heavier than air, he thinks, as she follows him around. 'Got a date. We've been chatting. Don't want to get my hopes up but he sounds *lovely*...'

'Oh, that's good.' Briefly, he eyeballs the dirty frying pan still sitting on the hob, and the plastic utensil which she seems to have melted beyond all recognition. It's only a spatula, he tells himself. And she'll be gone soon. This is not his life forever. His second urge – stronger than the window-opening one – is to send another message to Josie. She's been on his mind all day. Her beautiful, finely boned face filled his mind as he politely turned down the chance to buy a wheezy old accordion from a man emitting cast-iron confidence and whisky fumes. He thought of her while a teenage boy tried out seven different trumpets, assaulting his eardrums with a series of tuneless blasts. 'Not sure they're what we're looking for,' his mother trilled, and they left.

'Anyway, you'll meet him!' Elaine announces as he looks for a beer in the fridge.

'Meet who?' The beers have gone. Elaine must have had them.

'My man! Valter!' Hang on, is he *her man* already?

'Valter?' he repeats.

'Yeah. He's Brazilian. Gorgeous,' she adds.

Shane frowns, trying to make sense of this. 'But you haven't met him yourself, have you? In real life, I mean?'

'No, but he's coming round to pick me up. We're going to that cute little tapas place. The one I keep saying we should try, but you're always so *busy*—' She snorts and swivels her gaze to the small digital clock on the kitchen shelf. 'Anyway, he'll be here any minute, so—'

'Right! I'll let you get on then.' Shane smiles tightly and heads for a shower, more to try and wash away his irritation than anything else. In his cramped little bathroom, tubs of glittery body gel emblazoned with mermaids and unicorns have colonised every surface. There are fat tubes of fake tan leaking brownish goo, and several outsized, darkly stained mittens strewn about. He hasn't dared ask what they're for. A clear plastic pouch perched on his windowsill bears the words LAMINATING KIT. He doesn't understand what that's for either. Is it her face she laminates, or something else? He's asked, gently, if she'd mind storing some of this stuff in her room, but nothing has happened and he hasn't had the energy to pursue it. How had Josie signed off that first message to him again? Yep – that's it. He just needs to chill out and adopt some of those *best golden love* vibes himself.

From the sanctuary of his bedroom, Shane hears a sharp rap on the door and Elaine exclaiming, 'Hi! Hi! Come in!'

There's a low male rumble – 'Lovely to meet you at last!' – and a tumble of voices as they chatter over each other and then... silence. No, not quite silence. Shane has wondered sometimes if all of those years spent drumming in bands might have damaged his hearing a little. But apparently not, as it seems that his ears can pick up the tiniest sounds. He hears a long, drawn out *mmmmmm* from Elaine, followed by what are clearly kissing noises. So his hearing is fine – but Jesus! This is his home! A home he virtually bankrupted himself to buy, and a stranger is in it, snogging Elaine! Shane sits on his bed, staring bleakly at the wall and trying to figure out why this feels so wrong.

After all, they're only kissing – he *assumes* – and Elaine is entitled to do whatever she likes, with whoever she fancies. He's not going to police her. It's the fact that this is happening within earshot, alerting him to the fact that somehow, he has relinquished control over his own flat – and by extension, his life.

On and on they go, slurping and giggling, and Elaine lets out an ecstatic sigh: *aaaaaahhhh*. It's the first time they've met! Is this how it happens these days? You 'chat' for a while and the first time you meet in the flesh, you eat each other's faces off? He's become a prude, Shane realises with a flash of shame. A retired colonel from Frinton-on-Sea battering out a furious letter to *The Telegraph*.

She's young, he reminds himself. Hang on – forty-five isn't that young! Have some fucking decorum! At the sharp snapping noise, he flinches. That sounded like elastic being pinged. Is she taking her knickers off?

Shane jumps up from his bed, primed to do something. He just doesn't know what. He'd barge out and exclaim, 'Oh! Sorry!' – but what if Valter has his cock out? This is crazy. It's Shane's flat and he should be able to roam it freely! The thing about overhearing this kind of stuff is, you feel like *you're* the one who's in the wrong. That *you're* the perv for hearing anything, and you should magically transport yourself out of the vicinity, or at least possess noise-cancelling headphones, which Shane has never had any need for until now.

Go to your room, he wills Elaine. It's the room his kids slept in regularly until a couple of years ago, and it still has the lilac feathery lampshade which Liv chose from IKEA. However, no sounds follow to indicate that Elaine and her beau are relocating to a more appropriate 'space'. Then, suddenly: 'Shane?' she bellows. Ah, they've taken a break. 'Shane, come and meet Valter!'

'I'm busy just now,' he shouts back.

Silence. Then, 'He's a bit uptight,' Elaine hisses. Oh, is he really? His mobile rings and his heart jumps as he sees Josie's name displayed.

'Hello?' he barks, trying to sound calm and normal.

'Hi, Shane,' she says levelly, and he senses her hesitation. 'Is now a good time to talk?'

He is being summoned again by his housemate. He thought they were going for tapas! Why can't she leave him alone? 'Just on a call, Elaine,' he yells back.

'We're off, then. Don't wait up for us!' She hoots with laughter. 'See ya!'

The door bangs, and he clears his throat and tries to gather himself together. 'Yeah, it's fine,' he tells Josie. 'Sorry about that. So, erm, how did things go at work?'

She exhales forcefully. 'Not very well. I seem to have walked out on my job. Or been sacked. I'm not quite sure which...'

'Oh no! Because of the cheese?'

'Yeah.' She pauses. 'He's still convinced I sabotaged the order. As if I'd do that.'

'As if!' Shane exclaims, filled with outrage on her behalf. He strides out of his room towards the kitchen. It feels liberating, having his flat to himself for once.

'Anyway,' she says, 'I've been thinking.' He rubs at his chin, wondering what's coming next. 'About Ravi,' she continues.

'About her request – her instruction or whatever you'd call it – to us. And I wondered, perhaps we *could* actually do it—'

'You want to do this thing?' he cuts in.

She seems to hesitate. 'Maybe *want* isn't the right word. More like, I feel we should, for Ravi...'

'I feel the same,' he says quickly.

'Really? You do?'

'Yes, really. If *you* want to, I mean. That guy with the van popped into the shop today...'

'Boris?' she says, and he can't help smiling at that.

'You remember.'

'It's a memorable name, isn't it? So, d'you think he'd be okay with lending it to us?'

'Oh, yeah. Any time, he's always saying, as long as he's not away. I have no idea what it's like, but—'

'But it goes, doesn't it?'

'Yes.' He chuckles. 'It definitely goes.'

'And could you take time off from the shop?'

'I've been manning it a lot lately,' he replies. 'Fletch wouldn't mind covering a few days. But what about you? Are you having to work notice?'

'Doesn't look like it.' She pauses. 'I called him this afternoon. Rupert, I mean. Apologised for flouncing out. I thought we could figure things out, but he wasn't having any of it.'

'God, I'm so sorry,' Shane murmurs.

'Thanks. I'm okay, honestly. I'll find something else, even just to tide me over. Anyway, I'm paid till the end of the month, and I've done loads of extra hours, so...' She trails off.

Shane leans against the worktop, allowing all of this information to settle and wishing there was a chilled beer in the fridge. So it's actually happening. After all these years – and all that awful stuff he's tried to forget – they're going to be thrown back together again. Not just for an afternoon and an evening, like at the Kapoors' and in that hotel bar, but for *five whole days.*

What will they do all that time? What'll it be like?

He's trepidatious, of course. He doesn't know Josie at all – at least, not as a grown-up woman. Yet the prospect is also sort of... thrilling.

'Okay,' he says, trying to keep his tone light, 'so if we're going to do this, when would be a good time? I mean, when are you free?'

He senses her smiling and now Shane, alone in his kitchen, is smiling too. 'Right now,' Josie replies, 'I guess I'm free pretty much all of the time.'

12

TEN DAYS LATER

Josie

Incredibly, it's been agreed that I can visit Cora today. Perhaps she felt sorry for me over the Rupert business.

I have a nervy feeling in the pit of my stomach (ridiculous! I'm only visiting my *daughter!*) and a present for Poppy stashed in my bag. Just a few picture books I picked up, wrapped in cheerful bunny-patterned paper and tied with a bow. I know Zack said they were 'a bit overloaded' with books, but what else can I bring her? The cuddly lion and collection of plush Winnie the Pooh characters were greeted by Cora with a brief, 'Ah, nice!' and have never been seen since.

Theirs is a lively and interesting area – a mix of ramshackle grocers and takeaways with smart new coffee shops always popping up. Their flat, one of several owned by Zack's wealthy parents, is in a pleasant Victorian terrace, bordered from the street by freshly painted railings and small, neatly tended gardens.

Trying to quell my unease, I press the bell to their ground-floor flat. It's Cora who comes to the door, with a pink-cheeked, wide-eyed Poppy cradled in her arms. 'Hello, love! Hello, Popsy-baby!' I hug Cora – hug both of them, really – very lightly.

'Come in, Mum!' she says brightly, and I follow her into the living room. When Cora was a baby, my flat was an explosion of nappies and toys and splattered milk and baby food. Where did I go wrong? The impression here is that Poppy's arrival has been no more disruptive than buying a new cushion. The light tan sofa appears to be unmarred. Apart from her bouncy chair – spotless, parked neatly on the floor beside the coffee table – you'd never know a baby was resident here.

I lift off my shoulder bag and tug off my jacket, wondering where to put them. Placing them on the sofa would feel like tipping out the kitchen bin onto their fluffy cream rug. So I dart out to the hall, pull out Poppy's present and hang up my bag and jacket on one of the hooks.

I return to find Cora perched neatly on the sofa with Poppy on her knee, and sit beside them, placing my gift on the coffee table next to the Diptyque candle. 'So, how's it going?' I venture.

'Really well.' Cora smiles, although I detect a hint of tension in her pale blue eyes.

'She's grown so much,' I say truthfully. It's been nearly three weeks since I've seen her. Three weeks since I was last allowed through Border Control.

'I'm sorry, Mum,' she says, seeming to relax a little. 'It's been crazy lately. So many visitors, you know? We've tried to space them out...'

Is that what it is? I've been *spaced out*? 'Don't worry.' I touch her arm. 'I do remember what it's like, you know.'

She nods and smiles. 'You did it all on your own.'

'After a fashion.' I chuckle. 'So, is Zack around today?' I ask, in what I hope is a neutral tone.

'Yep. He's just on a call.' My heart sinks a little. I know he works from home as an IT manager a couple of days a week, but I'd hoped that this would be an office day.

I nod – let's hope it's a long call – and coo over Poppy's huge blue eyes and pink milk-plumped cheeks, her impossibly tiny fingers and wisps of soft blonde hair. She is so like Cora, it takes my breath away. 'Can I hold her?' I ask.

''Course you can, Mum.'

Cora hands her to me, and I'm overcome by a rush of happiness as I hold her close and breathe in her gorgeous scent. Poppy emits a sweet little gurgle and grasps at the cuff of my sleeve. I kiss the top of her head and nuzzle her cheek—

'Oh, hi, Josie!' Zack has appeared in the doorway.

'Hi, Zack.' I smile brightly as he comes closer.

'Watch her head!' he barks.

'It's all right.' I frown up at him. 'I do know how to—'

'It's just... her neck,' he blusters. 'You have to support it.'

'Yep! She's fine...' Fucking hell, mate, I have held a baby before. Or does he think Cora was made in a laboratory?

'Their muscles aren't fully developed at this stage.'

'No, I realise that,' I say, my smile set like cement. I alter my position to demonstrate how expertly her neck is being supported and address her directly. 'Popsy, darling, I brought you a little present...'

'Come to Daddy, then.' With a grimace, Zack bends to scoop her from my arms.

I clear my throat and try to catch Cora's eye, but she won't look at me. Zack is strolling around the bright, airy room now, taking Poppy to the window in order to soothe her, I assume, from the trauma of being cuddled by her granny for a couple of minutes. 'Look, sweetie,' he murmurs. 'The trees! See the branches blowing?'

I remember my own parents coming down to meet Cora for the first time, soon after she was born. How terrified of London they were: the crowds, the noise, the Underground as baffling to them as a wiring system for a nuclear submarine. Yet there they were, thrilled to hold their grandchild – even my gruff dad, who'd grafted away among men at the engineering works for fifty years. Seeing him being so tender with Cora had caused my heart to swell with love.

Trying to dispel the tension, I pass the gift to Cora. 'Just a little something for Poppy,' I say.

'Oh, Mum. That's kind of you.' Carefully, she peels off the Sellotape and eases off the bunny paper from the three picture books. 'These are sweet.' She smiles.

'Those two are just from a charity shop,' I say.

'Ah. Right.' Briefly, she examines them and places them on the table. They're in perfect condition, and I wiped down their covers just to be sure. But Zack grimaces at them as if I'd fished them out of a septic tank.

'I remember this one!' Cora exclaims, brightening now.

'Yes, you loved it,' I say, my spirits lifting. 'From when you were a baby right up until you were about four. We read it so many times—'

'The thing is, with charity shops, you don't really know where it's been,' Zack announces hotly.

Cora and I stare up at him. 'That one's actually new.' Blood rushes to my cheeks. 'I bought it from—'

'And I don't think she's quite ready for religious indoctrination yet,' he adds with an infuriating chortle.

For a moment, I can't form words. 'It's... it's not really religious,' I murmur.

'I think you'll find it is!'

'Well, yes, I know Noah's Ark comes from the Bible,' I say,

feeling caught out somehow, as if I'm trying to steal her away to join a sect. 'But it's just a sweet story, isn't it? That's the focus, really. Just animals!' I look to Cora for confirmation – or a smile, even – but she's got up and is asking, 'Does anyone want coffee or tea?'

'I'll make it,' I say, eager for an excuse to get out of the room, if only for a couple of minutes. 'The usual for you, Cor?'

'Yes, please,' she says tightly.

'Zack?'

'I'm fine, thanks.' In the kitchen I make two mugs of tea, aware of low muttering in the living room. I haven't told Cora about my forthcoming trip with Shane. I'd looked forward to a chat – and even if I hadn't got around to that, I wouldn't have cared. I just wanted some time with my daughter. Time without *him*, I realise now. Have I turned into one of those awful mothers-in-law who seems to cause an atmosphere just by being there? I didn't want it to be like this. I really tried, when they started dating – inviting them over for dinner occasionally, buying him Christmas and birthday presents, all that. Not to ingratiate myself – just to show that I was happy that... well, Cora was happy. But is she? I can't help wondering as I return with our teas.

Immediately, Cora springs towards the coffee table drawer and extracts two coasters. Poppy has been transferred to her bouncy seat and is watching us all with rapt interest. I place Cora's tea on one of the coasters and perch beside her, lifting mine to my lips. 'Careful with hot drinks around Poppy,' Zack says.

'Yes, of course.' I force a smile. Because I was thinking of sloshing hot liquid around like a manic.

'Zack, it's *fine*,' Cora says, throwing him a look.

'Right!' He nods. 'I'll leave you to it then. Gotta jump on a call.'

I'm relieved, of course, but the atmosphere he leaves in his wake is tense and stilted, and none of my attempts to lighten things, to chat about inconsequential matters, really takes flight. And even when my tea is finished and I'm no longer in possession of a scalding beverage, I daren't ask to hold Poppy again. She is sleeping anyway, and I realise that, for all her groomed appearance – blonde hair gleaming, light make-up immaculate – Cora looks exhausted. I stand up, and she does too, anticipating me leaving. 'I'd better get going,' I say.

'Okay, Mum.' She musters a smile and hugs me in the hallway.

I pull back and study her finely boned face. 'Please let me know if I can come over and help anytime. I'd love to take Poppy out. Or if you two want a night out, or even a day together, I could look after her here…' *You can X-ray my bag on arrival. I'll fill out the official paperwork.*

'Oh, Mum,' she says, shooting a hand to her mouth. 'We haven't even talked about you losing your job. I'm sorry, my head's all over the place at the moment.'

'Honestly, love, don't worry about that,' I say firmly.

She frowns as Zack's work voice – a deeper timbre than his panicky *support-the-head!* voice – booms from a bedroom.

'You're okay, though, aren't you?' she asks.

'What, me?' The woman who's about to embark on some crazy road trip with a man she knows nothing about, really? At least, nothing about the adult man he's become? 'I'm fine, hon,' I say, and then, seeing her face relax a little – perhaps because I'm leaving – I step out into the sunny afternoon.

It's true – I *am* fine. And Zack is just a nervous dad, I tell myself. Uptight and worried and that's perfectly natural, with a new baby. Maybe I was the uptight one today, with this trip looming tomorrow?

I really should take a leaf out of my boyfriend's book, I decide. Because nothing seems to bother Lloyd: not world events or health or money issues. He has the occasional ciggie without guilt, smokes weed daily and drinks as much as he likes (possibly less than I do, to be fair) and never seems to have a shortage of work. He can always make the mortgage on his little two-bed flat. Somehow, he breezes through life, as I will once this trip is over. Then I'll be throwing myself into job hunting; surely *someone* will employ me? I'm hard-working and versatile and will do pretty much anything.

I'll also plan a visit to see Mum and Dad up in Northumberland. Have a new, decisive haircut and sort my colour out – a total reinvention for this new, thrilling phase as an unemployed person. I have plenty of friends, scattered all over London, from when Cora was a baby and various jobs and the old school gate gang.

My life is full, I tell myself. I'm a lucky woman and I can handle this.

Next morning I'm up at dawn, lashing my ancient, bagless sleeping bag to my rucksack with an old pair of tights. It's a faded peach colour and decidedly musty, as if it's been trapped for a decade in a cupboard – which it actually has. What will Shane think of it? I don't care! We're not going to be in a competitive sleeping bag situation, I tell myself as I haul my rucksack onto my back.

It'll be *fine.* I have absolutely nothing to be worried or ashamed about. And so, with the tethered sleeping bag flopping about like a giant blancmange, I set off across town to a little musical instrument shop in south London.

13

SHANE

Shane hadn't expected a top-of-the-range motorhome. He hadn't envisaged one of those vast, gleaming vehicles with solar panels and a fully fitted kitchen and impeccable sound system. However, when he follows Boris out of the shop, he is alarmed to discover that it's not actually a campervan after all. 'It's... an old ambulance?' he blurts out.

'Hey, less of the old! The term is *retired,* I'll have you know.' Boris slaps its rear doors affectionately. 'Enjoying new adventures and freedom after many years of loyal service. Plenty of life left in the old girl yet.' He extracts a premade roll-up from the top pocket of his frayed denim jacket and lights it.

'An ambulance,' Shane mutters. Appropriate, considering how his heart is jolting alarmingly now.

Boris nods. 'Best vehicles ever built.' With some effort he wrangles the back door open, and Shane peers inside. 'See, there's plenty of headroom for a tall lad like you,' Boris continues as they clamber into it. 'And tons of space for moving around in your living quarters. Ambulances are big buggers when you strip all the stuff out. Obviously,' he adds, 'when you think about what's gone on in here. Medical emergencies and stuff.'

People have bled copiously in here, Shane realises. Countless medical procedures will have taken place in here. What's the worst thing that can happen in an ambulance? Death, he realises. *Death* has happened in here.

'Real bargain, she was,' Boris continues cheerfully, taking a puff of his roll-up. 'There are loads of these on the market if you're ever tempted.'

'Um, yeah! Maybe!' Deciding not to mention the dent in the side, Shane flits his gaze around the van's interior. It is entirely without permanent fittings. He doesn't quite know what Boris had led him to expect, or if Shane had merely *imagined* that this would be a fully functional camper to facilitate a life of luxury on the road.

Whichever it was, he didn't expect this.

'Don't look so worried. Old Doris is still roadworthy,' Boris announces. *Yes,* Shane thinks, *but am I*? 'And she's got so much potential,' his friend enthuses, more animated than Shane has ever seen him. His dark eyes are twinkling, his cheeks highly flushed. 'I'm gonna build fitted units along here and have a sofa bed that pulls out here.' He flails his skinny arms about to indicate their intended locations. 'And here's where the log burner's gonna be. It'll be so cosy. Can you imagine, getting all snuggled up in here with a nice glass of red in front of the crackling flames?'

No. Right now, Shane cannot imagine that.

'And jumping out of bed in the morning,' Boris raves on, 'cracking eggs into the pan, lightly scrambled, or maybe poached? Picture that! Pot of coffee brewing, toast on the go...'

Shane stares at him, waiting for him to stop. Already, he has had enough of being told what to 'picture.' He's not about to start rhapsodising about how he likes his eggs in the morning because there will categorically be *no* eggs.

'I made those curtains myself!' Boris indicates the mottled brown linen flaps stuck over the two small rear windows with masking tape. They look as if they have been roughly hacked from the shirt of a dead man. 'And look – here's your interior lighting,' Boris adds, grabbing a portable plastic lamp from a corner and clicking the switch. Nothing happens. 'Ah, you'll need to pick up batteries on your way.' He clonks the lamp back down and beams at Shane. 'It's gonna be amazing in here, mate, once I've kitted her out. I've got so many plans.'

Shane blinks at him. He doesn't need *plans.* He needs facilities *now* – a loo at least! What are they going to do about that? Shane has Josie down as a chilled-out and possibly spiritual type, but he can't imagine that she'd be terribly *spiritual* about having to poo in the woods. And what about washing and other basic human needs?

'Shower's gonna be up against there,' Boris continues happily, rapping the partition that divides the 'living quarters' from the cabin. 'But in the meantime, just enjoy old Doris as she is. Enjoy the *space.*'

Shane bites his lip and pushes his hands into his jeans pockets. No, he thinks, I can't enjoy the space. Because apart from everything else, there is another aspect that is concerning him. It's the unmentionable object that's lying on the van's floor, which the two men have been carefully stepping around, and which Shane has been trying to pretend isn't there. The thing that renders this trip impossible because, obviously, he and Josie cannot possibly share a mattress.

Shane clears his throat. 'So... there's just this?' he asks, feigning casualness as Boris pauses for breath. *Or is there a secret second sleeping facility cunningly hidden in one of the walls?*

'Yeah,' Boris replies. 'Don't look so worried. It's really comfortable.' Admittedly, it's a double, and it looks clean, at least – if a little thin. 'You can get all snuggly and cosy on that,' he adds with a grin.

Seemingly unaware of Shane's rising panic, Boris jumps out of the back of the van and flicks his damp-ended roll-up into the road. 'C'mere a minute. I'd better show you what's what, hadn't I?' He beckons Shane around to the cab, which he clambers into in order to demonstrate how to handle the vehicle. 'Driven one of these before?'

'Can't say I have,' Shane replies, gazing at Boris through the open driver's door.

'Vans, though?' He turns the ignition key. The engine coughs and splutters as if clearing out a dollop of phlegm and finally kicks into life.

'Yeah, loads of times,' Shane shouts over its roar. Not that this is relevant as he and Josie are categorically not going anywhere. He'll have to cancel the trip. What will he tell her? He's ill – that's the simplest option. He's been throwing up all night.

Quickly, he checks the time on his phone. Christ, she'll be on her way already.

Boris demonstrates the van's various functions – to which Shane is paying zero attention – and turns off the engine. 'So, what d'you reckon then?' As if he's just introduced Shane to his new girlfriend and is keen to hear his verdict.

'Really great!' Despite everything, Shane is fond of Boris and appreciates the £9.25 he's spent on plectrums over the past three years. And he doesn't have it in him to crush his enthusiasm.

'Been all over the country with me,' Boris adds as he climbs out of the cab. 'Tell you what, mate, you can't beat that feeling of freedom.'

No, you can, Shane thinks, as his gaze alights upon a sticker on the back door. *If this van's a-rockin' don't come a-knockin'*, it reads, with a crude illustration of a quivering VW camper. Catching him staring at it, Boris chortles. 'Historic artefact, that!'

'Ha! Yeah.'

'So, whereabouts are you planning to go again?'

Right now? Shane muses. A psychiatric facility might be appropriate because clearly, anyone who thought this might be a good idea needs professional help. 'Just a little tour up north,' he replies.

'Lovely. Do you good, I reckon. You're looking a bit strained, if you don't mind me saying. Putting in too many hours in that shop.' Shane shrugs, and then, because he can't think of anything else he can possibly do, he thanks Boris profusely as he accepts the van's keys and offers to book him an Uber home. 'Nah, mate. You don't need to do that. The walk'll do me good.'

'Okay, if you're sure?' Shane asks.

Boris nods and grins and pulls another roll-up from his jacket pocket. Giving Doris a final slap on her haunches, he lights his cigarette and saunters off down the street.

14

JOSIE

A scruffy white van with a dent in its side is parked at the end of the quiet side street. No, that can't be it. It looks more like an ambulance. The campervan mustn't be here yet.

Of more immediate concern is the fact that the moisture in my body seems to have gone to the wrong places. My mouth is so parched I can't swallow, yet my hands are soaked in sweat. Last night I was full of bravado, having had several boosting messages from friends: *It's an adventure! Have fun! What's the worst that can happen?* But this morning I woke up with The Fear, glad that at least I'd turned down Shane's offer to pick me up in the campervan. The prospect of him bowling up at my flat was a bridge too far. I'd have felt obliged to make him coffee, and have him check out my place and maybe judge me on it. To me it's home, and I love all my clutter and trinkets – but I'm not sure what Shane would make of it. And what if Lloyd had still been swaggering around in his extremely thigh-revealing shorts? It's not that I'm ashamed of my boyfriend – far from it – but I could imagine Shane thinking, well... *something* at least.

I breathe in deeply, trying to quell my rising sense of panic.

Hang on – did I take my pill this morning? I don't think so. It hits me that, in my haphazard approach to packing, and shuddering as I stuffed in Ravi's Polaroid camera, I've forgotten one crucial item.

My antidepressants aren't in my rucksack.

That's because they're still sitting in the bathroom cabinet at home.

Five days in a van with Shane and no head pills! Briefly, I consider rushing back home to fetch them. What does it matter if I'm late? We're not on a strict time schedule. I weigh up the hassle involved with the blessed relief of being in possession of my meds and decide I can't face it. I'll just have to self-medicate through this. As white wine is my preference, I hope the campervan has a fridge. But actually, I'm quite prepared to drink it lukewarm. This an emergency, after all.

My rucksack is weighing heavily on my back, my ancient sleeping bag billowing about like a badly tethered windsock. I cross the road, passing a low-rise maisonette block with small, scrubby gardens at the front. The street is filled with haphazardly parked cars bumped up on kerbs and jutting out into the road. Hopefully one of them will move before the campervan arrives.

Calm down, I tell myself. Whatever happens, I'm getting out of town, having a little break away from everything: being shunned by Cora, nagged about commodifying my feet and worrying myself senseless about finding a new job. And what was it that my friend Nisha said last night? *If it's really awful, you can duck out early, can't you? Catch a train home. I hate to say it, but Ravi will never know.*

And now, farther down the street – next to the ambulance, in fact – I spot one of those A-frame signs sitting on the pavement. *Back Alley Music*, it says, with an arrow pointing to the left. To an alley, in fact. So this is it. This is Shane's shop and any minute now the van will be here, and we'll be off.

A man emerges from the alley. It's Shane, in a black T-shirt and jeans, looking extremely preoccupied. I watch, hanging back a little, as he makes for the closed back door of the ambulance, bends slightly, and starts to scrub at something. Whatever it is, he's going at it furiously with some kind of scourer or cloth. Why is he doing that? Surely the ambulance can't be anything to do with him.

I take another fortifying deep breath and stop a short distance away. 'Hi!' I say.

He spins around and his face brightens. 'Josie. Hi! I was just, um—' He brandishes a Brillo pad at me. 'Just, er...'

'Doing a spot of cleaning?'

'Yeah!' He laughs awkwardly and rakes at the back of his head. 'Just thought I'd spruce it up a bit.'

My gaze falls to the spot he's been scrubbing at. Looks like the remains of a sticker, still clinging on. 'This... isn't *it*, is it?' I ask. 'This isn't the van?'

His jaw seems to tighten and he emits a small groan. 'It is, I'm afraid.' The wet Brillo pad drips onto the ground. 'Josie, I'm really sorry,' he says quickly. 'I feel like such an idiot. Honestly, I had no idea it'd be like this...' He looks away briefly and his cheeks redden. 'I realise I should've checked. Or at least found out what kind of van it was. I thought it might be a bit basic, but the way he talked about it, all the trips he's done—'

'And he definitely said it was a campervan?' I cut in.

'Well, yes. Yes, of course!' he says forcefully, then seems to catch himself. 'I'm sorry. I'm making this sound like Boris misled me, but he didn't. I just imagined—'

'A cute campervan?' I suggest. 'Like a classic VW in pale blue or pea green, with curtains?'

A smile flickers over his lips. 'There *are* curtains, actually. Of a sort.'

'Well, that's okay then.' I laugh dryly. 'Look, this isn't your fault. If someone offers to lend you their campervan, then that's what you'd expect, isn't it?'

Shane looks at me and nods resignedly. 'Okay, so we can just forget about it. Forget the trip, I mean. Explain to Pam and Kamal—'

'Is that what *you* want?' I ask. Because now I'm here – with no job to go to and having lugged my rucksack halfway across London – I'm not sure I want to duck out.

'I want to do what's right for Ravi,' Shane says with a shrug. 'But the thing is—'

'People convert all kinds of vehicles into campervans, don't they?' I interrupt. 'Who cares what it looks like on the outside? As long as it's fitted out, and we have the basics...'

'Well, that's the thing...'

'*What's* the thing?'

'Let me show you.' He sighs heavily and, with a firm wrench, hauls open the back door.

I stare in and my heart seems to plummet. 'Oh,' is all I can say. Because the vehicle hasn't been 'converted' at all – it's just an ambulance with all of its fittings and medical stuff stripped out, leaving nothing. There is a bed – a bed *singular*. Or rather, a mattress on the floor.

I stare at it wordlessly. It's not that I expected luxury; that's not the point. It's the fact that this arrangement would mean Shane and I lying together at night – *sleeping* together – which of course is unthinkable—

'Oh, hey!' A tall, rangy man with fine sandy hair and a small, neat beard has joined us.

'Josie, this is Fletch,' Shane says distractedly. 'My partner in the shop. Fletch, this is Josie.'

'Nice to meet you.' He grins, his eyes glinting with amusement behind chunky, black-framed specs. 'So, what d'you think of your accommodation?'

I choke out a feeble laugh. 'It's not quite what I expected.'

'Nope. Thought it might not be.' I catch Shane throwing him a quick look. *Please leave us alone,* is how I'd interpret it.

'So, what're you gonna do?' Fletch asks brightly.

'Not quite sure yet,' Shane murmurs. I sense him deliberately trying to exclude his friend from the discussion we clearly need to have.

'Could you hire an actual camper?' Fletch suggests. 'There must be loads of places—'

'Oh, no, I don't think so,' I say quickly. Not without a job, I can't. Not when I don't know how I'm going to get through the next month. Admittedly, Lloyd's foot-focussed enterprise is becoming more appealing, and didn't he say he'd take care of all the admin and the uploading of pics?

'How about booking hotels then?' Fletch asks. Clearly, he isn't up for being left out of this. He whips out his phone from a pocket and frowns at it. 'What's your first port of call?'

'Er, Grimsby,' I reply.

'Fletch, it's fine,' Shane says firmly, but his friend is already on booking.com, assuming the role of Trip Leader.

'Place here. Four-star average. Free hot breakfast.' He flashes the screen at me. 'Not bad, eh?'

'Yeah, we'll just have a minute, mate,' Shane says, at which Fletch nods, finally understanding that he's not needed, and he lopes away into the alley.

I look at Shane. 'What d'you think?'

'I guess he's right. One of us could stay in hotels. I mean *you,* obviously. This is all my fault, so I'll pay.'

'You're not paying for five nights in hotels,' I exclaim, 'while you sleep in the van. How would that be fair?' He shrugs. 'Look,' I add, 'I might as well be honest. I'm pretty broke at the moment. The only way I can do this is if we keep costs to the absolute minimum. So—' I tip my head towards the van '—how about we just do this as we planned? It's clean, at least. And we do have our sleeping bags.'

Shane nods thoughtfully, as if turning this over. 'Yeah, we do.'

'Although, obviously, as there's no shower or anything—'

'We'll have to stay on campsites,' he finishes.

'Yeah. But that'd be okay, wouldn't it? The van will just be somewhere to crash at the end of the day.' I'm trying to not even consider the many, many other hours we'll be spending together – the *non-sleeping* hours – which I have no idea how we'll fill. We haven't even discussed what our plans will be. Should I have brought Buckaroo?

'I guess so,' Shane says, seeming to relax a little now. 'Shall we have a quick coffee in the shop, then? Before we set off?'

'That'd be great.'

He bangs the ambulance door shut, and we head along the alleyway and into the shop, where I gaze around in amazement. 'Wow!' I exclaim. Gleaming guitars are hung along one wall, and rows of golden saxophones and silver trumpets are perched expectantly on stands. Everything is immaculate and beautifully displayed.

Fletch looks up from behind the counter and chuckles. 'Not what you expected?'

'The shop, you mean?' I smile. 'I wasn't really sure what to expect,' I add truthfully.

'It's a labour of love,' Shane says with a grin. Then, 'Any coffee on the go, Fletch?'

'Sure,' Fletch says, disappearing through a door behind the counter.

'Honestly, I think it's wonderful,' I say, remembering a couple of excitable women who'd tumbled into the bookshop last week. Clearly tipsy from lunch, they were obviously delighted to have discovered us. 'What a gorgeous little place!' one exclaimed. 'Thank God there are still unique little shops like this left in the world!' Shane and Fletch's place is just as special. Briefly, I wonder if Rupert has replaced me yet.

Fletch reappears with two mugs of coffee and hands them to us. 'So, you're sticking to the van option?' he asks.

I turn to Shane. 'Looks like it, doesn't it?'

He nods with a wry smile and sips his coffee. 'Yeah, I reckon we'll be all right.'

'You'll be fine,' Fletch asserts. 'But if anything untoward happens, you can always whack on the blue light.'

'It doesn't have a blue light any more,' Shane remarks.

'Pity, that,' I say, taking a gulp of strong coffee. Because the reality is, I'm about to share a mattress with Shane for five days. And if that's not an emergency situation, I don't know what is.

15

I have done so many things with Shane.

Some of these I've banished from my brain in order to survive five nights sharing a mattress with him. But now my head fills with less contentious memories – like all those hours we spent chatting, and the times we got drunk together, far more than I can count. All the gigs we played, and the night I laughed, rather cruelly, when a drumstick flew out of his hand and pinged right off the stage, hitting a man on the head. That time we lay together on the sparse, parched grass in the park, when he insisted he didn't need sunscreen because he 'never burned'. Because obviously, Shane wasn't a normal boy, but one with skin made from asbestos.

I have dabbed calamine lotion onto his tender back and shoulders. I have run to his house, yelling that he had to come over because my parents were out and a crow had somehow flown down the chimney into our living room. It was flapping around madly, crashing into Mum's prized shepherdess ornaments and hitting the window with a thud. Unfazed, Shane had cornered the bird and somehow wrapped it gently in a tea towel and carried it to the back door and set it free. I'd have been no more awestruck if he'd rescued a baby from a burning building.

'My hero!' I'd joked, and hugged and kissed him, our kisses growing deeper and hotter and then—*Don't even go there!* I command myself as I steal a quick look at Shane. It's all I can do *not* to keep watching him, as this is an entirely new experience for me. Because what I have never done is sat in a vehicle being driven by him.

Perhaps it's because I haven't had my pill today that everything seems sharper than I'm used to – as if my internal settings have been altered. Whatever it is, I cannot get over the fact that somehow, the boy with choppy home-cut hair and a love of charity shop overcoats and Findus Crispy Pancakes is now a properly adult man, currently driving an ambulance at a steady 60 mph as if it's *nothing*.

Dale, Cora's dad, didn't drive. (He didn't do much apart from getting stoned, drinking lager and wearing the same underpants three days running.) However, in my late twenties in London, I felt obliged to learn and bought a terrible old Fiat that belched thick black exhaust fumes, which caused people to stop and stare. The plan was to *force* some semblance of grown-upness upon myself, as if possessing these things – driving licence, car – would magically turn me into the sophisticated woman I yearned to be. However, I hated driving, and when Cora was around five, the rusty old heap finally expired, never to be replaced.

'Great,' my friend Gaby teased me. 'That's saved you cleaning it out!' Admittedly it had become little more than a receptacle for crisp packets and withered fruit.

Travelling in a vintage ambulance is an entirely different experience. 'D'you know how old this thing is?' I ask.

'Um... mid-nineties, I think,' Shane replies.

Ah, the era of listening to Supergrass with a bottle of Hooch. Kate Moss in that crinkly see-through dress, accessorised by Johnny Depp. Discovering I was pregnant after a brief reconciliation with Dale, my abject horror soon reshaping itself first into stoical acceptance, then quiet delight.

'Before mobile phones and the Internet,' I remark. 'Was that before suspension too?'

He laughs. 'Not exactly a smooth drive, is it?'

'It's like being rattled inside a gigantic tin.' Already it feels as if my fillings are being shaken loose, one by one. Yes, weirdly, this feels interesting rather than alarming. Perhaps that's also due to the lack of pills. I am hyper aware of every bodily sensation and wonder if this is the new me: tingly with nerves, yet somehow feeling fully alive.

We've slipped into silence now, and I gaze out at the endless flat, green landscape. For the last two hours on the road, we've been alternating light, inconsequential chit-chat with quiet spells over the whine of the engine. I've already decided that Shane is something of a closed book, and that I'm unlikely to get to know him as a fully-fledged adult on this trip. *Fine,* I tell myself. If this is the tone we're adopting for the entire five days, then I'm okay with that. It's not as if I want to spill out my innermost feelings – about our shared past, my life now or any of that. In fact, I'd rather not.

The silence stretches, beginning to feel a little taut. When the rain starts, Shane makes a brief remark about the windscreen wipers being a bit crap. More miles, more rain. The engine grinds along stoically. I mentally calculate that between now and the blissful moment when we arrive back in London and I bolt out of this van amounts to… something like *120 hours*. A full 120 hours of community service for my crimes! For telling Cora that Zack is 'such a great guy!' while secretly hating him.

For giving him the finger behind his back. For faking orgasms with Lloyd, yet saying the sex was 'amazing', even though I've often lost concentration part-way through the proceedings, wondering instead where my lost slipper might have got to (could it have fallen down the back of the radiator where I'd put it to dry, after spilling coffee on it?).

In the absence of playing I spy or listening to music (amazingly, this ancient van possesses no sound system) I continue to mentally list further sins.

'Borrowing' and then shrinking Lloyd's sweater and saying I'd never seen it.

Concealing said sweater under a load of vegetable peelings and cold spaghetti in my kitchen bin.

Nicking a big bar of Cadbury's Dairy Milk from the Co-op in 1986.

Me and Shane and Ravi guzzling my parents' Cinzano and smoking a copious amount of cigarettes while they were out and telling them we'd burnt some toast.

And at work, although innocent of the crime I've been accused of, I have done other bad things. Such as: throwing up in the back room sink after Gaby's fifty-fifth birthday party. Claiming to have 'no idea' about the source of the sour smell that lingered when Rupert returned from an errand, and blaming 'the drains'. Allowing an elderly lady to bring in her toy poodle, despite our strict no dogs policy, another time Rupert was out. After the pooch had leapt up onto his upholstered swivel chair and done a little widdle, I'd denied all knowledge of how the wet patch got there. Oh God – Rupert probably thought he'd done it himself, that he has a dribbling problem. I basically gaslighted him.

So I deserve this, really: being trapped with Shane in a van all the way to Grimsby. I am aware of yet more oestrogen draining from my body, down through the soles of my peasant trotters and the base of the van, finally dripping out onto the M1. And I wonder if Shane, a mere arm's width away from me, can sense this.

'Doing okay there?' I ask pleasantly, to break the lull.

'Yep, I'm good,' Shane replies. 'You okay?'

'I'm fine.' *Although I'm pretty sure that the effects of yesterday's pill have now fully worn off.* 'Let me know if you want me to take over,' I add recklessly.

'What, driving?'

'Sure!'

'Um... I'm okay,' he says. 'Unless you'd like to?'

'I'm fine if you are.' We settle back into silence punctuated by the odd inconsequential remark. It's as if we are work colleagues thrown together – tasked with driving to a retail park to collect some refurbished office chairs.

We stop at a service station for fuel, batteries for the lamp, plus coffee and cheese toasties, flattened to extreme thinness and oozing oil. The rain is heavier now, sheeting down the café window, and people are running to their cars with jackets pulled up over their heads. As I chew on my toastie I try to calculate how many of this particular kind of joyless snack or meal we'll eat together over the next five days.

I sip my coffee and glance at Shane, wondering if he's starting to regret this. 'So, what d'you remember about Grimsby?' I ask.

He gnaws away thoughtfully and then replies, 'Our first gig away from home, wasn't it? No friends to come and support us. We didn't know a soul.'

'Yeah, it was pretty scary.' Until then we'd stuck to our home town's familiar pub venues, where our loyal gang could be relied upon to show up and be disproportionately enthusiastic. But the tour had felt like something else entirely, and Ravi had insisted that we'd rise to the challenge. She was always in charge. She'd invented our 'style' (a mishmash of whatever we could fling together), wrote all our music and announced that, with six songs in our repertoire, of course we were a *proper band* now, ready to play at the world's most iconic music venues.

The Laughing Haddock in Grimsby! The Mucky Duck in Huddersfield! She was unstoppable.

Nerves aside, as the tour loomed, the thought of being 'on the road' with my best friends – with Shane especially – wasn't entirely terrible. We'd have a whole week away, the three of us together. How thrilling it would be to stay in ropey guest houses, Ravi's uncle's caravan, Shane's great-auntie's box room and on the living room floor of some distant family friend of mine. Ravi sprayed her hair neon pink from an aerosol can (we knew nothing about climate change) and Shane grudgingly let her hack at his floppy dark hair with kitchen scissors. My choppy crop – also home-cut – was bleached by Ravi in her impossibly glamorous bathroom (jacuzzi bath! Fluffy peach carpet that fitted around the loo!). She made our 'stage outfits' – spotty miniskirts worn with wide studded belts – that caused her mum to laugh and roll her eyes. We yearned for Chelsea Girl and Miss Selfridge, but these thrilling emporiums of style were a million light years away in Bradford. Meanwhile, Ravi forced Shane into a Breton top with a ripped neckline and persuaded him that a little make-up would look great.

What a ragbag we were, barely competent onstage, yet bubbling with the joy of all being together. Ravi made all of that happen, just as she is making this happen on this bleak, wet, Saturday afternoon. *She was so ill, and I didn't even know.* My vision fuzzes and I clear my throat. 'I don't remember much about the actual town, though,' I announce, checking Shane's set expression. 'Grimsby, I mean.'

'Neither do I,' he says.

I take another bite of my now cold toastie and swallow it down. 'Well, it *was* a very long time ago.' A lull settles. 'That was when Ravi did your make-up,' I remind him.

'Only eyeliner,' he says with a grin. 'And I thought it looked pretty cool.'

'It did! And she teased up your hair into a little quiff, remember?'

He chuckles. 'I do remember that.'

'"We're doing something with that barnet, Shane!"' I mimic her strident tones.

'"You look like a bloody geography teacher!"' he chimes in. 'And I did. So square and boring, compared to you two…'

But you weren't square and boring at all. You were adorable with your shy, off-centre smile and that choppy brown hair, constantly flicking into your dark eyes. I wanted to look at you so much that I had to keep telling myself: STOP LOOKING, YOU IDIOT! Or Ravi would realise, and the unspoken rule was that nothing would upset the dynamics of our little trio…

'…in those outfits,' he continues. 'Those matching skirts you used to wear. What did Ravi make them out of?'

'Pillowcases,' I remind him.

'Your mum was worried about you going out like that.' He looks across the table at me with a smile.

'Yes, but she was *more* worried about me electrocuting myself onstage. My parents were terrified of electricity, remember?'

'Oh yeah! All the plugs pulled out of their sockets at night…'

'They thought our appliances would catch fire. Even the kettle and toaster. They were worried about us being incinerated in our beds…'

Shane smiles fondly, and I catch a wistful look crossing his green eyes. As if, for a moment, he was right back there. I think of how we kissed, that day with the crow, and push the thought away again. We were just young and reckless, and everyone kissed everybody back then. I was only *thanking* him.

'Your parents were always lovely,' Shane adds.

I smile. 'You know they were so fond of you,' I tell him, and he flushes. Of course, everyone knew what Pete, his stepdad, was like, although Shane was always reluctant to go into any of that.

'You said they've moved to Northumberland?'

'Yeah. I was really surprised, actually. Maybe I was the one who'd held them back all that time.'

'They didn't want to uproot you?'

'Possibly.' To my shame, I'd always assumed that they weren't brave enough to relocate and make a new life for themselves. That they'd remain in our little terraced council house until the end of their days.

I finish my coffee and push my cup aside, relieved that we've managed these first few hours together at least. But something is niggling and now, before we're faced with The Mattress Situation, seems like the best time to address it. 'Shane,' I start, 'I was thinking... maybe we should have a few rules on this trip?'

He frowns. 'Rules?'

'Yeah.' I nod firmly. 'For one thing, we're going to be driving an awful lot. So I think we should share it.'

'Of course! No problem. Drive the next leg if you like—'

'Maybe not this bit,' I say quickly. 'Maybe later.'

'Fine. Just say, whenever you want to.'

'And if one of us wants to stop somewhere, or go off and do our own thing, we should say so. Shouldn't we?'

His eyes widen in surprise. 'Well, er... yeah. Of course. Absolutely.'

I take a breath, wondering why this doesn't seem to be coming out quite right. All I mean is, we should have the option to please ourselves – to take time out from each other if we need to. I push a hand through my dishevelled hair, wondering if I actually brushed it this morning. 'All I mean,' I blunder on, 'is that we should both feel we can say what we want, and what we need, because I don't think this trip is going to be easy.' It's all tumbled out in a rush, and something flickers in his eyes. He looks hurt, I realise, and a little confused.

'No,' Shane says quietly. 'I don't suppose it is.'

And with that, as we leave the service station café and hurry through the rain, I wish I could stuff my stupid words back into my mouth.

16

SHANE

Shane lied to Josie when he said he didn't remember anything about Grimsby. He remembers everything about that first stop of their tour. Every tiny detail is inked on the inside of his brain.

They'd been nervous, yes – but Grimsby wasn't *that* far away from home. Just a two-hour drive in the lumbering estate car, which Ravi – the sole driver among them – had borrowed from her uncle in Leeds. Devoid of style or class, by some miracle the tank-like vehicle contained all their gear (although the boot wouldn't shut properly).

They thought it was fantastic. Shane especially as, mixed in with nervy anticipation, was sheer relief to be getting out of his cabbage-smelling house for a week. In the lead-up to the tour, rehearsals had ramped up, and he'd been spending every available minute in the Kapoors' garage, where his drum kit was set up permanently (he'd never have been allowed to play at home). Pam was so good about that. 'You'll be great,' she assured them. And she'd given Shane that look – the look which said *we know, and we care* – when she'd noticed the bruising around his cheekbone and eye.

He was fine, he always insisted – even to Josie, who questioned him openly from time to time: *You all right, Shane? Want to stay over at ours? You can sleep on the sofa. Mum says it's okay.*

'Me and Pete had a bit of an argument,' he'd tell her. 'It was nothing, really. Looks a lot worse than it is.' What Josie and Ravi did know was to *never* phone his house, but to yell for him from the street instead. Because the wall-mounted phone in the hall was for emergencies only. Pete was very strict about its usage. The girls didn't know that after Pete had whacked Shane that last time, his mum had used the forbidden telephone to call the GP. Which meant, Shane realised, that she was actually worried.

Doctor Draper? Our Shane fell over and was unconscious for a bit. Will he be all right? Should I bring him in? Then, after presumably being reassured by the perpetually inebriated GP: *Right, okay. No, he's awake now. I'll keep an eye on him then.*

There would be none of that in Grimsby. And as the wide, flat Humber Estuary came into view, Shane realised that something monumental had switched in him. Something so big, he couldn't put it into words.

He felt happy and free – and more than that, he felt *safe.*

* * *

This time is different. Now he has nothing to run away from. But still, a little respite from Elaine is welcome, and from the rattly ambulance he takes in the undulating countryside on what's turned out to be a mild and pleasant afternoon. Despite his love of London, being surrounded by fields lifts something in him. He grew up roaming around in the scrubby woods and rolling farmland beyond the estate, and nature has left its traces on him.

They have turned off the main road, and Shane slows down as the narrow lane snakes back and forth, bordered on both sides by dense woodland. Josie has booked a night at a campsite called Paradise Vale, on the outskirts of town. He hopes it lives up to its name. 'How much further?' he asks.

'About a mile,' Josie replies, checking her phone. As directions follow – 'Next left, then the sign should be coming up' – it strikes him that this could almost be a normal scenario. Two friends after a lengthy drive, one consulting the map as they near their destination. A shared sense of relief that finally they are here for the night.

'D'you think it matters that we're not actually staying in town?' Josie asks.

'You mean, we're not strictly following Ravi's schedule?' He turns briefly and smiles.

'Yeah.' She nods. 'It does say Grimsby, not a campsite out in the countryside.'

'But this was the nearest one, wasn't it?' he reminds her. 'I don't think she'll be splitting hairs.' He catches a flash of her smile, and it warms something in him.

'No, that's true.' *This is going to be okay,* he thinks as he turns into the lane leading to the campsite.

'This looks all right, doesn't it?' Josie says as he pulls up beside the site office.

Shane takes in the rows of spotless motorhomes, a camping area dotted with a few tents and a lake gleaming in the distance. 'Yeah, it does,' he says. And it *is*, he thinks. They have survived being snared up in traffic, and five hours on the road, without anything difficult having come up. They are here for the night and, before that, they have many hours to fill – it's not even six o'clock. Following the rain shower, the air feels clean and fresh, and he breathes it in gratefully as they climb out of the van.

Shane can taste salt in the air. Gulls squawk loudly overhead, and he remembers the three of them making endless fish-processing plant jokes when they pulled up in town, all those years ago. Someone in his family had worked in one of the fish factories here, Shane had told them. It was his late father – this was the only fact Shane had ever been able to extract about him – but he didn't want to go into all that.

'What does that even mean?' Ravi had asked with a shudder. 'Process them into what?'

As he and Josie make their way into the little wooden office, he remembers the air smelling just like this, and how he'd filled his lungs with it. He remembers the guest house in town, and how they'd giggled after the owner – in her pink velour tracksuit – had shown them their room and left them to it. Bunk beds, as if they were kids, plus a double bed. 'My family room,' the woman had announced in her raspy smoker's voice.

That felt right, Shane decided later as he lay there on the bottom bunk. Josie and Ravi were his family; the family he'd chosen. Or rather, they'd chosen him.

He'd felt the luckiest boy in the world that night. But now, as an amiable man in a flat cap tells them where to park the van, he tries to ready himself for a very different sort of night.

He is trying not to think about that.

17

JOSIE

'So, I've been looking into it more and it seems like it's pretty crowded.'

I'm striding away from the van, across the damp grass towards the low stone wall at the edge of the site. When I saw Lloyd's name on my phone, I knew I didn't want Shane to hear any of this.

'What's crowded?' I ask.

'The foot market!' Lloyd exclaims. 'Y'know, when it started, you really could make a packet just with your basic pics.'

'How d'you know all this?'

He makes a *pfff* sound. 'Everyone does.' Do they? There are many things which apparently everyone knows but I do not. Like how to tidy my pubes without triggering a shaving rash. How to create a capsule wardrobe incorporating what the magazines term a 'crisp white shirt'. And why vintage trainers are so much more expensive than new ones. Lloyd has a vast collection, but even more mind-boggling is his highly organised tool store in his spare room. Screwdrivers attached to a board on the wall in ascending order of size! An enticingly named 'biscuit joiner' and several jigsaws, which until then I'd thought were only ever puzzles with lots of pieces! These days I'm hardly ever invited over. 'Much cosier here at yours,' he's insisted.

'So I'm thinking we need to go more niche,' Lloyd continues.

'Niche? What d'you mean, niche?'

'Well, for one thing, we can make a feature of your USP.'

'What's my USP?' I ask.

'Your unique selling point.'

'Yes, I know that,' I say impatiently. 'But what is it?'

'Um... your little *deformity*.'

'You're saying my feet are deformed now? I'm a deformed peasant?'

'I mean your little toes, babe.' Ah, I know what he's on about now. My tiny, *misshapen* little toes, he means – crushed up against the others as if cowering in fright. The result of cramming my hooves into shoes that were far too narrow all through the eighties, when Lloyd was a mere child. 'And we'll also need them in action,' he adds.

'My deformed little toes?' I lower myself onto the wall.

He laughs. 'No, your whole feet. We need them *doing* stuff.'

'Like what?' I ask.

'Anything. You can come up with some ideas—'

'What, like holding a paintbrush? Or beating the ingredients for a cake?'

He snorts. 'Maybe... but we could start with crushing things? That's popular.'

'Crushing what?' Crisps? Hula Hoops? Or grapes for wine – maybe *that* would work. I've already done a tour of the site, having told Shane I wanted to 'get my bearings', but really it was to check for licensed premises. My findings have revealed that there are none. 'I'm really not sure about this,' I admit.

'We'll think of something,' Lloyd announces, all jovial and

clearly revved up about the project. 'Don't worry, I'll do the videos.'

'You never mentioned videos!' I exhale slowly, aware of a dull, heavy feeling in my stomach that something isn't quite right. That I've made yet another mistake to add to my extensive list. That *this* is the reason why I can't lose myself, sex-wise, with him. It's not the head pills, or the fact that that part of me is broken.

I really tried to focus – to lose myself in my fantasy – that last time we did it. Emilio Estevez. Andrew McCarthy. *All* of the Brat Pack – even the one nobody fancied whose name I forget – were going at me as I clung helplessly to my fridge. It was rocking dangerously, banging so hard against the kitchen wall that my magnets flew off and clattered all over the floor (thank God I took out the extended appliance warranty!). I dredged up my filthiest perversions from my mental hard drive – the one that would be carried out of my flat, sheathed in polythene, if the authorities ever found out. Yet even that didn't work.

Seemingly unconcerned, Lloyd sprang off me, stretching out his arms and rotating his shoulders, as if that were his work all done and dusted. For all his pervy foot talk, it turns out he's a missionary man. Nice and straightforward – job done.

It was early morning and within seconds he was pulling on his clothes. 'In a hurry?' I asked, trying not to sound put out. I didn't want us to part on a bad note, and he's a kind man, really. He's offered to put up some kitchen shelves for me while I'm away. 'Got to get off to a new job,' he said by way of an explanation. 'Bit of a tricky one so I want to make a head start.' Something felt off, I decided. But I couldn't put my finger on what it was.

'Well, yeah,' he is telling me now. 'Videos are what the

punters like. And if they ask for anything you don't want to do, we'll just block them.'

I focus on Doris's sturdy front end as I try to process this. 'What d'you mean? What kind of stuff might they want?'

'Oh, you know,' he says blithely. 'Specific stuff. Custom stuff. Other body parts—'

'Lloyd, I'm not showing anyone my tits!'

'You won't have to!' he blusters. 'Not if you don't want to. You won't have to do *anything* you don't feel comfortable with...'

'Oh, won't I? Thank you!' I snap.

'You can just be firm,' he reasons.

'Right. Just say no?' I realise by the ensuing silence that my reference to the eighties anti-drug campaign is lost on Lloyd. I keep noticing that our points of reference are wildly different. When he spotted my ancient crimping irons he asked, 'Is that for waffles?' When I mentioned Curly Wurlys, he thought I was talking about my pubes. I know these things shouldn't matter. I never wanted a boyfriend for prolonged reminiscences over Beloved Confectionery of Our Past, and it's not as if I want to introduce a Space Hopper to our sex life (although maybe it would help?). But still, it highlights the gulf between us.

'So, what d'you think?' he asks. No *How's your trip been so far?* He hasn't even asked where I am.

'We'll talk about it when I get back,' I mutter.

'Could you just send me a few pics while you're away, in different environments? Just to get us started?'

'No, I can't,' I say wearily. 'I'm going now, I've got stuff to do—'

'Oh, c'mon, babe! You're in the country, aren't you? Some dirt would be good. Get your little tootsies all muddy and covered in soil—'

'Lloyd, I have to go. Bye.' Having ended the call abruptly, I get up from the wall, realising my bottom is damp. I find Shane in the van, sitting on the mattress, back against the wall, with a book on his lap.

'Everything all right?' he asks, looking up.

'Yeah, fine. Just my boyfriend.' I grimace.

He nods, raising a brow. 'Right.'

'Just something he wanted to discuss,' I add, conscious of my cheeks burning.

'Ah, okay.' I will him to not ask about my relationship, because right now, I'm not sure what I'd tell him.

'Are you starving?' Shane smiles. 'Because I am.'

'I am, actually,' I say, grateful to be pulled from the world of *feet-doing-stuff* to the practical matter of what we are going to eat. 'I did notice a chippy on the way,' I add.

'Did you? That'll do!' Shane says brightly.

So we leave the campsite, and as we stroll together along the lane, I manage to push all thoughts of Lloyd and our prospective 'punters' from my mind. We eat our steamy fish and chips with our fingers, discussing what we might do tomorrow and when we should set off for Bridlington, our next port of call. Basic, practical stuff, as if all of this is utterly normal. 'Have you checked the weather?' I ask.

'Yeah. Looks promising,' he says. 'We could tick off a few sights, couldn't we? The harbour, the castle...'

'And eat more chips?' I smile.

'Why not?' He laughs. 'And what about that pub we played at?'

'The Laughing Haddock.'

'That's it.' The smile crinkles his eyes. 'We'll need to find it. We have to take photos, remember? You did bring the camera, didn't you?'

'Of course I did!'

'Great,' he says, as we drop our cartons into a bin. For a few minutes, we walk in silence. Neither of us has mentioned our sleeping arrangements again. It's the elephant in the van, and dusk is only just starting to fall. We can't go to bed at 9 p.m., like children. 'D'you fancy a drink somewhere?' I ask.

'Oh, yes,' Shane enthuses. 'Good idea.' He consults his phone. 'There's a pub ten minutes away. Okay to walk there?'

'Yes, no problem,' I say. Anything to delay going back to the van.

Still on the outskirts of town, we pass the campsite entrance and a beleaguered-looking shop with rolls of carpet heaped against the dusty window. A squat brown dog is tethered outside and growls ominously.

For a minute or two we walk in silence and I wonder, briefly, how we're going to get through this trip. But now the pub is in sight, and although it's shedding its white paint, and looks as if it has seen better days, my spirits lift.

A drink is definitely required if I'm going to be able to get through the night.

18

Shane pushes open the door and we step inside. The tables are scuffed, the leatherette seats peeling, and everything looks as if it might be a little sticky. Apart from the young man behind the bar who's chatting idly to two elderly customers, the pub is otherwise deserted. But a real fire is flickering in the hearth, and through the frosted windows the sky is darkening. Once we're settled by the fireplace with our drinks, it's certainly cosier than the van.

Shane leans forward, looking thoughtful. 'Y'know, I could sleep in the cab,' he offers. 'Maybe that'd be better?'

'Don't be crazy,' I exclaim. 'You wouldn't sleep a wink in there.' So our nocturnal arrangements have been playing on his mind too.

'Honestly,' he insists, 'it'd be fine!'

'It wouldn't, Shane. There's no need for you to do that,' I say firmly. With that settled, we try to fathom out what we might do at each of our stops. 'Well, we need to visit all of our venues,' I remind him, 'if they still exist.'

He nods, looking relieved that, at the very least, this will give a sense of purpose to our trip. 'Should we check, d'you think? Look them up?'

I sip my wine, considering this. 'I think we should turn up and see.'

'Yeah.' He smiles wryly. 'Keep that element of surprise.'

'Exactly!'

'I did look up a few other things we could do,' he adds.

'Really? What kind of things?'

'Oh, y'know.' He shrugs. 'A museum, a gallery... but I don't want to—'

'It's fine,' I insist. 'We need ideas!'

'What would *you* like to do?'

For a moment this stumps me. For a normal trip, I'd have no trouble making plans – but this isn't normal. It's certainly not a holiday, so what is it? Lloyd jokingly called it 'a pilgrimage' and insisted that he had no problem with it at all. *Aw, I get it, babe,* he teased. *Off on a jaunt with your old boyfriend, reliving old times? As long as you come back to me, that's all that matters!*

Shane was never my boyfriend, I insisted (yes, stuff happened – but it was too complicated to explain, and Lloyd had swiftly lost interest in the subject anyway). I wonder now what Shane's girlfriend – Elaine, her name is, he called out to her when I phoned – thinks about this. If she was cool about him heading off for five days with another woman? No reason why she shouldn't be. Naturally, I want to ask him about her, to know all about his life now. But I'd rather he just told me, instead of bombarding him with questions. So instead, I pull out Ravi's letter from my bag, and we study our old itinerary, as if we didn't know it off by heart.

'I'd like to swim,' I say. 'When we're by the sea, obviously.'

'Yeah, me too,' Shane enthuses. 'Packed your swimsuit?'

'Of course! Like a proper tourist...' For a reason I don't fully understand, I've brought my most unalluring costume: a navy-blue one-piece, elasticity almost gone, effectively matronly.

I look at Shane, wondering how he really feels, being stuck here in Grimsby with me. If it was ever top of his wish list – ha! – or if he wonders what possessed him to come. Because it's still a little weird between us as we stroll back towards Paradise Vale, with that sole mattress awaiting us. I'd have suggested another drink, if only to put off that terrible moment of *going to bed together.* But I wasn't picking up the vibe that he'd be keen.

Back at the campsite, feeling grubby after the journey, I head for the shower block. After shivering beneath the feeble dribble, I towel myself briskly, telling myself it'll be okay. He's probably feeling as weird about all this as I am. Still, to avoid any getting-changed-in-front-of-Shane awkwardness, I've brought my night-time attire out with me. First, it's big knickers, which I'd never wear under PJs normally – I mean, who does? But to not wear any would seem... *unseemly.* Then it's pyjamas, selected for maximum plainness, baggy and faded and way past their prime. Lloyd has never witnessed them. For all he knows I *always* sleep either naked, or in a slippery, highly flammable cami set.

At the mirror above the basins, I brush out my wet hair, registering how drawn I look. The flickering strip light is harsher than my bathroom light, and I perform a quick inventory of the coarser grey that's pushing its way through my highlights. Seemingly deepening creases – geographical faults – run from my nose to the outer corners of my mouth.

Is this what I'm really like now? Is this what Lloyd sees when he wakes up next to me? No wonder he smokes a lot of weed. Leaning against the bank of washbasins, I ping a 'Night honey!' message to him. He doesn't reply and it remains unread. Now

I'm thinking I'll just go with his plan to monetise my feet. I could certainly do with the cash. My friend Gaby has been on at me, insisting that Rupert 'can't just sack you, especially for something you didn't even do.' I can get legal aid, she's assured me. As a high-ranking HR person, she can advise me on employment law.

I rub at my face, wondering how my skin has turned so papery in the few hours since we left London, and whack on a blob of cheap moisturiser. I clean my teeth and pull on a sweater over my PJ top. Finally, like a child trying to avoid bedtime, I take a meandering route back to the van.

On the lake, a lone duck is gliding slowly. The moon is high and bright, and I watch a gauzy cloud passing over it. I'm grateful for the slightly hazing effect of a single large glass of wine – although it's not enough to dampen the crackling sensations happening in my brain right now, like tiny fireworks ricocheting off my skull.

So this is what happens as the last traces of those magical antidepressants leave the body. If I focus hard enough, could I make those precious pills fly north to me and land in my hand? For his whole life, my father has been devoted to his homing pigeons. I try to picture the flat white packet as one of Dad's beloved birds, miraculously finding its way from a bathroom cabinet in east London, delivers it to a campsite on the outskirts of Grimsby.

When that doesn't work, I quicken my pace and climb into the van. 'Hey,' Shane says. He is sitting up on the mattress in a plain white T-shirt, his bottom half already tucked into what looks like a box-fresh sleeping bag. Although he appears to be immersed in that book again, I'm not sure how he is managing to read in the feeble glow of the lamp.

'Hey,' I say, shutting the door firmly behind me. I notice that already, he has positioned himself on the farthest edge of the mattress. If this were a raft, I'd worry about him toppling off. I tug off my sweater, feeling horribly self-conscious in my awful pyjamas (this is not how I dreamed I'd look, if our paths ever crossed again!) and rummage in my rucksack for my book. Once I've located it, I plonk myself down on 'my' side, shivering as I pull my own sleeping bag round me as best I can.

'Broken zip,' I explain.

'Ah.'

'Haven't used it since me and Cora used to go camping when she was little.'

A look of concern crosses his face. 'Bit chilly, isn't it? Want to use mine?'

'No, it's fine!' *Calm down, for God's sake.* He didn't say, 'Want to get into mine?' We play the pretending-to-be-reading game until finally Shane murmurs, 'Let me know when you want to go to sleep.'

'Yeah, I will.' I close my book and focus instead on the silvery moonlight struggling through the rank, brown material taped up over the two rear windows. 'I'm pretty tired, actually,' I add.

'Me too.' Shane reaches for the lamp and clicks it off, and in a flurry of self-conscious shuffling, we wriggle fully into our sleeping bags. Shane, I notice, has fashioned a sweater into a pillow, so I grope for mine and do likewise.

All is quiet, apart from the sharp cry of a bird and the whisper of wind tickling the trees. I close my eyes, breathing in the sleeping bag scent of long-ago camping trips with Cora. I'm not sure if I can really smell it, or it's like the way you sniff at your wrist hours after squooshing on that perfume you loved but couldn't really afford, hoping to catch a hint of it. But I think it's still there, embedded in the faded peach-coloured fabric.

We went all over, the two of us, long after our little car had died: to Kent, Somerset, Wiltshire, even Wales one time. Anyplace we could get to by train, and then walk or catch a local bus to a campsite. I inhale the sweet, warm smell of my daughter and me, happily cuddled up together in our tent on a warm summer's night. I picture us cooking plump pink sausages over a fire and heating up spaghetti hoops in a little pan over our stove. Calming thoughts of blissful days, once Dale was permanently off the scene.

He'd pretty much broken off all contact by then, which was something of a relief. Although friends urged me to chase him for regular money, we were managing fine without him. Better than fine, in fact – and I'd rather we were left to our own devices rather than having him muscling in. We'd created a new way of living, just the two of us.

All is quiet now, apart from faint, distant voices somewhere on the campsite. Trying not to breathe weirdly, I will myself to tip over into sleep. 'Night, then,' Shane murmurs.

'Goodnight.' I lie there, as still as a rock in the darkness, calculating how many hours it is until dawn, and how many further hours until I am home again in my little flat. Already, Shane's breathing has slowed and deepened. I flick a terse gaze in his direction. What is it about men and their ability to just conk out like that, even in the most bizarre situations? A wave of resentment surges over me. He's probably in REM sleep already, dreaming blissfully! Good for him—

'Josie?' he says.

My heart thumps. 'Yes?'

'You awake?'

'No.' I smile, and a pause hangs in the still night air.

Shane turns and looks at me, his eyes gleaming in the dark. 'What d'you reckon Ravi's thinking now?'

I can't help smiling at that. 'I think she's laughing her arse off,' I say.

He chuckles softly and I close my eyes, thinking about Cora and me, tucked up cosily in our little tent. And somehow a small miracle happens, because the next thing I know, it is morning.

19

SHANE

In his brand-new sleeping bag, bought to demonstrate to Josie how sorted he is these days, Shane didn't sleep a wink. Yet weirdly, it didn't seem to drag on for weeks like the normal kind of sleepless night. Compare, say, a shop day with virtually zero customers and bugger all happening, with one that's filled with complicated orders for strings for a ukelele group in Toronto and an orchestra in Belarus and a kid having a blast on every saxophone in the shop and various men of a certain age ambling in to try this guitar and that guitar, with endless permutations of amp and pedal.

Last night was that sort of night. It was hectic, and not with urgent requests from orchestras and string ensembles, but with thoughts bouncing chaotically around in Shane's head, such as:

My God, I'm lying on a mattress in an ambulance with Josie.

Is this really happening or just a bizarre dream?

So, what happens tomorrow? (He checked the time, taking care not to wake her with the glow of his phone. 4.58 a.m.)

Am I going to be okay to drive this thing tomorrow?

Of course I am. I'm so wired right now I could drive to the moon.

Am I taking over with the driving, though?

Does she think I'm a sexist twerp who doesn't like being driven by a woman?

Josie said she's happy to do it. But does that mean she wants to?

Am I acting weird? Was that mad of me, to offer to sleep in the cab? He'd sleep out there on the grass if she wanted him to.

We're being overly polite and not talking about the stuff that really matters. Do we need to go over it all? Or is it better to pretend that none of it ever happened?

And – while all of that was rolling around in his brain – another more pressing line of enquiry was simmering away underneath.

What was that stuff going on with her boyfriend last night?

While Shane wasn't eavesdropping, he couldn't help overhearing certain fragments. 'I'm a deformed peasant?' 'You never mentioned videos.' 'Lloyd, I'm not showing anyone my tits!' He knows that Josie is currently out of work, and he's furious on her behalf with that arsehole at the bookshop. He is also trying not to make any wild assumptions over alternative career plans that her boyfriend might have in mind for her.

However, at precisely 6.04 a.m., Shane decided that he had already taken a strong dislike to this Lloyd person. *Should I ask if she's okay?* his thoughts raced on. *Tell her how sorry I am about what happened between us?* Finally, at around six thirty, he knew there was no point in lying there any longer. The sun was already squeezing its way through the grubby sack-like curtains at the van's back windows. Shane eased his exhausted corpse from his sleeping bag and delved into his neatly packed rucksack for a notebook and pen.

He tore off a sheet and wrote a note.

Going out for a walk, won't be long, hope you slept well.

He thought about adding 'Shane' or even 'Shane x'. But who else would it be from? Father Christmas? So he left it like that, placed next to the still-sleeping Josie, and as quietly as possible he opened the ambulance's back door and blinked in the retina-searing morning sun.

He crossed the campsite, breathing in the cool, fresh air and marvelling at the quietness of the place. Seemingly, not another soul was up and about yet. In the rumpled T-shirt and joggers he'd slept in – he hadn't wanted to disturb Josie by faffing about with his clothes – he left the site and walked in the direction of the pub they'd stopped off at last night. From there he continued into town, where neatly kept terraced cottages soon gave way to small businesses. A pet shop, a grocer's and a post office, all closed. Then finally he spotted a greasy spoon café. He checked the sign listing its opening hours and decided to wait.

This is where Shane is now, his spirits lifting at the thought of hot coffee and something to eat. Finally, a blonde ponytailed woman appears, smiling at him through the glass door and beckoning him in.

'Thanks,' he says, conscious of his dishevelled state. He runs a hand over his unkempt hair and asks for a couple of takeaway coffees and bacon rolls, wrapped in foil to keep them hot.

'There you go, love,' the woman says with a cheery smile.

By the time he arrives back at the campsite, Josie is up and showered, judging by her still-wet hair. 'You needn't have done that,' she says, as he hands over her coffee and roll. 'But thanks.'

'No problem,' Shane says. 'I was awake early and fancied a walk. Also, I realise I don't know if you eat bacon, or if you're vegetarian or—'

'I eat bacon,' she says with a grin. They perch on the lumpy stone wall and as they devour their breakfasts, Shane glances down at his T-shirt and joggers. 'I really need a shower,' he says apologetically.

'The facilities are fantastic.' Josie smiles. 'Five-star.'

He chuckles. 'Compared to Doris's, you mean?'

She nods, knocking crumbs from the front of her sweater. 'There's hot water at least.'

'Glad to hear it. So, how did you sleep last night?'

'Actually, really well!' she says brightly. 'How about you?'

'Out like a light,' he fibs. Yet he feels surprisingly perky as he showers quickly and carefully manoeuvres Doris out of the campsite. It seems to be a muddle of ring roads and roundabouts until the town finally opens out into its docks.

Through the open driver's window, Shane catches the sharp, briny, unmistakably fishy smell. It's not unpleasant. This is a working town – no longer thriving, as he imagines it was when his dad lived and worked here, but still chugging along. They pass stout brick warehouses and a sagging terrace of shops, and park up close to the docks.

'Wow, look at that!' Josie exclaims as they climb out of the van.

Following her gaze, Shane takes in the sight of the tall, imposing red-brick tower. 'D'you remember that?' he asks.

Her clear blue eyes catch the morning sun. 'No, I don't. But we didn't do much sightseeing back then, did we?'

'Not that I remember.' He smiles and with no further discussion, they drift towards a little wooden-fronted café with a couple of tables outside, where they have a second coffee. Fat gulls shriek overhead, and boats bob gently on their moorings. 'So, I guess we'd better find it,' Josie announces.

'You mean the venue? The Laughing... Herring, was it?'

'Haddock.' She grins and pats the canvas bag slung over her shoulder. 'Ready for our photo shoot?'

'Oh God.' He sniggers. 'Do we really have to do this?'

'We do!' So off they go, with Josie leading the way with her phone map on this cool, breezy morning, and quickening her pace as the illustrious venue comes into view.

Without warning, a memory smacks him squarely in the face. For a second, he's no longer a middle-aged man with two teenage kids and an ex-wife and a special relationship with the Belarusian String Orchestra. He is twenty years old and has just arrived here in Ravi's uncle's massive car.

Ravi isn't dead. The cancer that cut her big, beautiful life short doesn't even exist. She is brimming with life, bossing him and Josie about, having booked their gigs and had fliers printed and even T-shirts made, for crying out loud. T-shirts with their faces on them, from a drawing she did! She's made him look like *Stig of the Dump*, but he doesn't care and wears it anyway. He's not bothered about his 'image' (a word frequently bandied about by Ravi) and anyway, he has bigger things to worry about. Although pretending that everything is in hand, he is worried about setting up his drum kit in an unfamiliar venue, and what the locals will make of their ramshackle brand of indie pop.

Josie is nervous too. She's admitted it to him, secretly ('Don't tell Rav!'). Shane also knows that she only settled on playing bass because she'd found one languishing among the frilly lampshades and Cliff Richard records in a charity shop. He was there with her that day. 'A bass? You sure?' he'd asked her. She'd laughingly said that, with four strings rather than a guitar's standard six, it was bound to be easier.

He flinches now as she touches his arm. 'Look at this place,' she murmurs.

'Jesus,' he breathes. The pub appears to be leaning tipsily into the street. Its painted sign – a cartoon fish clutching a tankard – is bleached almost to invisibility.

'Classy,' she says, turning to him with a smile as she pulls out the Polaroid camera from her bag.

'You've put the film in?' he asks.

Josie chuckles mockingly. 'No, I thought I wouldn't bother,' she retorts, and he tries to laugh off his embarrassment.

'She could have left us a digital one,' he jokes.

'Yeah. Bit thoughtless,' Josie adds with a wry smile. A silence hovers and he sees her eyes fill with tears and is overcome by an urge to hug her. 'Poor Ravi,' she adds softly.

He nods, not knowing what else to say. Josie examines the chunky device; it seems like an ancient artefact now. 'C'mon, then,' she says, brightening. 'Let's do it.'

'Okay!' Subconsciously, he straightens up and stands tall, ready for the paparazzi. She flops an arm around his shoulders, the simple act causing his heart rate to quicken, like when that kid came into his shop and fiddled with the metronomes, setting them click-clicking a manic beat.

'It doesn't have a selfie function,' Josie announces, holding the camera at arm's length.

'So how do we know if we're in the picture?'

'We'll soon find out!' Her cheek is up against his now, their faces touching as the wind whips at her fine blonde hair. Shane feels as if his heart could burst. 'Smile!' she commands, and he grins like a maniac as she presses the button and the picture slides out of the slot. Moments later, they are studying the photo as the image appears.

As he looks at it, he can hardly speak.

Him and Josie in the bleached, bluish tinge of the Polaroid print.

The two of them, just as they were. Before everything happened and he never saw her again, until Ravi died. Ravi who's brought them back to The Laughing Haddock on this blustery afternoon.

Josie smiles, tilting her lovely face towards him. 'Like it?'

'I love it!' The words fell out before he could stop them.

Josie blinks at him and quickly slips the photo into her jacket pocket, and the camera into her bag. 'Shall we go in then?'

'You want a drink?' Shane asks in surprise.

She laughs. 'It's a bit early even for me. No, just for a look. I'm curious to see it, aren't you?'

'Yeah,' he says truthfully. So in they go, hesitantly. Shane looks around the surprisingly cavernous room, taking in the smell of stale beer and an undertone of damp. The walls are deeply yellowed and strewn with frayed fishing nets, and Madonna's 'Like a Prayer' is playing quietly. There's not a soul in sight.

'Look,' Josie murmurs, indicating the 'stage' at the back of the pub. Barely any bigger than a dining table, it's wedged between the dartboard and the ladies' loo. Shane can see his younger self right there, hunched shyly behind his drum kit. A barrier between him and the audience that he was always grateful for. It felt as if he could truly be himself, behind his kit. No one could get at him there. It was a world that Pete, and his mum, knew nothing about, and whenever he played, his life at home faded away to nothing.

'God, this place,' he says softly.

Josie nods. 'Feels like yesterday, doesn't it?'

'It really does.' He looks at her, wishing he could take her hand and squeeze it. Wishing he could tell her how this feels, being here.

'Remember the trouser row before this gig?' she prompts him.

'Trouser row?'

She smiles. 'It *was* Grimsby, wasn't it? When Ravi bought you those outrageous trousers from a charity shop?'

Now it flashes back to him. 'Oh God, yeah! Made out of some kind of shiny black plastic?'

'And you refused to wear them, like a child.'

'Hey! Understandably, I think!' he says in mock defensiveness.

'So Ravi wore them,' she says, and as their eyes meet briefly, something sparks in him.

'To make a point, I think,' he adds.

'Yeah.' Josie nods. 'That was Ravi all over, wasn't it?' She pauses and he catches her glancing at the stage. 'Oh, Shane. I still can't believe she's gone.'

'Yes, I know.' *I'm thinking it too,* he wants to tell her. *You and me and Ravi with our lives ahead of us.*

'So,' she says, 'what d'you want to do now?'

Shane glances towards the pub's open door. 'I think we should go.'

She frowns, seeming momentarily confused. 'Go back to London, you mean?'

'Oh, no!' he exclaims. 'I meant, let's get on the road, shall we? To the bright lights of Bridlington?'

'Sounds good,' she says as they step out into the sharp, salty air. 'And you know what? I'd like to drive us there.'

'Really?' he asks in surprise. 'You're sure?'

'Of course I'm sure,' she insists. 'Don't look so terrified.'

'I'm not!' he protests. 'Honestly, I'm not—'

She grins, thrusting her flattened palm at him. 'C'mon, then. Hand over the keys.'

20

JOSIE

I'm driving because I don't want to be the pathetic ninny in the passenger seat. I'm driving because I want to show Shane that I'm capable of handling an ambulance from the era of Ginger Spice in her Union Jack dress.

And I can do this, dammit. *Feel the fear and do it anyway.* Don't be like dear, sweet Mum, too afraid to use the Soda Stream that had been presented to Dad as a long-service award from Smith & Parker, the engineering works. 'I don't like the way it gushes out, Billy. You do it!'

Actually, I'm not driving it properly yet. I'm manoeuvring the ancient heap extremely badly as we leave our parking space by the docks. It seems crucial, as I grapple and wrench the gear stick, to appear the epitome of calm. Although *obviously* I don't care one jot what Shane thinks of me! I'm not at all disgruntled that I packed only my ugliest clothes and no hair conditioner and one set of PJs which is going to be rank by the end of this trip.

I don't care that I have not one single attractive piece of clothing with me and no make-up whatsoever. Even though I love my make-up and have dutifully applied it daily since 1985! Why would I need a dab of concealer or a slick of lipstick on this trip? Why would I want to be attractive? *It doesn't matter what you look like,* I told myself this morning as I surveyed my bleak, scrubbed face in the dreaded shower-block mirror. *It's not a date.*

We lurch out of the relative quiet of the docks and through the confusing town centre where people appear to be driving normally, without fear. And finally, we are on the wild highway to Bridlington. It's like sex, I decide, gripping the gear stick with an iron fist. That first time with Lloyd, it had been ages since I'd last done it – eighteen months by my reckoning. I was worried that I might have 'changed' down there, that he wouldn't be able to get it in, or that my vagina would act like a grizzly bear, woken abruptly from hibernation, and bite him.

I glance at Shane, who's clearly pretending to be fully confident in my abilities as the engine revs and growls and the gears screech. But I can tell he's crapping himself by the way he keeps flexing his fingers, his gaze darting this way and that, as if he's assessing potential hazards. I suspect he is also formulating tips for me, and that at any moment these tips will be dispensed. He certainly looks on the verge of saying something.

'What?' I bark at him.

'Nothing! What?'

I shoot him a quick glare. *I don't need your tips, thank you very much!*

We reach the end of the road and I stamp on the brake, causing us to lurch forward. Shane does an excellent job of pretending that didn't happen, that everything is perfectly normal and we are just two middle-aged people enjoying a pleasant drive to the seaside.

I fumble for the indicator. 'Er, if you just—' he starts.

'It's fine!'

'The indicators are—'

'I know, Shane, I know!' Without indicating, I perform a clumsy right turn, the engine battling against the slight incline, then whining plaintively as we hit the straight, like a child tugging at his mother's skirt. But rather than wanting a biscuit, it needs me to change gears, urgently, triggering more gear stick grappling until I finally jam the fucking thing into the correct position.

In the event, that first-time sex with Lloyd was fine, if a bit nervy. Not the greatest I'd ever had, but the relief I felt made up for that. I could still do it! My vagina had not merely let him in, but also out again! I'd had visions of it spasming and us being stuck like that until the paramedics arrived.

And once I get the hang of the ambulance, it feels, if not fine, then not as if I am about to kill us both. I glance at Shane. His expression has settled into one of studied composure. At least he no longer looks as if he'd like to open the passenger door and hurl himself out on to the road.

See, I can do this! Nothing to it— My thoughts break off as I hit a pothole with a bang – 'Fuck!' – and I grip the steering wheel to return us to a steady course. Thankfully, the road is fairly quiet. Just the odd car, travelling at a respectable speed, and then an enormous lorry appearing out of nowhere and thundering past us.

'You okay?' Shane asks in a thin, tense voice.

'Yeah-I'm-fine,' I mutter, teeth gritted. Fields stretch into the distance on either side, and the sea is somewhere out there, waiting for us. I breathe slowly and deeply and make a conscious effort to loosen my grip on the wheel.

Shane consults his phone, telling me that we're on this road for half an hour or so, and look how blue the sky is now. Isn't it a beautiful day? I'd reply but something else is happening.

My heart rate is quickening and my hands are slick with sweat. There's no reason for it: no more thundering lorries, no wrangling of the gear stick as we're travelling at a steady fifty on a fairly straight road. Swathes of green unspool into the distance, and I catch a glimmer of sparkling sea. Yet my heart is thumping, hammering against my ribs, and my throat has tightened.

I blink hard, trying to keep the road in focus. It seems like a game now, one of those PlayStation driving games that enthralled Cora's boy mates when they were little kids. Although Cora wasn't really interested, she pretended she was, to be part of the gang.

Now I seem to have exited real life and I'm *in* that driving game, wiping the sweat off each hand onto the thighs of my jeans. Shane turns towards me. 'You sure you're alright?'

'I'm fine,' I say briskly, my tongue a dry cardboard flap. Behind us, a car toots as I waver too close to the verge. Panic surges up in me, and I can feel sweat trickling down my cleavage. I force my gaze on the white line in the centre of the road, exhaling forcefully now, still trying to maintain a rigid *I'm-in-control!* expression. But my hands are shaking, immediately wet again after each thigh-wipe, and I can't make them stop.

Never mind indicating. Never mind *mirror–signal–manoeuvre* as I swerve into a lay-by and bang on the brakes and slump forward, panting, with my head in my hands.

'Josie!' Shane's voice seems to float around my head.

'I'm so sorry, I could've killed us, I—'

'It's okay. You're all right. Take it easy, just breathe...' He touches my forearm, and then his arm is around my shoulders, pulling me close. I lean into him, crying now and wanting him to never let me go.

21

Gradually, I start to breathe normally again and peel away from him. 'Just give me a minute,' I whisper, pushing my damp hair away from my face.

'There's no rush,' he says gently.

I smile gratefully, and we sit in silence for a few moments. 'What happened there?' he asks finally. 'D'you want to get out? D'you need water or—'

'I'm sorry.' I rub at my face and exhale slowly. 'I just had... a *thing* there.'

He frowns, still looking a little shocked. 'Has that ever happened to you before?'

'No,' I mutter.

Then, instead of asking me more questions, he sits quietly and waits. 'Just say if you need anything,' he says.

'Thanks.' I open the driver's door and climb out, grateful for the cool breeze. Stepping away from the van, I look over the flat fields, still bewildered as to what just happened. A few moments later I'm aware of Shane standing a few feet away, casting me the odd glance.

'I think it might have been my pills,' I say quietly.

He frowns again. 'What pills?'

'Antidepressants. I've been on them for a while. I was just, um, having a bit of a tricky time. I didn't feel myself, you know? But I forgot to bring them with me.' I clear my throat, reminding myself that there's no stigma these days. I have nothing to be ashamed of. And I'm not going to start on to Shane about my menopause: my night sweats and dry, crispy hair and the fact that I seem to have *run out of orgasms* – like with library books, when you've taken out your full quota.

'Hey.' Shane comes towards me and touches my arm briefly, his eyes full of concern. 'I'm sorry to hear that. But are you sure it's okay? Just coming off them like that?'

I shrug. 'It was a low dose, and it mightn't even be that. I don't know. It was a sort of panic attack, I think...' I glance down at my battered trainers – my most unattractive trainers – and look back at him. 'Also, I haven't driven for years. Over twenty years, actually...'

'Really?' He feigns surprise, and I can't help smiling.

'Don't tell me. You're amazed.'

He rakes at his hair. 'I wasn't going to say.'

'So obviously, it was really smart of me to refresh my skills by getting behind the wheel of an ancient ambulance.'

He smiles wryly as we mooch back to the van, and I climb into the passenger seat. Shane puts the key into the ignition but doesn't start the engine. 'Sure you're okay now?' he asks.

'Honestly, yes.' I nod.

He seems to hesitate, as if turning something over in his mind. 'I'm not trying to pry or anything, Josie. But if there's anything you'd like to talk about...'

'Oh, I'm fine now, really.'

He looks at me levelly, those greenish eyes seeming to beam right into my head. 'You're sure?'

'Yes,' I say, even though it's not true. There's *so* much I want to talk about. And now we're together it's filling my head to the point where it feels like there's no room for anything else. Is that why I had that crazy freak-out there? Because my brain is just too full of him and me?

As Shane starts the engine and we pull away from the verge, I want to tell him that I remember *everything*. Every single detail that ever happened between us.

That kiss, for one – the day the crow flew down the chimney and into my house. His beautiful mouth on mine in my parents' living room. How we brushed it off like it never happened.

Then that hot summer's day in the park: me, Shane and Ravi lying out in the sun. Shane had pulled off his T-shirt and got sunburnt. I'd told him to use sunscreen, but he wouldn't listen. I rushed off to buy calamine lotion and when I came back he was waiting for me, and I tried not to stare at his beautifully shaped back, and how his arms were lightly muscled from all that drumming.

It was just the two of us then. Ravi had had to go for a music lesson or something (so supportive were her parents, they were happy to pay for a guitar tutor). Awful though it seems, I was almost glad that Shane was burnt as it gave me permission to touch him. He sat there quietly as I dabbed the lotion on.

We drank more beers, and he insisted he was okay now; that he could put his T-shirt back on without screaming. 'Idiot!' I teased him.

'I know,' he said, laughing.

We wandered around town, eating chips, and somehow we ended up at the end of the street, looking up at the derelict mill. 'Let's go in!' I announced.

'Okay!' As if it were the greatest idea I'd ever had. We clambered through a broken door, and once inside, took a moment to adjust to the gloom. As we prowled around, examining broken machinery and wrecked filing cabinets, he started telling me the history of our town. That once there were thirty-eight textile mills in the area, producing millions of yards of fabric to be exported all over the world. On and on he went, chattering happily, sunburn now soothed. Shane loved history – he was a bit of a swot, Ravi reckoned – and I loved to hear his voice, so animated as he told me stuff.

But at some point, I stopped listening.

'Did you know that?' He grinned at me.

'Know what?' I'd lost all track of what he was saying.

'Any of this! What were you doing when we did the Industrial Revolution at school?'

Thinking about you, I mused.

He started up again, about how in water-powered mills, the force of the water drove the turbine's blades, which powered the whatever-the-heck-it-was—

'Shane, stop it!' I commanded.

'What?' He stared at me.

'Stop the history lesson. Stop the turbines and water wheels—'

'What, and cut the power?' He grinned.

I laughed at his rubbish joke, and then I stopped laughing and we stood there, just looking at each other. And then we kissed.

I closed my eyes and everything else – the rusting machinery, the charred remains of fires and pigeons flapping around – melted away. It was just us. We kissed and kissed and kissed. The mill was smelly and damp, yet this is where we did it: up against a crumbling wall. My first time; his too. We were seventeen. It was hardly the location of dreams, but it was perfect.

In the days that followed we'd clicked straight back into our usual banter. The teasing was constant – it was just the way we were. His love of Hula Hoop sandwiches, the way he'd get drunk on two beers and the fact that he'd once bought a Rick Astley record; all of it was fair game. And he took it all so good-naturedly. Occasionally, he even threw it back at me. I loved that because it meant I had his attention, and that our bond was strong – even if it wasn't the kind I yearned for.

I never told Ravi what had happened, and I was certain that Shane wouldn't either. We knew the rules – that the band came first, and that she'd hate it if we were together. She'd never said it as such; it was just a feeling. And to admit to fancying Shane – to loving him, as I did – would have been unthinkable.

I wasn't even sure whether he wanted to be with me. We never talked about it – but both of us knew what had happened, that day of the sunburn and chips.

It happened one more time, three years later, and I haven't forgotten that either. These are the things I want to tell Shane as he drives the ambulance, competently and smoothly – at least, as smoothly as Doris will allow – towards Bridlington. That I remember every detail, and that none of it has faded over time.

However, I don't say any of that. Instead, I lower my window and breathe in the briny air, and focus on the road ahead.

22

SHANE

There was nothing she wanted to talk about, Josie assured him after the panicky episode. She didn't want to see if she could get a prescription dispatched to a chemist in Bridlington. She didn't know if you could even do that, and although he was tempted, Shane managed not to google it on her behalf.

He had a feeling that that would *not* go down very well.

Instead, he has driven them to a small, well-tended campsite on the outer edge of Bridlington. The sun has pierced through the clouds and, as they park up under the shade of a tree, things are looking good. A poster on the noticeboard announces a barbecue happening later, and Josie is cheered by the fact that they're within walking distance of the beach.

'Fancy a swim now?' she asks.

'Sure!'

She beams at him. 'I'll get changed in the showers. Put my swimsuit on underneath…' In the back of the ambulance she rummages through her rucksack, pulling out items chaotically until she finds her costume. Shane gazes down at the array of discarded clothing. 'Won't be a minute!' she says and scampers off, as if they're just two friends enjoying a trip to the coast.

Sometimes Shane almost forgets how bizarre this is, and that they are only together under Ravi's instruction. How he'd worried about what it would be like, and what they'd *do*, apart from drive from place to place. How on earth would they fill five whole days together? It wasn't as if he *knew* her any more – the kind of person she is, or what she enjoys. In panic, he'd done a bit of research and reassured himself that there were several places of interest they could visit along the way. However, even the thought of a trip to the Pontefract Museum, with its extensive display on the town's liquorice heritage, had failed to steady his nerves.

While Josie is in the shower block, Shane changes whippet-fast into his swimming shorts and pulls his sweatshirt and jeans back on. Then, fully dressed, with rolled-up towels tucked under their arms, they stroll across the campsite and follow the sandy path towards the beach.

It's a retro British seaside postcard come to life, Shane decides. There are candyfloss stalls, and a machine you can post a penny into and it'll come out flattened. With a flicker of pride Shane discovers that he does, in fact, possess a single penny in his wallet. 'Just what I always wanted,' Josie announces, laughing, as the coppery sliver drops from the machine.

On the long sweep of golden sand, children are riding on donkeys and screaming as gulls dive-bomb for chips. Kiosks are offering hot sugary doughnuts and waffles with every topping imaginable, and day trippers are posing for photos against the peeling railings, the backdrop a wash of milky blue sky.

'Oh, this is lovely!' Josie turns to Shane and smiles.

'Isn't it? Proper English seaside.' Shane remembers it vividly – being here with Josie and Ravi on day two of their tour. Playing the slot machines and Ravi trying to shake the Penny Falls machine to make money fall out, as if a handful of 2p pieces were essential to their survival – despite the fierce-looking woman presiding over the arcade from a raised booth.

Nostalgia washes over him, making him quite light-headed as they stroll past sandcastles at various stages of construction and decay. He's still concerned about Josie's 'turn', although he is being careful not to refer to it that way again, as she's scoffed, 'It wasn't a *turn*, Shane. It was just... a thing.'

Shane nodded, deciding she probably just wanted to forget it. With every passing minute he is enjoying her company more and more, and he doesn't want to annoy her. He knows this trip isn't about *them*; dutifully, they are just carrying out the instructions of their dead friend. But occasionally he forgets about Ravi's letter and the itinerary, and it's just him and Josie on a mad adventure.

She seems to flip, he's noticed, from quiet introspection to stand-offishness, with the occasional glimmer of the light-hearted sunniness that he remembers so well. Dare he even think it? Shane has detected a hint of the closeness they once had, seemingly buried but catching the sunlight occasionally – like a golden sweet wrapper peeking out of the sand.

'How about here?' Josie indicates an empty spot on the beach.

'Perfect.' They spread out their towels and sit down, facing the sea. The beach is busy despite the cool, bracing wind. There are babies in buggies and a big, jovial group armed with blankets and windbreaks and cool boxes, clearly revving up for a bit of a party. Dance music starts playing tinnily.

'Shane?' Josie turns to him. She has pulled off her jeans and T-shirt and is looking only mildly hypothermic in a sporty navy-blue swimsuit.

'Yeah?'

'I was thinking,' she says, looking hesitant, 'if you wanted to do any detours at all... I mean, if you wanted to add on anywhere else on this trip? I wouldn't mind at all...'

He looks at her, genuinely not understanding. 'You mean extend it?'

'No, no,' she says quickly. 'Not like that. I mean... visit your mum, maybe? Seeing as we've come up all this way. She's still in the same house, right?'

Shane nods, turning this over. 'Yes, she is.'

'And... she's still with Pete?'

'Yeah. But I don't want to visit. I mean, I haven't even thought about it—'

'I'm sorry,' she says, her cheeks flushing. 'I just thought I'd mention it.'

'Definitely not,' he says. 'But thanks for thinking of it.' He looks at her, and he knows what she's thinking – that she understands. She knew everything, he always suspected. More than she ever let on. He busies himself by pulling off his clothes and jumps up, shivering only slightly in his swimming shorts. 'So,' he says brightly, 'are we going in, or what?'

'Sure!' she announces.

'You feel okay to swim, do you? After the driving thing?'

'Stop fussing,' she exclaims, eye-rolling him like an adolescent, which makes him laugh as they stride towards the sea. In they plunge, with Shane pretending that the bitterly cold waters off Yorkshire's east coast are, in fact, *balmy,* and that he wouldn't have been quite content to watch other hardy swimmers from the beach.

'Great, isn't it?' Josie calls out.

'It is!' It's true – sort of. At least, he can barely remember a time when he felt so fully alive. He's still tingling all over as, shrouded by towels, they struggle clumsily back into their clothes.

'Fancy an ice cream?' Josie asks.

'Sure!' Because his teeth aren't quite chattering enough.

'C'mon, then.' She smiles, and he notices that she has already caught the sun across her nose and cheeks. Her blue eyes are shining, the precise colour of the sky.

Two older women – perhaps even as old as Shane's great-aunt Sylvia the last time he saw her – are strolling slowly, arms linked, along the promenade. It was Sylvia whose box room they had all stayed in here: Josie and Ravi crammed into the narrow single bed, and Shane on a partly deflated airbed on the floor.

He hadn't even known Sylvia, not really. But Shane and his big brother were in touch sporadically – by letter, it seems so antiquated now – and he'd suggested that she might be able to put them up for the night. Shane valued David's letters. There were seven years between them and straight after school, David had moved to southern Germany to work in construction, and rarely came home after that. Good for him, Shane had thought bitterly: having the means to get away from Pete. But he didn't blame him, really.

Shane didn't know much about his family background. He remembered his dad only as a faded image, strolling along a seafront somewhere, buying Shane a stick of rock, and holding his hand. Taking him on a big wheel and shooting a gun at a fairground side show. He'd 'gone away', Shane knew that much, and when he'd pressed his mum on it, she'd said he'd died. 'Just leave it in the past, Shane.' But he was just a child, and he didn't have a past to conveniently park difficult things in.

He and Josie queue at the kiosk, the breeze flapping the laminated menu tacked to a board. 'What would you like?' he asks.

'Can't decide. You go first,' she urges him.

'A vanilla cone, please,' Shane tells the girl behind the counter.

'Predictable,' Josie teases.

'No, it's a classic!'

Josie laughs, opting for a lurid strawberry/bubblegum duo, which she devours with enthusiasm. 'We've got to do our photo,' she reminds him, 'at our venue. The Marine Hotel, wasn't it?'

'Oh God, yes.' In the headiness of the day, Shane had forgotten. But now he remembers exactly where it is, and leads them straight to it, a little way back from the seafront. Or rather, to where it *was*. Because it turns out that the old-style seaside hotel, where the kindly owner had brought them platters of sandwiches as they ran through their soundcheck, has now gone. A retail complex sprawls over the area where the ornate whitewashed building once stood. Shane shrugs off his mild disappointment as they take their Polaroid in front of a featureless furniture store.

'I guess it'll do.' Josie slips the picture into her pocket.

'It'll have to.' Shane catches her gaze and smiles. 'That was a fun day anyway, wasn't it?'

'It really was,' she says as they make their way back to the campsite. 'The kind of seaside day we had when we were kids.'

Shane murmurs in agreement – although he never had those kinds of days. 'Oh.' She stops, frowns and touches his arm. 'I'm sorry, Shane. That was really insensitive of me.'

'No, it's fine,' he says with a shrug. 'I know what you mean. Remember that school trip we had to Morecambe?'

'Oh, yeah!' She grins, and he catches something flickering in her eyes. They'd sat together, Shane and Josie, on the back seat on the way home. There'd been some teasing from his mates, about how he always seemed to be near her. How there were plenty of other free seats on the coach. Naturally, he'd laughed it off.

They've reached the campsite now, where tempting aromas are already wafting from the communal barbecue set up next to the wooden reception hut. It's a golden, long-shadowed evening, and a full-scale feast seems like an awful lot of effort for the smattering of campers who have gathered around the trestle table. But everything is delicious, and as beers flow and the sky darkens, the atmosphere is touchingly jolly. By the time Shane and Josie repeat their getting-ready-for-bed routines in the van and shower block, he is overcome by the kind of pleasant drowsiness that only ever happens after a day by the sea.

When Boris said you can't beat the freedom of being on the road, Shane hadn't believed him. Perhaps it was because his joints hurt sometimes from lugging heavy instruments about. Or the fact that, since he's been a dad, he has always favoured Spanish holidays with the kids. Maybe he was also feeling a bit prickly about Rich Tony. Whatever it was, Shane suspected that 'van life', as Boris termed it, was overrated.

Now, though, as Josie sleeps soundly beside him, Shane replays the day in his head: the bitterly cold sea, gritty sand in his pants and a gull plunging down to steal his predictable vanilla.

It was perfect, he decides. So maybe Boris was right after all.

23

JOSIE

I'm feeling optimistic about Scarborough and we're not even there yet. I'm thinking hot dogs and ice cream (choc-mint chip this time) and jangling amusement arcades. Plus, it'll be another stage of the tour completed which means we're over halfway through, with just two stops left – Pontefract and Huddersfield. Then home! Mission accomplished! Although that doesn't feel quite as alluring as it had a couple of days ago.

Perhaps it's being by the sea, which I've always loved. When Cora was a baby, and things were rocky with Dale, she and I would escape for a day at the coast. Could I build a life without him, just for the two of us? Those breezy Brighton days made me believe that it might be possible.

Or maybe it's Shane, and being together isn't as torturous as I'd expected? Fun even, at times. So I have a feeling of quiet optimism about the day ahead.

However, by the time we reach the town's fringes, along with its sweeping coastal views, Scarborough has something unexpected to offer us. Torrential rain. It's gushing down, as if from a gigantic overhead shower, like the kind Cora and Zack had installed. She turned it on once to show me how powerful it was.

We pull into a lay-by where Shane goes to buy our now customary bacon rolls from a roadside kiosk. While he waits, I check my phone and see that Lloyd has messaged me.

LLOYD

Hope trip going well! Wanna see what I've built for you?

JOSIE

Of course!

I am picturing expertly constructed shelves, fitting snugly into my kitchen alcove. Lloyd might be annoying, in the way he fazes off sometimes when I'm chatting to him and I realise I might as well have been talking to a potato in the vegetable rack. But he's handy, and that's no small factor. Dale could barely operate a pepper grinder.

I glance out to see Shane waiting in the small queue, sheltered by a candy-striped awning from which rain is pouring, bouncing in puddles on the sodden ground. My phone pings: Lloyd has sent me a picture. It's not shelves, after all, but a kind of shallow rectangular wooden trough, filled with what looks like soil.

JOSIE

What's this?

LLOYD

Our first prop.

JOSIE

For what? Don't understand!

Lloyd is typing. I look out to see Shane being served by a large man in white overalls.

LLOYD

The idea is we'll get your feet in here, get them all muddied up and I'll film you—

The driver's door opens, and I plonk my phone face down on my lap. 'Thanks,' I say, as Shane hands me my roll and coffee.

'No problem.' We chomp away in silence for a few moments. That trough was in my flat, I noticed. Lloyd has built it there, and the thought of it awaiting my return causes my stomach to shift uneasily. *Videos are what the punters like. And if they ask for anything you don't want to do, we'll just block them.*

Have I turned into a prude? Am I the vanilla one now?

I catch Shane looking at me. 'Everything all right?' he asks.

'Yes,' I say quickly. 'Apart from the weather...'

'Yeah. Bit grim, isn't it?' he says. 'Hopefully it'll brighten up soon.' But as we drive to the campsite, the rain comes on even more heavily, if that were possible. Doris's antiquated windscreen wipers can barely handle the deluge. We pull up at the roadside, a little way from the entrance. I glance at Shane, wondering if he's thinking what I'm thinking.

'What are we going to do here?' I ask. 'It's quite a hike into town and we don't have umbrellas or proper rain gear. At least, I don't...' I think of my friend Nisha teasing me that I never have the proper attire for climatic conditions. 'That hike we did in the Lake District,' she's fond of reminiscing, 'when you wore your Converse!' I couldn't see what was wrong with that.

'We could wait and see how the day turns out?' Shane suggests.

'I guess so.' In the lull that follows, I sense him turning over alternative plans. I can *read* him, I realise. I've never been able to do that with Lloyd. Does he really think I remember Churchill as prime minister, or does he just enjoy winding me up?

Shane turns to me. 'Or,' he says, 'we could just head on to Pontefract?'

'You mean, miss out Scarborough?' I exclaim.

'Well, no,' he says quickly. 'We're here, aren't we? We're within the town's boundaries.' He pulls a mock-furtive expression as if Ravi might be watching us, beadily.

'We should do the photo, at least,' I announce. And so, with the distinct feeling of our old friend directing us, we drive into town. Cockles, our former venue, was once a tacky little club with feeble disco lights and a dry ice machine that nearly choked us. Now it's a bar called Ricky's, not yet open for business at 11.30 a.m. and looking rather sterile inside.

We take our picture outside it, huddled in the rain with Shane's arm slung around me, our hair plastered to our heads. 'Thanks, Ravi,' he chuckles.

Mild hysteria is rising in me and soon we're laughing at the absurdity of this. 'This is mad, isn't it?' I turn to him, grinning, as rain drips down my face.

'Just a bit,' he agrees.

But I'm glad we're doing this, I want to tell him. *I'm glad I'm here – soaked to the skin – with you.* How kind he was about my stupid panic attack I reflect as we head back to the van. And how willing and stoical he is, with not a moan about the mattress situation, even though I've caught him stretching out his lean body, as if easing out his knotted muscles, as I do. I've tried not to watch as he does this.

'So, what now?' he asks.

'Let's just stay,' I say.

'What, forever?' he teases.

'Of course!' I laugh. 'I want to spend the rest of my life here. It's my dream.'

Shane smiles. 'You mean stay at the campsite tonight, right?'

'Yes,' I say. 'We might as well do it properly, rather than skipping a night.' So that's what we do, parking up at the site, after which hot showers are necessary, followed by hot chocolates in the campsite café. We while away the afternoon there – it doubles as a games room – joined by a family with many children who delight in the extensive selection of board games.

'Buckaroo!' I exclaim, as the dad sets it up at the next table. 'It was our favourite,' I tell Shane, 'when Cora was little.'

In turn, he tells me about Ryan and Liv, and how fiercely competitive they were at games; the stakes sky-high, even with seemingly innocent KerPlunk. 'How are things now?' There – I've dared to ask. 'I mean, how d'you manage things with Paula and your kids?'

He glances towards the café window, although it's opaque with steam. 'We've managed okay, I think. She has a new partner now and their lives are pretty full…' He trails off. 'You know what kids are like with their hectic schedules.'

'I do,' I say, detecting the stoicism in his voice. He misses them, is what he means.

'D'you have any pictures?' I ask.

'Sure.' He opens his photos and hands me his phone across the table. 'That's a recent one of Liv,' he adds. 'Her eighteenth birthday.'

'Oh, she's gorgeous!'

'And also appalled that her brother's shoved his way in,' he adds. I chuckle, noticing the side-eye directed at her goofily grinning brother. Both Liv and Ryan are a merger of Shane and Paula: her dark auburn hair, high cheekbones and aquiline nose; his soft greenish eyes and full, expressive mouth.

'Can I see some more?' I ask.

''Course you can. Scroll away.' And so I do, through all the sports days and holidays and Liv playing an acoustic guitar, perched on a stool in a garden. Big smiles, wistful gazes and *don't-you-dare-take-a-photo-Dad* glares. Then a picture of Paula and the kids, all three attractively tousled by the wind on a boat somewhere.

While Shane is up at the counter, perusing the cakes on display, I study Paula more closely. She was easily the best-looking girl in our school year. A giant photo of her was displayed in the window of Headlines, the hottest hair salon in town. As their model, she had her hair cut for free; to me and Ravi, this seemed on a par with being a minor celebrity. She is still a beauty, but in a more polished way. Her bouncy auburn mane is slicked back now, and her teeth appear to be bright white and neatly aligned, rather than being the normal, everyday teeth that she – in fact, everyone – used to have.

I'd been surprised when I'd heard that Shane and Paula had got together. Not because he wasn't good-looking, or a lovely person; just that normally, she'd gone for slightly older guys in their mid-twenties, with cars and well-paying jobs and even *mortgages*, which seemed unthinkable. But then, what did I know? Having convinced myself that Dale was the love of my life, I'd already moved to London. It felt good to be away from all that; the gossip and constant reminders that I'd messed up. Anyway, if Paula loved him, then I'd never have stood a chance. That's what I told myself because she – the hair model! – was queen.

I look up as Shane reappears at our table and hand him his phone. 'Your kids are lovely,' I say.

'Thanks.' He smiles warmly and cuts the last remaining brownie in two, so we can share it. Having shown him a photo of

Cora – 'She's the image of you,' he insists – I rub a patch of condensation from the window and see that the rain has eased.

'Fancy a walk along the coastal path?' I suggest.

'Sure,' he says, so we head out, grateful for the cool freshness after the downpour. Fuelled only by sweet hot chocolate and that tiny brownie, we are relieved to finally spot a pizza place. It's really nothing special. Yet somehow, as we devour hot dough and lashings of cheese, I sense this faded restaurant imprinting itself indelibly on my mind.

'So, after tonight,' I remark as we stroll back to the campsite, 'there's just Pontefract and Huddersfield, and then we're done.'

'Yeah,' he says. 'God, we're over halfway through.'

'Are you pleased?' I prompt him.

He shoots me a quick glance. 'Actually, not really,' he admits.

I blink at him in surprise. 'You mean you're not keen to get home?'

We've reached the campsite and pass an ebullient family gathered around a table on the grass, and realise it's the group from earlier in the café. After a brief exchange about the break in the rain, we cross the site towards Doris. 'There's just a bit of a situation in my flat,' Shane explains, as he opens up the back door. 'The, erm... the woman I'm living with—'

'Elaine,' I cut in without thinking.

He looks at me curiously as we clamber in. 'That's right, Elaine.'

'You said something to her, that time we spoke? When I called to say I was up for doing the trip...' *Obviously, it's totally normal behaviour for me to have lodged her name in my head all this time.* I will my cheeks to stop burning as I pull my pyjamas from my rucksack.

'Oh, did I?' he says.

'Yes, I just wondered, I—'

'Well, um... it's a kind of housemate situation,' he explains.

'Really?'

He smiles grimly. 'Yeah, I know that sounds ridiculous at this age.'

'You mean she's your lodger?' I ask.

'No, no. It's not really that either.'

I nod, still unclear about the kind of situation he's talking about. 'She's a friend then?'

'Um, not really. Well, I guess so.' He starts delving into his rucksack. 'We worked together in a pub a few years ago,' he adds. 'The shop was going through a shaky time, and I'd picked up a few shifts.'

'And?' I smile.

'I ran into her again and she was in a bit of a state about being evicted. So I said she could move into my spare room as a stopgap.'

'That's very sweet of you,' I say. *Why am I pleased that she's not his girlfriend?*

He shrugs, pulling out the black joggers and white T-shirt he's been sleeping in. 'Well, it was only meant to be a short-term thing.'

I study his face, detecting a hint of relief that he's told me. Three days ago, he had a perfunctory, *let's-just-get-this-done!* vibe. Beyond the basic facts – the shop, his kids and his split from Paula – I'd known virtually nothing about his life now. 'How long has she been at your place?' I ask.

'That's the thing.' He scratches at the back of his neck that's a little tanned, I've noticed, from our Bridlington day. 'It's been six months.'

'Six months! Do you mind? Is it okay, or—' I break off, realising that he might not want to go into it all. But as he tells me how it is, with Elaine frying onions at all hours, it's clear that it's far from okay.

'So what are you going to do?' I ask.

He pulls a face. 'I really don't want to ask her to move out, but...'

'You want her to go, though.'

Shane nods slowly. 'I'm sort of feeling that it's time.'

'Tricky,' I say. 'Is she seeing anyone?'

He brightens. 'Yeah, she is actually. Seems pretty keen. But it's very new—'

'But you're hoping they'll rush into living together?' I smile.

'It has crossed my mind!' He laughs.

Later, lying side by side on the mattress, we continue to concoct a scenario in which Elaine and her new love are not only flat hunting, but browsing the IKEA website and picking a sofa as we speak. And by the time we say goodnight, we have convinced ourselves that everything will resolve itself brilliantly.

Shane is sleeping now. I can tell by his slow, steady breathing. The way it's been tonight, I reflect, it's as if all the bad stuff never happened. Somehow, everything has been made better, just by us being thrown back together in a rattly old van.

I never imagined we'd be friends again, and tonight, on this campsite in Scarborough, I barely sleep a wink. My head is full of it all; full of Shane and me. And I'm right back there, with him, on the night that changed everything forever.

24

This time it isn't a derelict mill. It's a shabby guest house in Huddersfield, in which the three of us are staying on the last night of our tour. The whole time we've been away, it's been simmering between Shane and me. We are older now – I've just turned twenty – and things seem a little more serious. I catch him looking at me. I see it in his eyes, and it thrills me to know that he wants us to be together.

Although we don't discuss it, I know we both have the same thing in mind. So on a dark, wet night, I send Ravi out for beers, insisting that it's her turn. Shane and I are always the ones to do all the errand stuff, the fetching and carrying and running about.

We couldn't get a family room this time, so we had to book two rooms – a double for Ravi and me, and a single for Shane. As soon as she's gone, we fall into bed together, in his little room next to ours. We're kissing, then we're naked and I'm wrapped around him, wanting him so much. 'I love you, Josie,' he says. 'You know that, don't you?'

'I do,' I say, 'and I love you too.' He's inside me then, and I cry out as three years of longing seem to burst from my heart. Afterwards, we dress quickly. But we want to hold each other, to eke out every last minute, so we lie down again together. Just a few minutes more, we're reckoning, before Ravi comes back. Then we'll get up and straighten ourselves out and act like everything's normal—

The door flies open and Ravi marches in, clutching a carrier bag of beers. Her mouth drops.

'We were just sleeping,' I insist as we jump up.

'Yeah, looked like it!' She shrugs it off, and we're about to head to The Mucky Duck, our venue for the night, when she beckons me into our room. We've left Shane in his, to change and get ready.

'What's going on with you two?' Ravi exclaims.

'Nothing!' I don't want to spark off anything that might spoil the last night of our tour.

'Why are you lying?' She looks incredulous. There's no way she believes me.

'Ravi,' I say – and if I could take those words back, I would – 'd'you honestly think I'd do it with Shane?'

She frowns at me, then breaks into a loud, booming laugh and hugs me. 'That's up to you. Honestly, I don't care what you two get up to!'

It's too late to backtrack now. 'You *are* joking,' I say. 'Jesus, Rav.' She grins and everything is normal again, until a small movement snags my attention. Shane is standing in our doorway. His hair is dishevelled, and rather than looking at me, he is staring blankly into the middle distance. 'What are you doing?' Ravi asks.

He doesn't answer. His face is like stone.

'Aren't you getting ready?' she prompts him.

'No,' he replies.

She looks at him, then at me, as if I might be able to shed some light on what's going on. 'Shane, you need to,' she says. 'What's up? D'you feel ill, or—'

'I'm going home.'

Ravi stares at him. 'What? You can't do that! We have a gig tonight—'

'Yes, I can,' he says defiantly.

No, she's telling him; that can't happen. Tickets have been sold and we're finally getting somewhere, after all our years of hard work. Rob Jessop from the record company is coming to see us. This is our big chance. She's right – it really matters that we not only play tonight, but play our *best.*

'Please, Shane,' I start. 'We've just got this one last gig—'

'He'll play,' Ravi says, marching across our room and picking up her guitar, the beloved instrument her parents bought for her eighteenth birthday. Perhaps hoping to deflect things, she sits on the edge of the bed and begins to strum softly, working through one of our songs.

For a few moments Shane and I watch her in silence. Then he turns and leaves the room. Ravi leaps up, guitar still strung across her body. 'Fucking hell, Shane, what are you doing?' she blurts out. 'You're *not* walking out on us!' She charges after him into the hallway and there's shouting out there.

'Ravi, stop it!' he cries out. I rush out and see it happen: Ravi grappling with Shane, and him trying to break away. Angrily, she pulls off her guitar. Perhaps she drops it, or maybe she flings it down because this *matters so much;* for years it's all she's cared about. And now she's yelling at Shane, and he's stormed into his room and slammed the door and Ravi's guitar is lying on the lino floor, its neck broken.

There's no gig that night. We don't stay at the guest house.

We just pack up our stuff, and Ravi drives me and her home, and we barely speak the whole journey. She is *furious.*

I never find out how Shane gets back. Because that's it; we never hang out together after that. There's no band, no friendship. No gang of three any more, hanging out together in the Kapoors' garage. It's all over.

It seems crazy now that we couldn't patch things up. But I was too ashamed to even try. In fact, before I left for London, I went out of my way to avoid Shane, which was challenging with him living in the same street. But then, understandably, he seemed to be steering clear of me too. As for Ravi, she had always been the strong one and I guess she didn't want to back down.

Whatever the reasons, it was all so stupid and unnecessary, and surely we could have worked things out? We could have even clubbed together to buy her a new guitar! But I guess that's how it is to be young. You think you're right about everything; that you know it all. Or you realise you're wrong – but don't know how to fix it. My instinct was to run away.

I open my eyes, realising they're crusty, perhaps from crying in my sleep. So I *have* slept a little. As my vision grows accustomed to the gloom, I notice several things. Daylight is struggling into the van now, and rain is pattering gently on Doris's roof. I realise to my horror that I have snuggled close to Shane, that we are lying face-to-face – close enough to kiss. And my arm is slung over him, as if holding him close.

My heart thuds. What did we do last night? *Nothing!* I reassure myself. Absolutely nothing! We must have somehow drifted together like this in our dreams.

Thankfully, he seems to be sound asleep. Slowly, I lift my arm off him, and ease myself away until there's a respectable distance between us. His eyes open, and he looks at me a little blearily and smiles. 'Morning,' he says.

'Morning!' Instantly, I am scrambling up and pulling on a sweater over my PJs, as if that will cover up my mortification.

Shane sits up and stretches out his long, lightly muscled arms. 'Good sleep?' he asks.

'Erm, not really,' I admit.

'Rain keep you awake?'

'Yes, something like that.' I look at him, sitting there, gazing up at me, on a mattress that's only a little thicker than a pancake. Perhaps he's fully aware of how we were lying together when I woke up. I just have that feeling. But I also know that it's okay between us; that *everything* is okay. And as he smiles his beautiful smile, I realise that, right now, there's nowhere else in the world I'd rather be.

25

Rather than booking into a campsite – because none have been busy so far – we've decided to chance it and arrived in the middle of town. 'Aren't we wild?' Shane jokes.

'Totally!' I agree, gazing around at the busy shopping street. Pontefract is liquorice town, as it turns out. It's emblazoned on shop signs, in window displays, even on a mural of a smiling cartoon man clutching a bag of sweets. 'They used to grow the stuff here,' Shane tells me.

'Yes, I've sort of gathered that,' I remark.

He grimaces, as if having been caught out patronising me. 'D'you like liquorice?'

'Love it,' I say, so we veer into a sweet shop, the air thick with a dark, earthy sweetness, jars lined up on the shelves. I buy a paper bag of the famous black discs, and as we leave the shop, I offer them to Shane.

He picks one out, chews thoughtfully and makes a face. 'Bit medicinal, isn't it?'

'Vanilla man,' I tease him, fuelling myself with more as we mooch around the streets of shops, and then the castle ruins, and finding them oddly addictive. Then, remembering Paula's bright white smile – a perfect row of dazzling tiles – I nip into a public loo, relieved to find a mirror there. Miraculously, the local confectionery hasn't blackened my teeth.

We wander on, taking larky Polaroids of ourselves that Ravi hasn't even required of us. We're adept now at managing to both be in the picture without a selfie function. When we run out of film, we track down a tiny photographic shop, tucked down an alley a little like Shane's place. I've stashed all of our photos in my bag. I've been sneaking the odd look at them, noticing our demeanours changing day by day. Relaxing, I suppose. No longer appearing as if we are here under duress.

In the museum we marvel at the mechanics of liquorice production until my head is swimming with the stuff. From there, proper tourists now, we do a quick whip round of the town's main art gallery and then make our way to the bustle of the market square. The afternoon is warm and muggy, and pewter rain clouds hang ominously. 'Oh, look!' I exclaim, zooming in on a stall piled high with soft toys. 'I should get something for Poppy,' I add.

'Which one would she like?' Shane asks. A memory flickers: of Lloyd looking blank when I mentioned my granddaughter's name recently. Yet he expects me to remember the extensive cast that he used to party with, back in the day! Someone called Mad Max, who'd spiked a water cooler of blackcurrant squash with ecstasy!

'Hmm, I'm not sure…' I scan the garish selection.

'This fella?' Shane picks up a sparkly purple giraffe, and I laugh.

'I think maybe this,' I say, opting for a demure beige llama, hoping it'll be deemed acceptable.

'You said they live near you,' Shane ventures, as we stroll onwards. 'You must see a lot of them. I bet that's lovely.'

I'm poised to trot out my stock reply – 'Yes, it's wonderful' – but instead, I admit that it's a bit more complicated.

'Really? Nothing bad, I hope?'

I pause, my attention caught by a cheerful-looking café, its butter-yellow interior blurred by steamed-up windows. Inside, once we're seated, is where I tell him: that it's not how I thought it would be. That Cora seems to be intent on keeping me at bay, and that Zack regards me with mild shock/horror as if I'm the cleaner who's shown up at precisely the wrong time.

'That must be hard for you,' Shane offers, and I nod.

'It is, but maybe it's me? Maybe I expected too much.'

'But she's your only child. Your first grandchild,' he adds. 'Of course you want to be part of it all.'

'Yes, I do.' Without thinking – because surely he doesn't want to see *baby photos?* – I go to pull up a picture of Poppy on my phone. Only it's not my granddaughter who appears, but the soil-filled trough that Lloyd built.

'What's that?' Shane asks, peering more closely.

'Oh!' I quickly shut it down. How stupid of me to save it for my friends' amusement next time we meet. 'Just something my boyfriend built. For the garden,' I say quickly.

'You have a garden?'

'Erm, no. Not personally. It's a communal garden and we're going to grow, um...' My mind empties itself of all the vegetable names. 'Sweet peas,' I announce. 'No, I mean *peas*. Regular peas.'

'Right!' He looks a little baffled and not entirely convinced. 'So, d'you live together, then? You and—'

'Me and Lloyd? God, no. I mean, he's a nice guy but I couldn't live with him. Not with his violent drama thing...'

'What? You don't mean—' Shane breaks off.

'Oh, no,' I say quickly. 'I mean watching them. I can't stand it. I annoy him by constantly asking who the baddies are.'

He smiles at that and seems to relax again. 'So that's his thing, is it?'

'Very much so,' I reply, still rattled by that brief sighting of the soil trough picture. Am I up for doing this – flaunting my muddied feet – as long as my face isn't pictured? What if someone (Cora and Zack, for example) found out? I'd be banished not merely from their home, but their *postcode.*

Shane's mouth flickers with amusement. 'In among making raised beds,' he says.

'Raised beds?'

'Yeah.' He nods, expression neutral. 'The one in the picture. You said he's into gardening too—'

'That's right! Blood, gore and gardening.' I look at him, wanting very much to change the subject now. And as we sip our builder's tea, I wonder in fact if he *knows.* Whether he's figured it out somehow – the trough thing, and what it's really for. Did he hear me talking to Lloyd that evening, back in – where was it again? Bridlington, I think. It's all blurred into one, all of the tiny incidents bringing us to where we are now.

'Shane?' I start.

'Yeah?'

'I… I just wanted to say, I'm glad we're doing this,' I tell him.

He blinks in surprise. 'You are?'

'Yes, I really am.'

The smile reaches his beautiful eyes, and I yearn to lean over the table, in this steamy little buttercup-yellow café, and kiss him. 'Well, I am too,' he says.

'I'm glad about that.' As a warm feeling seems to fill my heart, it feels as if that's all we need to say on the subject as we leave the café. It's true; I really am happy to be here, with Shane. However, by the time we reach the car park, where Doris awaits us, I'm starting to think that perhaps we could up our accommodation standards, just a little. My broken-zipped sleeping bag might have served me perfectly well twenty years ago, but our relationship is flagging a little. Shane has mentioned Boris rhapsodising about freedom and life on the road but – controversially, and perhaps I'm being terribly feeble – wouldn't an actual *bed* be nice?

'Shane?' I say. 'I know this is a bit nuts, and I really do need to do this trip on the cheap. But I was thinking...' I catch his expression flicking from quizzical to bemused, as if he knows exactly what I'm going to say. 'But sod it,' I add. 'That mattress is doing my back in a bit and every morning I've woken up hardly able to turn my head.'

'Have you?' he exclaims. 'Why didn't you say anything?'

'There was nothing you could do about it, was there?' I smile. 'And I'm sure it's not been great for you either.'

He shrugs. 'It's been... okay!' Obviously, it hasn't.

'Even so, would it be terrible to cheat a bit, and stay in a hotel?'

Shane frowns, appearing to be giving the matter serious consideration – but I know he's faking. 'Well, I guess Ravi didn't stipulate the van part,' he remarks.

'No, she didn't.'

'So we wouldn't be breaking any rules,' he adds.

'Shall we do it then and book a twin room? We could stretch to that, couldn't we? In some ramshackle little hovel...'

He laughs, already stepping away from the van. 'You make it sound so tempting.' Then, suddenly serious, 'But wouldn't you miss the freedom?'

I chuckle, thinking how far we've come. Not merely in miles but the way we are together, doing this bonkers thing. 'I think we'd cope, wouldn't we?' I reply. 'Just for one night.'

26

SHANE

Shane had been thinking the same. He just hadn't wanted to wimp out. Now, though, he is immensely happy at the prospect of a little respite from the miserly mattress and chilly nights. So, having abandoned Doris in a car park, and with their rucksacks on their backs containing just overnight essentials, they roam the streets of Pontefract in search of a hotel.

'A hovel will do', Josie had said, but surely they can do a bit better? Shane is aware that she'll rail against him offering to pay – not that he's Rich Tony, but he knows she's on a tight budget. They stop at a somewhat bleak-looking B & B, jammed between an upmarket antiques shop and an artisanal pizza place. A jug of plastic roses, bleached of all colour, sits on the windowsill in front of a less-than-sparkling net curtain. They look at each other, shake their heads and stroll on.

Josie's phone rings, and he hangs back a little, anticipating the boyfriend nagging her about this thing they're doing (Shane still doesn't understand what it is and doesn't feel it's his place to pry). As he feigns interest in the window display of yet another sweet shop – Pontefract seems to be powered by confectionery –

he hears her say, 'I'm good, Mum. I'm actually in Yorkshire! No, Pontefract. Yeah, I know. Just a little road trip with a friend...'

Of course, Josie's parents knew Shane, back in the day. She probably doesn't want to go into it all, he decides. While Josie chatters on, Shane studies the window of another shop, this time displaying professional cooking equipment, as if he's in the market for something called a cast-iron steak press, £47. 'We're in a campervan,' she continues. 'No, Mum, I haven't bought one! Don't you think I'd have told you?' She has a wonderful warm laugh, Shane thinks. After their horribly awkward meeting that day, at the Kapoors' celebration for Ravi, he'd forgotten about that. 'We've borrowed it,' Josie explains. 'Yes, it's lovely. So cosy and it has everything we need... Yeah, okay. Put Dad on...'

In the pause that follows, Josie glances at Shane with a fond, *Parents, eh?* eye-roll. 'Hi, Dad. Yeah, of course we're driving carefully. Yep, we're properly insured...' There's more chatter as, endearingly, she seems keen to impress her dad by detailing their cultural and historical highlights: the castle, museum and art gallery. Shane picks up on the affection in her voice, and it stirs a sense of guilt in him.

Perhaps he should have factored in a visit to his mum. It's been a couple of years since he last saw her – way too long, really. However, even though his stepfather is an old man now, bald as an egg and somehow shrunken into himself, he's still Pete and his mum still fusses around him and apparently, he can do no wrong.

On Shane's last visit, the fridge had housed a miserly sliced white loaf and several teacups containing unidentifiable leftovers. He'd concocted a fib about popping out to see an old schoolfriend, and with his old buddy sitting invisibly beside him, he'd necked three large whiskies in The Grey Mare. Back at his mum's, he'd packed up his records that had been put away in the attic and left at the crack of dawn the next morning.

They are passing a record shop now and, although Shane feels the pull of it, he manages to resist.

'Shane?' Josie touches his arm and points across the street. 'How about checking that out?'

The Sweet Jar, the candy-striped sign reads. 'Just another sweet shop,' Shane says.

'No, it's The Sweet Jar Hotel,' she corrects him. 'Look – "hotel" is in tiny letters underneath.'

'So it's a sweet-themed hotel?' Shane pulls up his jacket hood as the rain comes on again, with almost comical force.

'Looks like it,' Josie says. So they hurry across the road towards what looks like two Victorian terraced houses knocked together, and exchange a quick smile as they step into the reception area. It's a sherbet explosion: pink curtains, pistachio rugs and vases of frothy peach blooms. There are dishes of cellophane-wrapped boiled sweets on the reception desk, on a couple of low side tables and even on the windowsill.

They wait expectantly. The sound of voices and the clink of crockery drifts out from another room, and Josie whispers, 'It's setting my teeth on edge.'

'I can feel a diabetic coma coming on,' Shane remarks, and she sniggers. They wait some more, and he eyes the bell on the reception desk. As if to prove that she is unintimidated by it, Josie gives it a decisive ding.

The sound of clacking footsteps grows louder. 'Oh, hello. I'm so sorry!' A young woman with glossy dark curls clamped under a rigid polka dot hairband has appeared, hot-cheeked and looking a little harassed. 'We're short-staffed today. How can I help you?'

'We were wondering if you have any rooms,' Josie says.

'A *twin* room,' Shane blurts out, louder than is strictly necessary.

'Hmmm, let's see...' The woman presses her lips together and peers at a computer screen. 'We just have a double, I'm afraid.'

'Oh.' Shane frowns and turns to Josie.

'Are you sure?' she asks the receptionist.

'Yes, sorry. For one night, is it?'

'Yes, that's right,' Shane replies. She tells them the price – it's surprisingly low – and turns back to her computer as if to allow them a moment.

Shane looks at Josie, who seems to be weighing up what to do. He doesn't want anything to spoil today, as it's been wonderful for him. For one thing, it's chimed in with his love of history (there's nothing he couldn't tell you about liquorice production now!). But more than that, he's loved just wandering around with Josie with no particular plan.

He still has her down as a spiritual type. He'd hovered, bemused, as she enthused at the market over tinkling wind chimes and dreamcatchers and fridge magnets bearing various affirmations. Stuff he still thinks – rather old-fashionedly – as 'new age'. Despite the procession of hippies who come into his shop, he doesn't know the first thing about that world. In contrast, Shane battles with what Elaine teasingly refers to as 'old-age stuff': that rogue eyebrow hair, his cricked shoulder from lugging instruments around, and the peculiar clicking sensation coming from his left knee from time to time.

However, despite the joys of Josie's company, he now is overcome with an urge to lie down – even briefly – on something springy and comfortable, in an actual heated building. Plus, it's still bucketing it down out there, and the thought of further hoofing around town makes him sag a little.

How big is the bed? he wants to ask. Surely it's huge, as seems to be the norm in hotels these days. But what are its precise dimensions? Could she show them a scale plan? Shane inhales the scent of synthetic strawberry, which he assumes is coming from the nearby reed diffuser, and looks at Josie. 'What d'you think?' he asks.

She pulls a *not-ideal-is-it?* face. 'I guess it'll be all right for one night. I mean, it'll be nice to have a break from the van.'

'I think so too,' Shane remarks.

'You'd like to take it, then?' the woman asks pleasantly.

'Yes please,' Josie says. Minutes later the receptionist is trotting up a short flight of stairs, each one painted in a different pastel colour, with Shane and Josie following in her wake.

As they pass along the corridor, Shane exchanges an amused glance with Josie. The rooms, too, are all sweet-themed. The Humbug Snug. The Dolly Mixture Den. The Parma Violet Suite. *What's ours going to be?* Shane muses.

'Just along here,' the woman trills, rounding the corner in clicky heels. She stops at the last door in the corridor and beams expectantly. 'Here we are. I have to say, it's my favourite room. You're very lucky, as couples often request it specially.'

Shane senses his chest tightening and realises his back teeth are clenched together. He looks at Josie, seeing her healthy flush fade, as the woman swipes a key card and opens the door to The Love Heart Boudoir.

27

JOSIE

It's a long time since I've eaten a Love Heart. I'd forgotten how many different phrases there are on the sweets. TRUE LOVE. HUG ME. YOU'RE FAB. BE MINE. And the colours! If you'd put a gun to my head, I'd never have been able to list them. But I know them all now, as one entire (pink) wall of our room is covered in polystyrene Love Hearts the size of extra-large dinner plates.

As soon as the woman leaves us, Shane bursts out laughing. I look at him, hand clamped over my mouth, hysteria rising in my chest. KISS ME. I LOVE YOU. YOU'RE HOT. We simmer down and then start up again. Like the time we saw our maths teacher – Mr Groocock with the sandy wig – roaring past the bus station in full leathers on a Harley. We'd clutched each other then, our eyes streaming. Shane had had to cling to a lamp post for support.

'They're definitely committed to the theme,' he manages now, gazing around at the matching curtains and duvet cover – also patterned with Love Hearts – and at baskets of the ubiquitous sweets set on the wicker bedside tables.

In an attempt to wrestle myself together, I'm trying to think about non-funny things. That Dairylea slice in the art book! My impending financial woes and another night in my disgusting pyjamas! At least the bed is of a generous size – far bigger than the van's mattress – and the bathroom is plainly lined in white brick tiles, perhaps for retina-soothing purposes.

'Can we actually stay here, d'you think?' Shane asks.

'I guess so. But it's making me queasy. Will you hold my hair back if I'm sick?'

'I'd be happy to,' he deadpans. 'I mean, I've done it before.'

I smile, filled with a rush of warmth for him – a sugar rush, possibly – and perch on a spindly lilac chair at the table by the window. Now Shane is studying the outsized Love Hearts wall as if expecting the slogans to magically rearrange themselves and spell out the meaning of life. 'So, what are we going to do now?' I ask.

He strokes his chin and smiles. 'We haven't done our photo yet, so I guess we'd better do that?'

'God, yes. The Black Bull, isn't it? Shall we head out and find it?'

He nods, looking keen to get out. 'I think so,' he says. 'I'm guessing it'll be more appealing than the bar here.'

'You mean you don't fancy a sherbet cocktail?' I grin. 'No, me neither. Let's go.'

Perhaps that night, back in 1988, had ended up an especially boozy one. Because when we arrive at the huddled little pub on an otherwise deserted street, we have no recollection of having played here at all. Still, we take our Polaroid, dutifully – old hands at this now – with his arm around my shoulders, my face pressed next to his. Then we step inside and order drinks, plus a selection of bar snacks entitled 'Picky Bits' on the laminated menu.

When the small, indistinguishable brown nuggets materialise, our hunger seems to have dwindled. In the corner, a fruit machine beeps and flashes and a loud group of young men are holding court around the biggest table.

I look at Shane, wondering now if booking a room was the right thing to do. I'm certainly conscious of it *awaiting* us: that enormous bed, overpopulated with cushions and pillows, and that huge puffy duvet emblazoned with KISS ME motifs. A room we have booked and paid for and are therefore committed to. Whereas Doris's flat mattress is just *there.*

I drink my wine, and Shane sips his beer, without either of us saying much. The walls are almost entirely covered with framed photos of what's presumably the local football team – the classic line-up of lads on the pitch – plus yellowing newspaper clippings celebrating their successes. Enthusiastic football talk fills the room. Pontefract Collieries – 'The Colls' – are having a moment, it seems. The bald, portly man behind the bar is enthusiastically trashing a recent performance by another northern team.

I catch Shane's eye. 'So, our last night tomorrow,' I remark.

'Yeah.' His expression is unreadable.

'Then home! We've almost done it.'

'Yeah.' That's it: just *yeah.* He wipes a touch of froth from his upper lip, and we slip back into silence. Of course he's fully aware of our itinerary. I don't know why I'm spelling it out to him.

'I'm quite proud, actually,' I go on. 'At the Kapoors' place, I never imagined we'd actually do this, did you?'

'God, no,' he admits. *You want to go home now,* I decide, *even though Elaine is there. You've made the best of it but you've had enough.* He does agree to another drink, which I insist on getting up to buy, if only to be able to chat to the barman – I assume he's the proprietor here – instead of sitting there with my thoughts swirling. *He'd rather be at home with Elaine's stinky fat fumes than here with me!*

In contrast, the bald man seems fascinated by our reason for being here. 'Amazing. So you were a proper band? With a record deal?'

'Not exactly.' I smile.

'You got close though?'

'Kind of close... *ish*,' I concede.

He chuckles. 'So it's Huddersfield next?'

'Yep,' I reply. 'The bright lights await us.'

'Like the Rolling Stones!'

I laugh and make my way back towards Shane, hoping I'm also bringing a little of the man's *joie de vivre* to our table.

'Hello, Huddersfield!' calls out one of the men from the big group, mimicking a frontman with a mic.

'We have fans,' I tell Shane as I sit back down opposite him.

His face softens and I catch a hint of a smile. 'Nice place, this,' he remarks.

'It actually is. Very friendly...'

He looks around, as if trying to figure out something. 'We must have set up over there, in that corner?'

'Guess so,' I say. And then I add – because I can't help it – 'I'm a bit sad, Shane.'

His forehead furrows and his gaze settles on mine, unwavering. 'Are you?'

'Yeah,' I say quietly. 'I mean, after tomorrow, this will be over—'

'I know,' he cuts in. 'I'm sad too.'

My heart quickens. 'Really?'

There's a proper smile this time. A big, warm grin that crinkles his eyes. 'Yes, really!'

'It's been all right, hasn't it?' I ask.

He bites his lip and the moment seems to shimmer between us. 'No, not really,' he says.

'What?'

'I mean, it's been *better* than all right,' Shane says quickly.

'You really think that?'

'I do!'

I look at him, and my heart seems to swell. 'Shane, I know we haven't talked about this,' I blurt out, 'but I wanted to say, all those years ago, that night in Huddersfield—'

'Hey, it's okay.' He stares at me.

'No, it's not.' I clear my throat, trying to wrestle myself under control. 'What I said that night—'

'Josie, it's all so long ago. We were young, it doesn't matter.'

'I know, but—' I stop and then I lean towards him over the little circular table, and throw my arms around him, and his arms are around me and we're hugging tightly, narrowly missing knocking over our drinks.

Finally, we pull apart. 'You don't still feel bad, do you?' he asks softly.

'I do a bit,' I admit, aware of my cheeks burning.

'Well, yeah.' He forms a grim smile. 'I do too.' I inhale, looking around the pub, at the bunch of men all clustered around the big table, who have fully resumed their football chatter. 'We don't need to, though,' he adds, 'any more.'

'No, we don't,' I say as we get up and leave the pub, amidst a flurry of good lucks and 'Hello, Huddersfield's! And once outside I link my arm in his, simply because we are friends, and it feels like the right thing to do.

28

Back at our boudoir I shower and change into my terrible PJs and examine my face in the bathroom mirror. Is it the sun I've caught, from our Bridlington day, or an alcoholic flush? The wine has rushed to my head tonight. Not enough carbs – those 'Picky Bits' weren't exactly tempting – to mop it up.

I emerge from the bathroom to find Shane lying on his side of the bed, shoes off, but still in his jeans and a sweater. He jumps up. 'I'll have a shower too,' he announces. I watch him disappear into the en suite and lie on my side of the bed, on top of the duvet. How funny, I reflect, that in just three nights together we have 'sides'. But not for much longer because very soon, all of this will seem like a bizarre dream.

He reappears in his joggers and a T-shirt, and we sit side by side on the bed, backs against the quilted headboard, legs stretched out. Like an old couple, I reflect, fiddling about on our phones.

I glance over at his mobile and smile. 'I know,' he says, catching my look. 'Liv says it's an embarrassment. An ancient artefact.'

'I'd say she's right,' I remark.

'It's all, "God, Dad. Put that thing away!"' He hands it to me and, although I have already registered the state of it, I examine it more closely this time. It's welded together with sticky tape and possibly powered by steam. I chuckle and pass it back.

'Well,' I say, 'if it *works*—'

'—then why bother upgrading?' he finishes.

'Very sensible.' As Shane reaches for his book, I switch my attention back to my own phone, about to message Lloyd, just to see what he's been up to. It feels slightly odd to be about to text my boyfriend when I'm stretched out on a king-size bed, emblazoned with Love Hearts, with another man. But he's not 'another man' – he's Shane, my companion on our *pilgrimage* – and Lloyd isn't the jealous type.

In fact, I'm wondering now if he's been a bit under the weather these past couple of days. He's certainly been quiet – but then he's not a big texter at the best of times. And perhaps he's a little huffy about my lack of enthusiasm over the soil trough. *It's just a bit of fun!* was his last message on the subject. *No big deal. We don't have to use it if you don't want to.*

I start to figure out what else I could use it for, seeing as it's sitting there, waiting for me in my flat. Yes, the block has a communal garden but it's firmly under the control of Deena from upstairs. The one time I added a pretty pink hydrangea in a pot, she swiftly moved it, tucking it away in a corner like a sleazy uncle at a family gathering. 'I thought it'd be better there,' she said tartly, 'out of the way.'

Would Cora like the trough, I muse, for her tiny back garden? But then how would I explain what it was originally for, and why I came to own it? It's not the kind of thing you just have kicking around. I'm turning all of this over, conscious of Shane at my side, so close to me on an *actual bed*, when my phone pings.

Weirdly, as if he can magically see the Love Heart bed situation – and he does mind, after all – Lloyd has messaged *me*.

I read it once, and then close my eyes and lean fully back against the padded headboard. Vaguely aware of Shane turning a page of his book, I open my eyes and read the message again. My heart is thudding, my hands trembling a little. Suddenly, so many things fall into place.

Shane reaches for a tiny packet of sweets from the bowl on his bedside table. 'Want some?'

I shake my head. 'No, thanks.'

His forehead creases as he sets down his book at his side. 'Are you okay?' he asks.

I swallow hard and try to steady my breathing. 'Um... not really,' I mutter. 'No, I'm not okay. Not at all.'

His gaze fixes on mine. I take a deep breath, knowing what the message means. And that there's no going back from it. 'What is it, Josie?' Shane asks gently.

Wordlessly, I show him my phone. He squints to read the screen.

'Who's this from?' he asks.

'Lloyd. My boyfriend.'

Shane frowns hard at it. 'Sorry, I don't get it...'

'He didn't mean it for me,' I tell him. 'It was... supposed to be for somebody else.'

His expression switches. 'Oh, God. Are you sure?'

'Yes. Yes, I'm sure.' That's when the tears well up and overflow as, in a room bedecked with giant Love Hearts, Lloyd has messaged:

Thanks for gorgeous pics you horny minx. I'm at J's flat still finishing that job here. Hurry over now.

29

We are drinking cocktails in the hotel bar. Or rather, I'm glugging mine (lilac, slightly fizzy) and Shane is sipping his gamely (violent green). His is only a third down by the time I'm slurping my sugary dregs, and I'm unembarrassed by this.

Obviously, further alcohol was needed after that message. The thought of Lloyd not only doing it but doing it *in my flat!* Are they swinging from my multicoloured plastic chandelier? Banging against my fridge? Doing it in my bed, even? I hope he warns her about the dodgy slat!

I have tried repeatedly to call him but it's just rung out and of course he's *busy* right now. Busy drinking my cheap white wine with her and laughing at my fridge magnets! 'Who's this mouse?' Lloyd asked once, jabbing at one of them.

'It's not a mouse,' I retorted, 'it's Madame Cholet.'

'Madame who?' The lady Womble! What a dope! I should have *known.*

A minor positive is that the hotel bar is still open at this late hour. We found the clamped-headband receptionist manning it, and she uttered the magical words, 'Yes, no problem. What would you like?' I could have torn that Love Heart off the wall of our room for her. The one that says I LOVE YOU.

The cocktails are fierce, and this is a good thing. No pissing around with weak alcohol when your so-called boyfriend has been receiving photos of an intimate nature from an unknown woman and is likely to be shagging her at this very minute. I wonder if he's Missionary Man with her too, and if she can orgasm that way? If she can name all the members of the Brat Pack, with extra points for Ally Sheedy? Bet she can't.

'What a time to come off antidepressants,' I remark, and Shane smiles grimly. We are on our second round now, and he is sticking to the lurid cocktails, in solidarity. 'You're absolutely sure that message wasn't meant for you?' he ventures.

'Definitely not. I haven't sent him any photos, although he's been asking for them...' I catch Shane's surprised look. 'Of my feet,' I add weakly.

'Er... right!' He sips his caramel negroni.

'It's a thing he wants us to do,' I start, any lingering scraps of embarrassment having long been dissolved by my Dolly Mixture martini. So I spill it all out: Lloyd's insistence that we'd 'make a packet', that he'd take care of the visuals and all I'd need to put into it was my time and a wide array of nail polish options.

'Wow,' Shane murmurs. 'How did you feel about that?'

I shrug. 'I'm not a prude, but it kind of weirded me out.'

'I can imagine.' We let this settle, and then he looks at me and asks, hesitantly, 'So... that wooden box thing in your photo? The thing for growing peas in, was it really—'

'I'm sorry,' I cut in. 'That was a foot thing, for getting them muddied up. Apparently, the punters like that.' I laugh dryly.

Shane reaches across the candy-striped table and touches

my arm. 'Christ, Joze.' That's what he used to call me: *Joze*. 'I'm sorry this has happened to you,' he adds.

'Oh, I'm all right,' I say dismissively. 'It's good to know, at least.'

'I s'pose so. Still very hurtful though.'

I nod, conscious of the prickle of tears gathering at the back of my eyeballs, and flinch as my phone rings on the table.

It's Lloyd. I tip the remaining pink martini down my throat and jump up from my seat. 'Better take this,' I announce, already marching away from our table.

'Hey, hon!' Lloyd says.

'Hi, Lloyd.'

'So, how's life on the road? Got the band back together yet?' He sniggers.

'Not exactly,' I reply as I step outside into the cool, damp night. 'It'd be tricky, seeing as Ravi died.'

A brief pause. 'Oh, babe, I'm sorry. Just a joke.'

I breathe out slowly, trying to steady myself. 'I... got a message from you,' I blurt out.

'Did you?' The silence hangs between us. A ginger cat, eyes glinting in the silvery glow of the street lights, peeps out from under a car.

'Yes, I did. Obviously, it wasn't meant for me.'

'Shit,' he murmurs.

'It was a bit much, to get that,' I continue. 'Who did you mean to send it to?'

Lloyd exhales, as if my pesky trivial questions are irritating to him. 'It doesn't matter.'

'It matters to me!' I cry as I stomp down the street, away from the hotel. A sliver of moon shines hazily through the fine drizzle. I think of Shane, sitting alone at our table, with his caramel cocktail – 'liquidised Caramac!' he joked, being of the same vintage as me. And I realise just how much I want to be back there with him, in the bar's cosy warmth.

'So, what's her name?' I ask, as Lloyd is still not being forthcoming.

'It's not really relevant,' he replies.

'Actually, it is!' Fury rears up in me. 'I'd like to know, especially as you invited her to my flat.'

'No I didn't, I just—'

'Have you fucked her in my bed, Shane?'

'Hey!'

'If you have, would you strip the bedding and put a wash on? A hot wash, please. Ninety degrees with softener—'

'Stop it,' he snaps. 'No, I haven't. What d'you think I am?' Hmm, where to start? 'It wasn't meant like that,' he goes on. 'She's just... a friend. It's just a place to meet, with you being so close to the Tube—'

'In the middle of the night?'

'It's not that late—'

'It's nearly midnight!' I yell. 'Hang on – is she there now?'

'No, of course not.'

'Not yet.'

'Josie, *please*,' he says in a calmer voice. 'Look... it's nothing. Really. Just someone I see now and again. Just occasionally.'

'What, like, all the time we've been together?'

'No! Not really. I don't know,' he says hotly. 'I'm sorry, I guess we should have talked about this...'

Something dawns on me now as an attractive, entwined young couple approach, their voices tumbling together. That even though there's 'only' a decade between us, Lloyd and I view dating very differently. I mean, call me stupid, but I thought he was my boyfriend! I even took the fucker to Lanzarote last summer for a birthday treat! However, I realise now that, like Cora's bewildering clean beauty routine compared to my 'cakey' powder, Lloyd and I are from different eras. For him, it's all about talking to people on the apps and calling them horny minxes and apparently having sex with them. That's how it is now. Why didn't I know this?

'Anyway, what about you?' he counters.

I stop abruptly, realising I've arrived at The Black Bull pub where Shane and I were earlier. Now it's firmly shut up for the night. 'What *about* me?' I ask.

Lloyd snorts. 'Going on a little tour around the country with your old flame. Reigniting the spark.'

'He's not my old flame!' I splutter. 'There isn't any *spark*...'

All right, your honour. All *right*. I won't deny that I've experienced stirrings at certain points on this trip. When I had that panic attack, and Shane put his arm around me. I was still sweating like a horse and felt like I might vomit. But even then, a single thought – *Don't take your arm away! Keep it there forever!* – ricocheted around my brain.

When his hand brushed against mine, as we examined a scale model of a liquorice factory at the museum, I wanted to hold it. *People must think we're a couple*, I thought ridiculously (of course 'people' didn't think anything). As he sat opposite me in that campsite café, sipping his hot chocolate with a fleck of cream on his lip, I wanted to kiss it right off him. I've tried to dampen it down and get a grip on myself. But the truth is, I've been a pan of milk on the verge of frothing over from the minute we pulled away from Back Alley Music.

'Oh, come on,' Lloyd scoffs, factory settings fully restored. 'The two of you cosied up in a campervan together?'

'I'm telling you, it's not like that!'

'Really.'

'Yes, really.'

Lloyd sighs, as if trying to figure out where to go from here. 'Look, I'm sorry. I didn't want to hurt you, babe.'

I turn back towards the hotel. 'I guess we didn't have that *conversation*, did we?' I say dryly.

'What conversation?' he asks.

'The one I think you're meant to have, where you decide that you're going to be exclusive?'

I hear him clear his throat. 'Um, no. We've never had that conversation.'

I stop outside The Sweet Jar Hotel, feeling stranded and utterly stupid, and also decidedly tipsy, in this unfamiliar town. Silly Josie, assuming that seeing each other regularly, and going on holiday together and, latterly, him embarking on home improvements for me meant that we were actually a couple. I feel sometimes that the world is speeding ahead of me and I'm blundering along in its wake.

'So we're *not* exclusive,' I remark.

Lloyd has the decency to wait a moment, possibly to choose his words with care. 'Josie, look... I like you a lot. I really do. I think you're lovely and sweet and—'

'Sweet?' I bark at him.

'But I think we're at quite different stages.'

'Fine,' I snap. 'It's fine.'

'I'm still doing your kitchen shelves,' he adds quickly. 'They're looking great so far! I'll get them finished in the morning, you'll be so pleased when you come home—'

'No, just leave them,' I cut in.

'What?'

'Get out of my flat right now, Lloyd.'

'But—' I sense him frowning, perplexed by my unreasonableness. 'Don't want me to finish them properly?'

'No, I don't!'

'Okay, okay, no need to shout—'

'Just lock up and put your keys through my letter box.' With a gulp, I finish the call and scrunch up my eyes as if, when I reopen them, I'll have turned into a sensible woman fully in control of her life.

30

Ridiculously, the hotel bar has closed. I consider firing off a furious letter to the Pontefract Gazette, if such a paper exists. But instead, I grab Shane's arm as we make our way, a little woozily, up to our room.

As we navigate the stairs, I'm trying to figure out how upset I really am, and what I'm feeling. It's not heartbreak, I know that much. It's not even on the fringes of it. Viewing the situation through a blur of sugary booze, I'm not sure *what* it is. It seems funny, almost, as Shane and I make our way along the corridor. How slapdash of Lloyd, to missend a message! He's so meticulous with his work, and how he stores his tools and shaves in the morning and rolls a joint perfectly – like they've been factory-made. Yet with messaging – even though he double-thumbs like a youngster – it's all typos and half-written nonsensicals, or they're not sent at all: 'Sorry babe, I thought I'd replied!' In a wider sense, his communications skills aren't the best, and I realise I don't actually *know* the man, not really.

Shane swipes our key card and we step into the room. 'Well, it's not the van, at least,' I announce.

'No, it's not.' A pause settles, and he looks at me as if he wants to say something else.

'What is it?' I ask.

'It's just—what we said in the pub.'

My breath catches. 'About what happened?'

'No, not about that. I mean... it just feels a bit weird, that's all.'

I look at him, not understanding. 'You mean being here? Staying in a hotel together?'

He looks away and my heart seems to thud. 'No, it's not that either. I don't know. I s'pose it's sunk in, that's all. That soon we'll be heading back south—'

'Yes, I know.'

'And this'll all be over.'

His words seem to float around us. So he hasn't had enough of this, after all. Something new wells up in me and my heart quickens. 'It needn't be,' I say quietly.

'Needn't it?'

'No.'

The hotel, the street outside – the whole of Pontefract, it seems – is silent. We stand, facing each other, surrounded by Love Hearts. And then I step towards him and I slide my arms around his waist and reach up and kiss his beautiful mouth.

Like that time in the derelict mill, among the flapping pigeons, and in my house that day with the crow. And one more time, when I'd sent Ravi out to buy beers in the guest house in Huddersfield. I'd hatched that plan, so that Shane and I could be alone together – even for a few minutes. I'd wanted him that much.

And I want him now as we kiss deeply. I am melting like sugar as he holds me close. We pull apart, and I wrangle my top off over my head, and he does likewise. Our clothes fall onto the carpet of the Love Heart Boudoir, and now, drunk on wine and sweet cocktails and three days together in a van, we are naked in the confectionery-patterned bed.

I don't know how much time spins by. Hours, possibly, as we kiss and touch and hold each other in the dark. It's as if we know there's no need to rush. Unlike that mad scramble in Huddersfield, tonight we have all the time in the world. Then, finally, I can't hold back any more and I'm on top of him. I don't care that I'm so much older and differently shaped, and not how he might have remembered me. Because we're the same people, me and him. He *knows* me – he doesn't think I was born in 1937! – and I want him more than I have ever wanted anyone.

I lower myself to kiss his mouth, when he stops. 'Is this okay?' His gaze bores into me. 'Are you sure?'

'I'm sure,' I say. And then it happens and he is deep inside me, and every cell in my body is shimmeringly alive. I come with him, crying out. My face is wet with tears, and my head is filled with shooting stars – no fantasy needed, no flying fridge magnets or any of that.

My heart is thumping steadily as he wraps his arms around me and pulls me close. For a few moments we lie in silence together. And then Shane reads one of the Love Heart mottos aloud, and I do likewise. We do this, reading out every sweet on the wall, in between kissing and giggling until finally, wrapped up together, we tip over into sleep.

31

We sleep in a tangle, I think. I wake sporadically, aware of the warmth of him, and I breathe in the delicious scent of his skin. It's so familiar to me, but thrilling too as I don't know him like *this*. Shane, who's lived a life and driven Doris for hundreds of miles and cared for me when I had a driving freak-out. I don't know him at all, and yet I do, more than anyone. I want to wrap myself around him and never let go.

Then, rudely, daylight beams through the flimsy curtains, and just as I'm de-crusting my eyes, an unfamiliar ringtone fills the room. Shane peels away from me and reaches for his phone, then climbs out of bed. Still naked, he stands by the bathroom door, taking the call.

'Hey, you okay? Oh, right!' He grabs his boxers, jeans and T-shirt from the floor, as if caught out, and steps into the bathroom, leaving the door partly open. 'Yeah, I get that... You remember I'm away, don't you? I'll be back soon. Oh, that sounds a bit shit... We can talk about it then? When I'm home?' He clears his throat, and something falls over me like rain. The reality of what happened last night. How drunk we were, and whether *that's* why it happened, and whether he regrets it now.

I sit up in bed, mentally slotting together the jigsaw pieces. Lloyd's message. All those cocktails. The way I instigated this – launching myself at him like a missile. The way I climbed on top – oh God!

Still in the bathroom, Shane finishes the call. He reappears, looking a little sheepish with a bath towel wrapped around his waist. 'Sorry about that,' he says.

'Everything okay?' I ask, duvet pulled up to my chin.

'Just Ryan. My son.'

'Yes, I know.' *I know your kids' names,* is what I mean.

'Stuff at home with his—well—with Paula's partner.'

'Oh?'

'Nothing serious,' he adds, then disappears into the bathroom again. This time he shuts the door. Perhaps he even locks it! Who knows? What I do know is that the mood has changed, and I feel lost and stranded and utterly foolish in this giant bed.

I hear the shower blasting, and then, what feels like moments later, Shane emerges, fully dressed. I blink at him, trying to figure out how he has managed to do this so swiftly while I'm still lying naked beneath the billowing duvet. And why this is more crushing to me than Lloyd's missent message.

'Shane... is something wrong?' I ask.

'Ryan's just a bit upset.'

Anything you'd like to talk about? I want to ask him, but I don't.

I watch him opening the curtains a chink, examining the complimentary biscuits, filling the kettle and switching it on. And then he stops, as if he has run out of things to do. Neither of us says anything. At the sound of footsteps in the corridor, my whole body tenses, as if the clamped-hairband receptionist/bartender is about to burst in on us. When that doesn't happen – when *nothing* happens – I slide out of bed, feeling horribly naked, somehow *more* naked than I was when I was wrapped round him last night.

I dart to the bathroom and shut the door. I shower quickly, failing to be charmed by the sherbet gel, wrap myself tightly in a bath towel and come out.

Perched on the bed now, Shane looks at me and motions for me to sit beside him. I study his face, trying to read his expression, and sit a good metre away. He clears his throat, and this is how it starts, the joy swilling out of me like bathwater down the drain: 'Josie... I just wanted to say I, um... I realise you were pretty upset last night.'

I stare at him. 'I didn't do it just because I was upset!'

'It's okay! You don't have to explain it. You're hurt, and he hasn't been honest with you. And you thought—'

'Shane?' I cut in.

'Yeah?' His eyes widen.

'Can you stop telling me how I feel?'

He reddens and looks down at his hands. 'I'm sorry, I didn't mean—'

'You think I slept with you to get back at Lloyd? Like some kind of revenge?'

'I don't know, I—'

'Why are you saying all this?' Tears spring to my eyes and I jump up from the stupid bed and turn away so he doesn't see them.

Back in the bathroom, having gathered up my clothes and brought them in with me, I dress quickly and sit on the closed loo seat. Thirty-seven years it's been since the last time we did it. How many times have I thought about him since then, wondering where he was? And who he was with? Peeking at his Instagram, gathering clues – Paula's too. Like picking at a spot, I couldn't resist. In a recent one she was grinning at a restaurant table, with her and Shane's teenage children (they looked so like him, they had to be his), and an extremely buffed-looking bloke in a black polo neck. I checked the caption: *Copenhagen, you've been a blast!*

I've trawled Shane's account for pictures of him and Paula together, or him with any woman who might be a girlfriend or a wife. Home alone, after a bottle of wine, I've considered dropping him a message. *Hey, just stumbled upon you here! How are you? DON'T DO IT, YOU STALKING LOON!* I've actually said that out loud. *STOP IT! PUT YOUR PHONE AWAY!* It's a benefit of living alone, being allowed to shout at yourself. And this is what he thinks? That I only had sex with him because I was upset by a missent message from a man I'm not in love with – or, worse, that I wanted to pay him back?

It's true. I liked and fancied Lloyd, but I wasn't in love with him. The man I love is right here, on the other side of the bathroom door.

I stand up, readying myself to do this, fully aware of how mad it is. Could it be the meds? They warn you that you shouldn't come off them abruptly, but taper down. I haven't tapered. I've gone from the prescribed dose to zero and as part of the process I've had wild, thrilling sex with the only person who's ever made me feel that way.

Clutching my washbag, I step out of the bathroom and stuff it into my rucksack. 'What are you doing?' Shane exclaims.

I look at him, and then I gaze down at the bed. Just like at that guest house – the last place we stayed on our tour – the sheets are rumpled. Only this time it's different. We won't even get there because this is where it ends.

'I'm going home, Shane,' I say.

'What?'

'I can't do this any more. I want to go back to London.'

'But why?' He gets up and puts his arms around me, but I pull away. 'What about Huddersfield?' he asks, looking distraught.

'We'll always have Huddersfield!'

He stares at me. What made me do that? Make a terrible joke at a time like this?

'I don't think it's funny,' he mutters.

'No, I know. I'm sorry. I didn't mean—'

'So we're leaving now? You really want us to go back to London today?'

'No, I'm taking the bus.'

'The *bus*? Why?' His face pales and his beautiful eyes fill with hurt.

'Because it's cheaper than the train and—'

'I mean, why are you doing this, Josie? Why d'you want to leave without me?'

'I just think it's better,' I say firmly, hating myself already.

'So... you won't travel back to London with me?'

'No,' I say firmly.

'But why not? Please tell me!'

Because I can't bear it, is the answer. *Because I loved you so much back then, and all these years I haven't been able to shake you off me. It's why I fell into a thing with Dale Watson and moved to London with him. It's why I stayed with him, when it should only have been a fling, if that – all the better to push my love for you right out of my brain. And right now, the thought of five hours in the van with you is more than I can bear.*

'I'd just prefer it,' I say.

Shane rubs at his eyes and exhales loudly and finally regards me with a look of resignation. 'Okay then, if you're sure.'

'I am sure. I'm sorry.'

His mouth twists and I see that his eyes are wet. 'Fine,' he murmurs. 'I guess it doesn't matter about Huddersfield, does it? It's not as if Ravi will ever know.'

32

SHANE

The stupidest man in Britain is driving south at a steady 60 mph. The biggest twat in the known universe is telling himself that it's okay, it was her choice – and Josie knows her own mind.

It was bound to be a one-off, he'd decided, when he'd woken up with her snuggled close, her arm flopped across his chest. They'd had a ton of booze, and she'd literally just broken up with her boyfriend. She was upset, her emotions running high. That's why – thrillingly – she'd grabbed him and kissed him like he'd never been kissed in his life.

Last night had been incredible. For a short while this morning Shane had lain there in the Love Heart bed, replaying it all in his mind like a wonderful dream you don't want to fade from your consciousness just yet. But then had come the wake-up call: his son phoning him *on the actual telephone.* What terrible thing had happened? Who was injured or dead? Ryan despises making phone calls, and avoids them at all costs. Shane would be no less shocked to see him writing a cheque, or expressing enthusiasm over broccoli. So it had to be something major.

In fact, it turned out that all he'd wanted was a moan about Rich Tony establishing a 'Rota of Responsibilities' in their home, with stickers awarded for goals achieved. Shane gets it that, at sixteen, Ryan no more wants a sticker than a Thomas the Tank Engine pencil case. But he couldn't understand what he expected him to do about it at 8.15 a.m. from a hotel in Pontefract.

So all of that had rattled Shane. Then he'd had to switch from dad stuff back to the scenario with Josie. He didn't want her to feel awkward, or feel she had to explain anything to him ('Look, Shane, that was lovely but...'). *Pre-empt it,* his stupid brain had urged him. *Tell her you understand it was just a drunken thing in the heat of the moment, and that you're fine with that.*

Obviously, that went brilliantly.

As Doris's engine acquires a new, higher pitch, as if mocking him, Shane tries to shake off the terrible feeling that he's screwed everything up. As a distraction, he makes a concerted effort to focus on shop matters instead. What's been happening there, he wonders? He's barely been in touch with Fletch, as his mind has been very much elsewhere. However, these days, Back Alley Music is where he tends to feel at his most content. It had seemed like an impossible goal, at one time – to build a music-related business. He'd done years of session playing and teaching drumming, supplemented by a ton of bar work, but he'd known he couldn't keep doing that forever. Aside from the financial peril that engulfs him sporadically, things have turned out pretty well.

Only they haven't really, have they? Never mind the shop. Never mind sourcing an elusive brand of strings for a banjo orchestra in Bristol. What about his personal life? His relationships and his family – the things that really matter?

He stops at a service station for a coffee and sandwich and

wonders if he should message Josie. But what would he say? If she couldn't even bear to travel back to London with him, will she really want to be pestered by him now?

Maybe it's him, Shane reflects as he climbs back into the ambulance. When he and Fletch set up the shop, working all hours in order to refit the place and set up the website, he'd still been with Paula. Back then, he hadn't even realised anything was wrong. The kids were great – still at that age when they were generally happy and relatively uncomplicated and thrilled about the shop. In school holidays they'd loved to hang about there and 'help.' Liv played drums and Ryan played guitar. Music was a thing he had with his kids, something that bonded the three of them.

Had Paula felt excluded? He had no idea. So when it all came out – that she had a keen interest of her own – he was blindsided.

'I've met someone,' she announced one bleak, wet afternoon just after Christmas.

He stared at her. 'What d'you mean?' Of course, he realised she didn't mean, 'I met Mrs Lamar in the street, she wonders if you could help her drag her old mattress out for the council collection?' Nor did she mean she'd 'met' someone who might invest in the home storage business she'd set up with a friend. In fact, she didn't mean 'met' at all but was sleeping with.

'I'm sorry,' she said, tears spilling from her big brown eyes. 'I've dreaded telling you. I don't know what else to say.'

They were standing face to face in the living room. The kids were out, thank God. 'So... you mean this person, this person you've *met*...' Shane broke off. He knew what he wanted to ask – what he needed to know – but he was finding it hard to place the words in the right order. 'Does this mean you're... with him?' he choked out. 'You mean, you want to be with him and not me?'

Paula nodded. Tears continued to stream down her cheeks without dislodging her make-up. 'Yes, I do. I'm sorry, Shane. I really am.'

'But... why?' He stared at her.

She wiped her face briskly, and seemed to click into a business-like manner, as if faced with a particular challenge in the home storage arena. A request for a foldable hanging system for a child's room that could be reconfigured as they grew older, perhaps? Jolly butterfly motifs, attachable by Velcro, that could be switched for more sophisticated adornments as their tastes changed? In his reeling shock, Shane found himself *picturing* that storage system – and Paula demonstrating how to assemble it – and had to haul himself back to the matter in hand.

Following her announcement, Paula explained, curiously dry-eyed now, that their life together had taken so much out of her, she had 'nothing left to give'. All those years of trying for a baby and then finally going through IVF, resulting in their much-wanted baby girl. Then – miraculously – Ryan being conceived naturally and born when Paula was forty-one. Did Shane have any idea what that had been like for her? Being an older mother?

Not that old! he'd wanted to protest, but a rare flash of common sense had told him to keep his mouth shut.

Further details were spilled. The 'someone-she'd-met' wasn't Rich Tony (he came along later) but a man she'd got to know through her business. A man called Marcus who'd wanted a bespoke system for his *headquarters.* 'Honestly, Shane, it was a professional relationship until—' Until they'd taken their clothes off, presumably.

He'd grilled Paula some more about how long it had been going on, aware of the life they'd built falling away from him. All that history they shared – together since they were twenty, after the band had imploded and Josie had run off (that's how he'd viewed it. Shortly after the terrible end to their tour, he'd heard that she and Dale Watson were an item, and next thing they'd moved to London).

All he could do was leave the room, and their family home, and climb into his car and drive, drive, drive, finally ending up at the shop which was still closed for the festive season. He'd let himself in and then gone to the pub – a grimy old boozer down the road – and got royally pissed. Early next morning, he'd woken up in the shop, lying on the scratchy carpet behind the counter. *Well,* he thought as he hobbled outside to put the A-frame shop sign in the street, *I handled that maturely.*

He was fifty-one years old, and a father of two, and nothing would ever be the same for his children again. It wouldn't be the way he'd dreamed of and had wanted with every cell of his being from the moment Liv, and then Ryan were born.

Shane hadn't expected perfection. He realised that raising a family would be hard. But he'd known, more strongly than he'd ever known anything, that he'd wanted the very opposite from the family life he'd experienced with his mum and Pete. Warmth and kindness where what really mattered, he'd decided. From out of nowhere, a scene had popped into his mind: when Pete overheard Shane asking his mum if she'd buy him a hot-water bottle. *What does he think this is? The fucking Ritz?* Shane hadn't even known what the Ritz was, but he deduced that it was posh – like the salty crackers.

'You don't need one,' his mum had said firmly.

As a parent, he had to do better than that.

And now Shane is driving home alone, back to Onion Elaine, wondering how he could have handled things so much better this morning. What is it about him and his ability to mess things up? And why on earth had Ravi sent him and Josie on this ridiculous trip? Maybe it was to pay them back for something. That's all he can think of. But then, what could it have been? Surely she hadn't still been pissed off about what had happened in that Huddersfield guest house, back in 1988?

Whatever it is, Shane can't fathom it out at all. All he does know is that somehow, in a pretty major way, he's made a terrible mistake.

33

JOSIE

My bus journey back to London has taken an even darker turn.

The man sitting next to me has pulled out a crisp packet from his bag and is noisily crunching some kind of powerful-smelling snack. Monster Munch, I realise. Beef flavour, judging by the stink.

What kind of middle-aged man eats Monster Munch on a bus? It has to be an offence. *Section 67 of the Aggravating Snackery Act 1982.*

I shoot him a quick look. He smiles, wet-lipped, before sucking each finger clean (mustn't waste that salty dust!). Finally, he *licks* a finger and slithers it around the bottom of the packet to mop up any remaining bits.

Once finished, he scrunches up the packet and swivels fully towards me. 'Been on a holiday, love?'

'Um, no, just a short trip.'

'Ah, right. Back home, huh?' He's picked up on the traces of my West Yorkshire accent.

'Kind of,' I fib, hoping that will shut him down.

'Have a good time?'

'It's been fun.' Yeah – fantastic! Apart from sleeping with a very old friend, and then acting so badly this morning, leaving him there after what happened last night. I close my eyes briefly, trying to blot out the horror. One more town and we'd have finished what we'd set out to do. We'd have done it for Ravi, for her parents – for ourselves.

'No place like home, eh?' the man remarks.

'No.' I force a smile.

'So, d'you live in London?'

'Yes,' I reply, wondering why I am programmed to make conversation with strangers like this. Don't they say that, as your oestrogen dwindles, you stop caring what anyone thinks of you? If anything, I care *more.*

'Oh, I couldn't live there,' the man declares, scowling. 'So busy and dirty. I'm only going on a quick visit to see a mate.'

I shrug. 'Well, I like it.'

'Do you?' he exclaims, as if I'd said, *I absolutely love to roll in manure.*

'Yes, I do.' The beef odour is lingering and I need something to mask it. I delve into my shoulder bag, thinking peppermint will do it – but there's no gum. Not even a loose pellet kicking around among the cheap lip balms and ageing make-up.

In weirdly mirroring behaviour, the man has started to rummage in his own bag. Finally, he extracts a roll tightly encased in cling film. He unwraps it carefully and takes a bite. Of course it's an egg roll – not even egg mayo but *sliced* egg, pungently sulphurous and mingling with the beef. I know this because a slice has tumbled out and landed on his right thigh. How can he leave it sitting there on his trouser leg? Is he hoping it'll sink in, like spilt water on a rug?

I eyeball the egg slice. It seems to be eyeballing me back, mockingly. *See your life?* it sneers. *It's a mess. Look at you, travelling home by bus. How does that make you feel? What must Shane be thinking now?*

The bus rumbles on. Apparently sufficiently fed, Monster Muncher has nodded off and is snoring throatily. Many moons ago, when Cora was around twelve – and apparently still *liked* me and wasn't determined to keep me away from her – she did a school project on the world's remotest settlements. I still remember our giggles when she told me about a chilly little town in northern Norway. 'Is that where the cake comes from?' I'd asked.

'Not Battenburg, Mum,' Cora spluttered. '*Barentsburg*.'

That's how far home feels right now, with the egg slice having travelled roughly a hundred miles on the man's sheeny-trousered leg. But I can handle it. I'm a hardy, peasant-footed northern girl and I can survive a lengthy bus journey with a stranger belching quietly beside me. I just need to grit my teeth and banish all thoughts of last night from my mind.

It was a big mistake, I tell myself firmly. Topping off the night with a gallon of liquidised sweets, and then sleeping with Shane when I was messed up over the Lloyd stuff? It was never going to turn out well.

The only thing for it is to slip the episode into the already over-stuffed file in my brain, labelled *Josie's Grave Errors of Judgement*. But instead, my head floods with images of me and him last night, loving each other that way, in our hotel bed. All I want now is to jump off this bus, wherever we stop next, and call him.

I want to ask him to meet me in the ambulance or, if that's not possible, in London. I want to tell him that I lied to Ravi that night of the broken guitar in Huddersfield. That I hadn't meant what I'd said to her; that I'd loved him madly. After he'd gone, I'd glanced into his little single room, at the bed that was still rumpled from us, a lone pillow lying on the floor.

Glancing briefly at the egg slice, I go to pull my phone from my bag and check for messages. But instead, my hand snags on our Polaroids, bundled together with one of my ponytail bands. I pull them out and remove the band and study them, one by one.

Hello, Grimsby, Bridlington, Scarborough and Pontefract! I think of the jovial publican in The Black Bull: 'What, like the Rolling Stones?'

No, I think: like two people who really only ever wanted to be together. Reaching for my phone, I go to our message thread. With Monster Muncher still snoring erratically at my ear, I try to find the right words to say to Shane. *Best golden love* – that would do! But he feels so far away now, I just can't do it.

He feels as far away as Barentsburg.

34

SHANE

On this warm and humid evening, Shane tries to appreciate the shabby charm of his street. He is lucky to live here he reflects as he parks Doris as close as he can to his block.

It's not the London of artisan bakeries and speciality coffee shops with *tasting notes* on their various bean varieties. (He can't fathom how they can have 'bursts' of citrus, clove and jasmine. And if he's honest, Shane doesn't fully understand what matcha is.). But it's his London, and he loves it. From the very first day when he and Paula landed here, he felt as if he belonged.

Even so, he's been putting off going home – to the point where he stayed away for an extra night, at a campsite in some random spot in the Midlands. He just needed a little more time to try and get his head together. All was fine with the shop, Fletch said. 'No need to hurry back. Glad it's all worked out so well, mate!'

Shane wouldn't have put it that way exactly. He'd sat there alone in the van, drinking beer, missing Josie with an actual ache, and trying to piece together exactly how everything had gone so wrong.

The other reason for being in no hurry to get back is the fact that his home doesn't feel the same to him any more. As he approaches his block, with his rucksack on his back, Shane's chest is taut with tension. It's not that he is afraid to enter his flat; that he is primed to intercept an intruder or find blood on the walls. More that he is hoping with every cell of his being that Elaine won't be there.

He needs, more than ever, a bit of time to himself. Just to sit and think in a quiet room, without Elaine chattering about her Crafternoon sessions and what does he think of her polka dot gel nails and thrusting her phone at him with a picture of an outfit she wants to buy.

What was the last thing she wanted his opinion on? Something green and pink, emblazoned with peacocks? 'Jesus, Shane, it's a co-ord set,' she'd cackled. He'd thought they were pyjamas.

Thoughts of this type always make him feel guilty, as Elaine can't help her situation. In recent years she's lived in terrible flats and done some pretty grim jobs. She's worked in shabby clubs and cleaned budget hotel rooms favoured by stag and hen crowds. Of course she's entitled to kick up her heels and have some fun. And this situation is only temporary, he reminds himself as he climbs the short flight of metal stairs, lets himself into his flat and steps into his hallway.

Setting down his rucksack, he looks around and listens and inhales. The door was only on the Yale lock – no Chubb lock – but that doesn't mean anything. Elaine never bothers to double-lock it. Still, no TV is blaring, and no one is clomping about or singing loudly in the bathroom. There is no smell of burnt fat hanging in the air.

'Hi?' Shane calls out tentatively. No reply comes. He still expects her to bound out from her bedroom, or the bathroom, in her pink satin pyjamas with her face slathered in some kind of creamy mask. It's almost noon, but it's not unlike her to lie in until lunchtime after a heavy night.

The realisation that he has returned to an Elaine-free home triggers a small wave of relief. He wanders into the living room and sees that, instead of lying all over the room, as if tossed about by a gale, her puzzle magazines are sitting in a neat stack on the coffee table.

Curious behaviour, he notes, making his way to the kitchen where – shockingly – there is no chopping board left out, no dirty frying pan left on the hob. All that's out on the draining board are two wine glasses, washed and placed upside down to dry.

He registers the vase of carnations on the table, their pastel colours reminding him of Love Heart sweets, and for about a billionth time he checks his phone.

Still no message from Josie. He feels stupid for even thinking she might contact him because she'd made it absolutely clear that she didn't want anything more to do with him. That's why Shane hasn't messaged her. And anyway, what would he have said? With a heavy feeling in his chest, he makes himself a mug of builder's tea and a slice of toast with the lone, stale crust that's left in the bread bin.

Again, he studies the carnations. Weird, he thinks. Elaine has never bought flowers for the flat before.

Carrying his tea and toast through to the living room, he places them on the coffee table and stretches out on the sofa, a little achy from driving the rattling biscuit tin. Without Josie at his side, even with his stop-off in the Midlands, the drive home had seemed interminable.

He chews on his toast, remembering those motorway toasties they'd had, when it had still felt so weird and awkward between them. Yet even then, he'd felt glad that they were doing this mad thing together. He'd had a feeling about it, even then. That it might heal things somehow – perhaps even repair their friendship.

He reaches for his phone and messages Boris, confirming that he's back in London, and would he like him to drop off the van at his flat, or the shop?

BORIS

Shop's fine. Did the old girl behave herself?

Then, in quick succession:

I'm talking about Doris, not your esteemed lady friend!

Shane picks up his mug and blows across it, wondering what Josie is doing now. Whether his *esteemed lady friend* is busily searching recruitment sites, and has given that cuddly llama to her granddaughter yet? She'll be cracking on with things, he reckons. Getting on with her life. He takes a sip of tea.

SHANE

All good, mate. Really appreciate it—

He breaks off and sits bolt upright. He heard something there – a heavy thud. Just somebody upstairs, he decides. The walls and floors of this building are paper-thin. He often hears the ping of a microwave in the flat above.

No, it's not upstairs, Shane realises. Someone's here in his flat – in the hallway he thinks. 'Who's there?' he calls out sharply.

Another thud. He leaps up, still clutching his mug, his heart banging hard.

'Whoa, sorry, mate!'

'What the hell—?' Shane reels back, sloshing tea onto himself as a man appears in the doorway. It takes him a moment to register that this tall, powerfully built individual is entirely naked.

'Didn't realise you were here!' the man exclaims.

Shane stares at him. 'I fucking live here, mate! Who are *you*?'

'So you're Shane,' he says, ignoring the question. *It's my flat! Who else might I be*? Casually, the stranger tugs earbuds from his ears, reaches for a pair of black joggers from the back of a chair – Shane had assumed they were Elaine's – and, seeming in no particular hurry, pulls them on. His man bun, Shane notices, is secured with what looks like one of Elaine's glittery scrunchies. 'I'm Valter,' he adds belatedly. 'Didn't mean to shock you there. Also, I think you're out of cereal. Sorry, mate.'

He's been strutting around with his cock out yet is apologising for eating the last Weetabix. 'Where's Elaine?' Shane barks at him.

'She's away for a couple of days,' Valter says blithely.

'*What*?'

'Yeah, some friends of hers are having a girls' thing in Brighton,' he explains with a throaty chuckle. 'Livin' it large.'

Shane baulks at the phrase he hasn't heard since circa 1998. 'Right,' he says as Valter lands heavily on the armchair, swipes the remote from the coffee table and flicks on the TV. Shane watches him with a blend of amazement and quickly rising fury.

If there's anything he finds difficult in life, it's confrontation – a legacy from keeping his head down as a child, never wanting to anger Pete or rock the boat. He's too soft on the kids, Paula is always telling him: rushing over to school that day Liv had forgotten her packed lunch. Replacing Ryan's football boots after he'd left them on the bus. However, he knows with absolute certainty that, on this occasion, he will not be 'soft.'

Picking up his plate and mug, Shane heads for the kitchen where he stands at the sink, exhaling fully and staring down at the scrubby playground below. Then, even though it's not even lunchtime, he reaches into the cupboard for the bottle of whisky that Fletch gave him for Christmas. He pours himself a generous measure and studies it, holding it up against the light.

This is too much. Not the measure – he might even have another after this one, a *triple* – but Elaine. She's overstepped it this time and he's about to go back in there and switch off his telly and tell Valter to get his stuff together and leave his flat.

But first, Shane lifts the glass to his lips and takes a huge swig of Scotch. And then, without pondering it or wondering what to say, he taps out a message to Elaine.

35

JOSIE

I'd expected to feel weird, coming home to my flat. After all, Lloyd had been here, possibly with his 'friend' she of no name ('not relevant!'). But I hadn't been prepared to find that he had actually finished my kitchen shelves, and extremely professional they were, too!

That didn't make up for the fact that there was no wine. Just one lone bottle sitting in the door shelf of the fridge – of *apple juice.* What use was that? Disgruntled, I took myself off to bed and slept terribly, craving Boris's pancake-thin mattress, because then Shane would be there with me.

And now, as I wake up all scratchy and groggy in my second-worst pyjamas, I slope through to the kitchen to inspect the shelves again. They're so beautifully made, I can't help admiring Lloyd's handiwork and attention to detail. However, we weren't exclusive. I'd guess that there are other shelves like these – in kitchens all over London, probably. Lloyd always seemed to be on the move, driving here and there, bemoaning the parking in Vauxhall and Camden and Battersea. I wonder if he's been on at other women to start up foot fetish side hustles. Maybe they show more than their feet. How square I must have seemed to him – squeamish about stomping about in a box of soil!

The day stretches bleakly before me, the newness of the shelves somehow highlighting the shabbiness of my flat. When will I own a sofa that I don't feel the need to shroud in a variety of throws? I launch into a whirl of cleaning and even thoroughly de-gunk the fridge, repositioning my magnets neatly. In Cora's room – what I still think of as her room – I dust, hoover and polish the mirror at her dressing table. Cora moved out eight years ago. I can still hardly believe she's a mum herself. Why am I preserving her room like this? It's not as if she'll ever move back.

When there's nothing left to clean, I settle at the kitchen table with my laptop, checking out the website of Rupert Featherstone Fine Art Books, realising how dated it looks. I guess at work, I was always too busy keeping on top of orders to consider how it could be improved. Yet we – or rather, Rupert – specialise in books about the world's most beautiful objects! And this site looks like it was designed by a kid in his bedroom.

I eye my phone, seized by an urge to call Rupert, just to tell him I'm back from terrifying Yorkshire and that I survived my mission. That, apart from ill-advised sex with my oldest friend and behaving abominably the next morning (and, as a final flourish, nearly choking on Monster Munch fumes on the journey home), it's all been fucking fantastic.

I'd also like to tell Rupert how sorry I am that things ended so horribly. Yes, he was wrong – but we all make mistakes, don't we? I certainly do. Briefly, I think of Shane and wonder what he's doing now. Happily working away in his shop, I'd imagine. Getting on with his life.

I fiddle with my phone, wondering how Rupert would react if I asked if I could pop in sometime, just to say hi. Plus, I'm fond of that initialled china cup he gave me. I'd like to pick it up. I'd also like a look around the shop, just to make sure the window display is up to standard – because I know he's lax with it, forgetting to fill spaces whenever books are sold. The place could look so much more welcoming, I've always thought. Parked there at the desk, he looks like he's guarding the shop against undesirables. I've noticed countless people glancing in, clearly intrigued, but lacking the courage to enter. 'You're a bit intimidating,' I've told him.

'Nonsense! Why would anyone be afraid of me?'

I bite my lip, building myself up to calling him. What's the worst that could happen, really? If he's offish with me – well, at least I'll have tried. Aware that Rupert never answers his mobile, I call the shop number. 'Hello, Rupert Featherstone Fine Art Books?'

'Hello?' I say hesitantly, unable to place the male voice.

'Can I help you?' the man asks pleasantly.

'I, um, wondered if Rupert's there today?'

'He's off at the moment. If there's anything—' He trails off. 'Is this Josie?'

'It is, yes.'

The man chuckles. 'Ahh. I was hoping you'd call. It's Charles.'

'Oh, Charles, I'm sorry! I didn't recognise—'

'That was my posh phone voice,' he admits.

I laugh obligingly, trying to reconcile the fact that Rupert has replaced me already with his old boarding-school friend. That's up to him, I tell myself. But is Charles really up to running the online order system, created by me?

'Is Rupert away?' I ask.

'Umm... not exactly. He's just taking a bit of... *time out*, I think you'd call it.'

'Time out?' I ask incredulously. Rupert rarely takes so much as a day off. I've wondered sometimes if this is because he gets lonely in his Notting Hill flat, and that really, the shop *is* his home.

Charles clears his throat. 'He's been a bit down actually, Josie. Realised he'd said some things he shouldn't—'

I blink in amazement. 'To me, you mean?'

'Yes, that's right.'

'You know about that?'

'I do,' he murmurs. 'But now you're back from your trip, if you did feel like dropping by...'

'I'm just not sure how he'll be with me,' I admit. But perhaps I could take a trip to town at some point, and have a browse around the big Waterstones? Maybe a wander through the streets of that rarified corner of London that I've grown to know so well? I mean, Rupert doesn't *own* it.

'See how you feel,' Charles adds kindly. 'I think he'll be in tomorrow and, well, if you're in the area—'

'I might be,' I say.

He coughs dryly and I hear the shop door ding. 'The thing is—'

'What is it, Charles?'

'We have a new printer.'

'*What?* Oh my God.'

'And neither of us can work it,' he says.

36

SHANE

Shane is grateful to Fletch for manning the shop while he was away. However, certain aspects have slipped in his absence: emails, accounts stuff, chasing up an order for saxophone reeds that was expected while he was away. Buzzing with caffeine, he works steadily all morning, pausing to re-read the message thread with Elaine last night.

SHANE

Back from trip, bit of a shock to find Valter here. We need to talk about things.

ELAINE

Sorry, should have said. He's a sweet guy. Hope you liked the flowers! Did you find the cakes I made? Cupcakes in the red biscuit tin. Help yourself xxx

Shane is not a cupcake person and steeled himself to push on through her generous gesture.

SHANE

Thanks. Thing is, I didn't know he was here and I don't even know him. Basically came home to a stranger in my flat.

(*A naked stranger*, he almost added.)

ELAINE

You need to get to know him! He's lovely. Having fun here in Brighton! See you soon! Xxx

He'd glanced briefly at the attached photo of four women, all crammed around a table, cocktails brandished aloft. And he'd thought of that little bundle of Polaroids of him and Josie, taken at various stops on their trip, and wondered whether she'd post them to Pam and Kamal. Would they even notice that they'd never made it to Huddersfield?

It doesn't matter now, he supposes. They tried, at least. What he needs to focus on is getting through the day, and leaving the shop on time for once, as Elaine is due back tonight.

The first potential customer of the day offers a welcome distraction – although it turns out he's only here with a flyer for the shop's noticeboard. When he's gone, Shane inspects it: *Tambourine lessons for all levels. Beginners to advanced.* Is this a joke?

Something else is snagging his attention now, wafting in the periphery of his vison. That bloody eyebrow hair! He tries to grasp it between his thumb and forefinger and yank it out. It won't budge. He delves into the cupboard behind the counter, hunting for scissors among the selection of tools that he and Fletch keep in there. No joy. The chunky pliers, frequently used for snipping off excess strings on a newly strung guitar, will have to do.

He has an exploratory poke, but trying to plier out the rogue hair feels like something of a risky endeavour without being able to see what he's doing. There's no mirror here – not even in the tiny bathroom. He's seen Liv put her phone on selfie mode in order to check her appearance, but no way is he doing that. What if a customer were to walk in?

His gaze lights upon the cymbals, displayed vertically on a stand. The effect is something like a metallic Christmas tree. Shane removes the top cymbal and props it up on the counter to act as a mirror. While not ideal, it will have to do. He peers at his distorted reflection, clutching the pliers, wondering if he always looks as wired as this as he moves in on the eyebrow region.

There it is, the fucker! He clamps it between the pliers and tugs. It still won't come out. He pulls harder, the pliers' metal jaws gripping tightly. Still, it won't move. Is it cemented in? On the third go, as the hair comes out sharply, the sudden movement causes his elbow to shoot forward, sending the cymbal toppling over the counter and landing on the wooden floor with a metallic crash.

'Mate, what's going on?'

Shane swings round and straightens up. 'Just, uh, rearranging things a bit!'

Boris smirks. 'I'm used to a drum roll when I make an entrance, but I've never had a cymbal clash…' Shane laughs obligingly. 'So how did it feel being back on the road?'

'Brilliant!' he enthuses.

'Glad to hear it.'

'Really appreciated the van,' Shane adds. 'Thanks a lot. It was so generous of you…' He fishes the keys from his jeans pocket and hands them to Boris, along with a paper carrier bag containing a bottle of Jack Daniel's – his tipple of choice – plus a box of Pontefract cakes.

'Aw, mate! You needn't have. But thanks. So, she handled all right?'

'Like a dream,' Shane says, feeling as if he's on autopilot as he follows Boris out of the shop and along the alley to where the ambulance is parked in the street. His friend wanders around it, as if checking for – what? Scratches? Dents? He bends to peer closely at the back door and beckons Shane towards him. 'Where is it?' he asks.

Shane frowns. 'Where's what?'

'My sticker.' Boris gives him a quizzical stare.

Feigning bafflement, Shane inspects the spot. All that's left are a few whitish traces that he hadn't been able to pick off. 'No idea. Must have fallen off,' he says.

Boris sighs heavily. 'Weird, that. All those years, it's been there. Misty bought it when we met at the Isle of Wight Festival.' He seems to go off into a sort of reverie.

'Misty?' Shane prompts him.

'Yeah.' He sighs. 'What a trip that was! And me and Misty – the sweetest thing, she was. Me and her in the van...'

'Well, look, I'm really grateful,' Shane cuts in. He's not up for hearing about sexual antics that happened in Doris back in 1996.

'Glad you had a good time,' Boris says, recovering himself.

Shane smiles. 'Honestly, the best.'

It's not even a lie, he realises, as Boris clambers in and starts the engine with a metallic roar. It was great, really. As weirdly brilliant and amazing as that tour, with the three of them, all those years ago. Like the first time, it ended messily but then, what did he expect? That he and Josie would end up somehow – magically – together? He should have known better than that.

Boris lowers the window, an unlit roll-up already dangling from his mouth. 'You've got the bug now, right?' he says with a chuckle. 'Told you there's nothing like it! Any time you want to borrow her again, just give me a call.' And with that, he lights his roll-up, gives Shane a sort of salute, and drives off down the street.

37

JOSIE

I set off next morning straight after breakfast, with the hopefully non-controversial cuddly llama in my bag. Realising it's too early to visit, I take an indirect route, dawdling with a takeaway coffee and watching the ducks on the lake in the park.

Yesterday – my first day home – was a bit of a write-off. Post-cleaning and mustering the courage to call the bookshop, I'd spent most of it alternating between Shane's Instagram and our Polaroids, and was determined that, from now on, I'd structure my days and be *purposeful.* And this had seemed like a great idea, when I'd set off. However, as I near Cora's flat, it occurs to me that I'm not thinking straight.

I haven't been, really, since I came back to London. Is it the Shane business, or the lingering effects of coming off the pills? *See another GP,* my friends keep telling me. *See someone who'll listen and understand.* But perhaps this is just me now? Impetuously calling the shop when Rupert sacked me (I think), and about to turn up at Cora's with no prior warning, with an unapproved cuddly toy? Better message her, I decide.

JOSIE

Hi love, back from trip. What are you up to today?

CORA

Hi Mum! Just hanging out at home.

I study it for a moment. A quick visit won't hurt, I tell myself. To show them that I come in peace, I take a small detour to a fancy little deli I've been to before. But as it's closed, I have to make do with an ordinary mini-market where there's nothing terribly posh – nothing of Cora and Zack's standards anyway. Gripped by indecision, I roam the two short aisles and select a small box of milk chocolates and a bunch of tulips, streaked like raspberry ripple ice cream. And then, because I think my offerings look a bit cheap, I do that thing of piling on more items – a packet of salty crackers, a tin of olives and for some reason a pineapple – in a quantity-over-quality approach.

As I arrive at Cora's smart, leafy street, I remember that I haven't actually told her I'm coming. *Wondered if I could pop over?* I message her. *Just for a quick hello?*

I stand, waiting, pressed up against the brick wall.

You mean now? I can sense the agitation radiating off her.

Yes, just in the area, love. What would I be doing 'in the area' other than coming to see her? *Promise I won't stay long!* I add.

I wait. Minutes pass and then: *Mum, we're a bit caught up at the moment. Poppy v colicky. See you soon, I promise!*

I stare at the message and then look down the street, towards Cora's place. I check the time – 12.04 p.m. – and wonder how I'm going to fill the day. Then something catches my eye.

The main door to Cora's building has opened. A cluster of people are chattering jovially as they descend the short flight of steps to the street. All booming voices and hugs, these four adults are clearly at ease with one another. 'Thanks so much!' That's Zack, addressing the older couple. They are his parents, I realise now – whom I've only met a handful of times. Martine and Douglas Bleasdale who have an enormous house on the Kent coast.

'Any time, darling!' his mother calls back. 'You know we love staying over. It's such a wonderful change for us.'

'You've really helped us out,' Cora announces, and I can see her beaming smile, even from here.

I shrink backwards, wishing that the brick wall would suck me in, along with my flimsy carrier bag of cheap crackers and flowers and a stupid pineapple.

A car door closes. 'Bye!' Zack calls out, and the engine starts and off they go. Zack and Cora, with the baby in a front-loading carrier, disappear back inside.

I turn and walk towards the Tube, my heart thumping and my eyes flooding ridiculously. Outside the station I toss the carrier bag into a bin where it lands with a thud. I'm crying silently as I stand there on the pavement. Crying like an idiot who's lost all control of herself. What am I doing? I want a cigarette – and I gave up smoking nearly thirty years ago! Christ, no wonder they don't want me around the baby. No wonder they've never asked me to stay over and look after Poppy, although I've offered. Did they think I'd ransack their booze cupboard and break their rain shower?

'We just feel she's still a bit young, Mum,' Cora explained, 'to be left with someone else.' Someone else! Someone who turns up with a cuddly llama from a market stall. It's probably not even made from natural fibres. I should have checked. Peering into my shoulder bag, I glimpse its fur, aware of a sharp pang as I remember Shane being there when I bought it. What is he doing now? Why hasn't he messaged me?

I'm gripping my phone, trying to calm myself down as I scroll through my contacts. I need to talk to someone – Shane, really! – and stop when I see my local surgery's number. Without thinking, I call it.

The holding music has changed since last time. Someone must have thought that a banging beat, distorted by feedback, would be more soothing than the classical music they used to have. *You are number 8,627 in the queue...* That's what I'm expecting, all revved up for a fight. The sudden human voice startles me. My God – an actual person! 'I'd like to make an appointment with a doctor,' I say quickly.

'We have nothing left for today,' the woman says. Of course, I expected that too. You have to call, on the nail, at 8.30 a.m. One second over and you have no hope. In a splurge, it comes out: how I stopped taking my pills and don't know whether to go back on them. How that doctor I saw last time, I'm not sure he was the right person for me – at least, if there's someone else I could see—

'Oh, we have a dedicated weekly clinic now,' she cuts in smoothly, 'with a specially trained female doctor.'

I blink as a fat pigeon lands on top of the bin. 'Oh!'

'If you go on our website,' she continues, 'you can book yourself in.'

I thank her, still a little taken aback, and head down into the station. The train approaches and something switches in me. I don't want to go home. What would I do there? Sit and stare at my new shelves? Take a hammer to them and smash them to bits? Or, more likely, arrange my numerous trinkets on them? (No, Cora, I do *not* like clean lines!)

No, I decide, I won't do that. Instead, I cross to the opposite platform and take a train to Holborn. From there, I march along the street, feeling somehow lighter, towards a specialist shop I've never been to before. I know it, of course – everyone does. *Established 1830,* the sign says. *Umbrellas * Walking Canes * Shooting Sticks.*

For a minute or so, I hover outside, wondering if this is the right thing to do. Then a smartly dressed woman comes out and holds the door open for me. 'Thanks.' I smile and step inside and gaze around at the display-cases, bewildered by the array of patterns and styles.

'Can I help you?' asks a wiry young man with a slick moustache.

I clear my throat and try to stand a little taller. 'I just wondered,' I say, 'if you have a man's umbrella in a burgundy tartan, with a maple handle?'

38

'Well, this is a beauty. You needn't have gone to the trouble! But thank you.' My heart lifts as Rupert admires the fine workmanship, the subtle burgundy pattern and the handle's graceful curve. I don't tell him that opening an umbrella indoors is supposed to be bad luck. I'm just relieved that he is apparently happy to see me, full of blustered apologies – no, not apologies exactly, just a muddled explanation: '...perhaps a bit hasty, Josie. Neither of us were at our best that day... You understand the importance of excellent customer service...' Which, I suppose, could be interpreted as 'sorry' in Rupert's language.

Having closed and thoroughly caressed the umbrella, he beckons me through to the back room. Here the new printer sits, apparently awaiting my return. 'I know I'm being silly, but it's bringing me out in hives...'

I blink at the supposedly baffling object and make us a couple of instant coffees, experiencing a small sense of satisfaction on being reunited with my special cup. 'Did you make some changes to the ordering system before you left?' he asks. *Left?* I didn't 'leave' – I was pushed! At least I think that's what happened.

Already, as I explain the basics of how the system works – and is unchanged – I sense his attention wavering. And when I quickly figure out the printer's basic functions and run through those with him, I might as well be talking to the tape dispenser. Rupert is *me*, I realise, as the teacher droned on about West Yorkshire's pivotal role in the Industrial Revolution while my mind wandered to more interesting matters. Such as Shane Calvert sitting a few desks away.

'Honestly, Rupert,' I say, snapping him back to attention, 'it's all quite simple.'

'Oh, it's easy for you!'

I laugh. 'Why d'you say that?'

'You're young, you're so much better at this kind of thing.'

'Young,' I repeat, smirking. Rupert is well educated; he went to some private school in Scotland, and then Cambridge. Not that I think it makes him *better* than me. But he didn't attend a seventies-built comprehensive, all polystyrene tiles hanging off the classroom ceilings, and that RAAC concrete that apparently caused the entire building to collapse a couple of years ago. I wonder sometimes if his bluster is an act, a role he enjoys playing. He is a smart man, obviously – he established this shop, although Charles has expressed amazement that he managed 'before you came along, Josie.'

And it seems that I'm back. Perhaps – as far as Rupert's concerned – I never really went away. We get on with our respective tasks, although when lunchtime comes around, something is different. 'No, I'll go,' he insists. 'What would you like?'

'Oh no, I'm fine,' I say quickly.

He fixes me with an avuncular look. 'My treat. Salmon and cream cheese bagel?'

I stare at him. As I'd only popped in, I haven't brought a packed lunch. 'That'd be lovely.' Maybe we should fall out more often? 'Thank you,' I add with a smile.

There's a flurry of customers while he's out. A few casual walk-ins who opened the door with a hesitant, 'Is it all right to just come in and have a look?'

'Of course,' I say. In fact, Rupert welcomes anyone, even if he doesn't give that impression. He'd hate to be viewed as stuffy and exclusive. But even after a short break, I can see that the shop's layout – with his giant desk at the front – is off-putting, and I'm formulating plans to switch things around, to give the whole place an overhaul. Once I've worked through the backlog of orders that he's allowed to build up, I can do that.

Will he let me? When he dropped by earlier, Charles hinted that he would. 'I think you can pretty much do anything you want to around here,' he murmured with a smile. 'So strike while the iron's hot.' I'll have to be diplomatic, as Rupert likes to think he's good with the 'common people', switching effortlessly from yacking with friends from his gentlemen's club to a bunch of women down for the weekend from Manchester. But actually, 'The North' scares him. And when he returns with our bagels, and we eat them companionably together at either side of his fancy desk, it becomes apparent that something is causing him no small degree of concern. That it is, in fact, more alarming to him than the new printer.

'I'm not sure I even want to go,' he announces, crumpling up the cream cheese-smeared bag in his fist. 'It's not as if I'm an expert in the field.'

I look at him in bewilderment. 'You're not an expert on selling high-value art books, in an independent bookshop, in the digital age?'

'Well, yes, I know a thing or two,' he blusters, 'but I'm really not much of a public speaker these days.' I go to put on the kettle, and by the time I've returned to his desk I've just about figured this out. I know that Rupert belongs to several booksellers' associations, and that there's the occasional conference that he likes to swan along to with his pocket square just so. But it seems that this one is different.

'What's *really* bothering you?' I ask. 'It's not just the thought of giving a talk, is it?' He never seems short on confidence, and I've always imagined he grew up being well-drilled in debating and the like.

'I just feel a bit rusty, that's all.' He shuffles a sheaf of papers on his desk.

'Rupert...' I start. 'Is it because this conference is happening in the North? Is that why you're so reticent about it?'

'It's just an awfully long way to travel,' he says with a dismissive flap of his hand.

'Whitby isn't that far.'

'It's far enough!' He laughs and fondles his glass paperweight.

I glance around the shop, trying to maintain a neutral expression. 'Do you *know* anything about Whitby?' I ask.

'Only that Dracula came from there.'

I can't help smirking at that. 'You do know that Dracula wasn't real?'

'Of course I do,' he splutters. 'I mean, the people it attracts – that connection with the macabre. I've been reading up on it. There's a whole... *goth* thing going on up there and I'm not sure how to deal with those sorts of people.'

I stare at him. 'What, goths?'

'Yes, you know. Those people.'

'I don't think they'd be at the booksellers' conference,' I

venture, but he waves me away to signal that the conversation is finished. I turn my attention to smartening up the window display, and have just removed a fat, dead bluebottle as two women breeze in. Somewhere in their sixties, they launch into a commentary as they browse the books. *This artist behaved despicably to women. Look at how he objectified his mistress! D'you know what he really got up to?*

I turn from the window and one of the women catches my eye. 'Not much escape from it in here, is there?' She picks up a coffee table book on Picasso.

'From what?' I ask pleasantly.

'The male gaze.'

I'm not an art history expert like Rupert. Perhaps I am also a terrible feminist, because at this very moment I *crave* the male gaze. Shane's gaze, to be specific; the way he looked at me when we woke up together in the Love Heart Boudoir. 'I guess not,' I say. But as the women leave, I want to cry after them: 'I want it! I want the male gaze!'

I look at Rupert when they've gone, and he laughs. 'Gosh,' is all he says.

'They're right, though,' I add, 'about pretty much all male painters.'

'Don't you start!' He feigns irritation.

I smile, about to return to the back room where a whole load of customer queries awaits me. 'You know it's... *all right* up north, don't you?' I add.

'You would say that. It's where you're from!'

I laugh. 'We don't bite, you know. Some of us are pretty friendly.'

'Hmmm, I'm sure.' There's a trace of doubt in his voice and I wonder now if this is something he genuinely needs my help with – along with the printer and ordering system.

'Rupert,' I say, 'are you trying to tell me that you'd like me to go up to Whitby with you?'

He tweaks at the tuft of wiry grey hair above his left ear. 'Of course not. That would be ridiculous.'

I shrug, watching him align his small collection of fountain pens on his desk. 'I will, if you want me to?'

He looks up, his light blue eyes softening. 'Would you be able to do that?'

'I don't see why not,' I reply. 'But what about the shop?'

'Oh, I can ask Charles to hold the fort for a couple of days. He's enjoyed helping me out. I don't imagine it'll be a problem.' His shoulders lower, as if in relief. 'So, if you're sure, I'd very much appreciate it.'

'I'm sure,' I say firmly. 'In fact, I'd like that very much.'

39

THREE WEEKS LATER

Shane

As he arrives in his home town, Shane reminds himself that he's doing the right thing. His mum is sick and Pete is a useless bag of shit, so of course he has to be there with her. No question about that. But his feelings about his mother are complicated, and when she texts to say she's been discharged from hospital and is now back home, he feels he can justify not heading over to see her right away.

Instead, he parks in the town centre. How weird, he thinks, to be back here again so soon. It struck him last time how much had changed, on the surface at least. But now he realises that the bones of the place are the same.

When his big brother hotfooted it to Germany, Shane knew – even at eleven years old – that he too would get away at the first opportunity. At least, out of his mum and Pete's house. At first, he and Paula had moved into a tiny flat above a dentist's on the other side of town. However, it was only when they arrived in London that he felt like he actually belonged. Somehow, the huge, sprawling city both fuelled and soothed him. It still does. He has always loved how you can be anyone there.

He buys a takeaway coffee and passes what was once Billy Hardacre's newsagent. Shane had done his paper round from here, handing roughly 90 per cent of his earnings straight back to Billy as he bought all the music papers: *Sounds*, *Melody Maker, NME.* It's now a vape shop, its window crammed with products in dazzling hues. Around the corner his attention is caught by a shop he hadn't noticed last time. It's a record store. This is probably very wrong of him, with his mother having only been sent home this morning, following her heart attack. But Shane can feel it, even through the shop's closed door: a strong gravitational pull which he is unable to resist.

Once inside, he starts to browse the boxes of records, imagining what Pete would say if he could see him now. Pete, who'd mocked his skinny build and once threw a baked potato at him – a Maris Piper grenade – sending baked beans flying across the living room. *Waste of bloody space, that kid!*

Shane glances over at the man behind the counter. In his checked shirt, with silvery close-cropped hair and glasses, he is the archetypal record shop guy. 'Has this place been open long?' Shane asks.

'Just a couple of weeks,' he replies.

'Wow. Good to see it.' Shane scans the wall display of album covers. 'What was it before?'

'Been lying empty for years. But it was a café a long time ago. The Milk Bar, I think it was...'

'Oh, yeah. Mary's Milk Bar.' Shane smiles. Just six weeks ago, when he was here for Ravi's celebration, the original signage was still up. 'It was a big favourite back in the day,' he adds.

He catches the man studying him now, as if trying to figure something out. 'You grew up around here, right?'

'Yeah.' He nods.

'You were in a band, weren't you?'

Shane chuckles. 'That's right.'

'With Ravi Kapoor? And, uh...'

'Josie. Josie Metcalfe, yeah...'

'I saw you!' The man grins. 'You used to play at the Royal? Down in that horrible old basement bar?' Shane confirms that that's correct, and the reminiscences floodgate is flung wide open. Yes, the man knows that Ravi has died – he's a friend of her brother's. Of course, Shane reflects – everyone knows everyone around here. On and on they chatter until finally, the man apologises, saying he'll let him browse in peace.

'It's been really good to chat,' Shane assures him. He is aware, as he flips through box after box of records, that any decent bloke would be rushing to his sick mother's bedside, but he's nearly done. It's in the last box that he spots it. The bargain box: everything for a quid. He pulls it out and examines the cover which depicts a handsome young man with a mop of dark curls, a roll-up clamped between his lips.

He takes it to the counter and hands it to the man. 'Boris Gilmore,' the man murmurs. 'Can't say I've ever played this...'

Shane smiles, fishing a pound coin from his pocket. 'I've heard it's pretty good.'

He leaves the shop with his purchase, tempted to take a picture of it and send it to Boris, but remembers he's away at a wedding this weekend. After forty years together, a couple of his muso mates are finally tying the knot. 'Fools rush in,' he chuckled to Shane.

And now Shane's chest is tightening because he too should get a move on. He climbs into his car and drives through town and out to the estate where, instead of parking right outside his mum's place, he stops outside Josie's old house. He remembers the day a bird flew into it, and how petrified he'd been as he'd caught it, but hadn't let on. He remembers more birds, out the back: where Josie's dad kept his beloved homing pigeons. Off they'd fly, far above the huddled terraces and mill chimneys and green, undulating hills.

Sometime, Shane decides, he must bring the kids up here. It's been years – there's no bond between his mum and her grandchildren – but they could do a tour, make it a bit of a holiday. West Yorkshire might not top his kids' wish lists but it *is* where Shane is from. It's a part of him that he's tried to push away, but which seems to keep calling him back.

Having always lived in south London, Elaine used to mock his accent. Shane didn't mind, not really. What got to him in the end was feeling that his home wasn't his any more. That's why he'd gritted his teeth and explained that it was time for her to move on. He'd expected things to drag on interminably, but in fact, a friend of hers had a room going and Valter had helped her to move her stuff, and that was that.

Having a reason to reclaim his spare room had made things easier. Because soon, Ryan would be coming to stay for an unspecified period, just for a bit of respite from Tony. Shane is fine with it – of course he is, it's his son! – and naturally, his loyalties will always be with his kids. But he knows it's not quite as clear-cut as Tony being a pain in the arse.

Having been round to discuss the whole thing with Paula, Shane learnt that Ryan's real issue is being expected to help around the house. 'Tony's always on at me,' he's complained. Well, yes – the success architect might be irritating, but he's a good man, really. He tries with Ryan and Liv – there's no doubt about that. And Shane won't allow Ryan to strew his stuff all over the place as Elaine did. In contrast, Shane and Ryan will be two adults living together in a mutually respectful manner. He won't be running around after him as if he were a little kid.

At least, that's the plan! It feels a little like the time Ravi asked Shane if he'd like to be in a band with her. He was trepidatious but also knew, deep in his heart, that it was going to be great.

Outside his own front door now, Shane takes a deep breath and presses the bell. When no one comes, he opens it and steps inside, ready to fix on a clenched smile – the kind you give the doctor when he makes a bland remark ('It'll be over before you know it!') before the rectal examination. 'Hello?' he calls out.

No reply comes, so he shouts, 'Mum?' And then, with his heart thumping dully, he climbs the steep flight of stairs. 'Hello? Mum – it's me!'

Her bedroom door is shut. He swallows hard, wondering if this is it. That, while he was raking through boxes of records and merrily reminiscing about that gig at the Royal when Ravi tripped off the stage, his mother was—

'Is that you, Shane?'

His breath catches and he pushes the door open to find her sitting on the edge of her bed, coat buttoned up to her chin. 'Mum!' Relief surges over him and he hugs her.

'Ooh!' She smiles, lips pressed tightly together, as if she hadn't expected that.

'I was worried,' he announces.

'What for?'

He looks at her, wondering where to start. *Because Pete called to say you were in the acute cardiology ward. Because until about forty seconds ago I thought you were dead.*

'Well, I know you've been through a tough time,' he says.

'Fuss over nothing,' she declares, getting up.

'Mum, I've just driven all the way up from London to see you—'

'Did I put you out?'

He shakes his head, exasperated. 'No, of course not! That's not what I meant…' Her face softens and she does something she has never done in his life: she links her arm in his. And then, with Shane still reeling in shock, she announces, 'I thought we could go for a walk, son. I could do with some air. I've been sitting here waiting for you.'

'Sorry I'm a bit late,' he says, flushing.

'Ah, that's all right.' She peers at him, seeming to study him properly, perhaps for the first time. 'I've got rid of Pete. Did I tell you that? So now I've got all the time in the world.'

40

JOSIE

I'm not what you'd call an expert packer. With Cora and me, even though it was only ever the two of us, we always ended up lugging way too much baggage on our trips. Toys, books and once, at the peak of our obsession, I'd brought Buckaroo all the way to a campsite in the Chilterns. However, this time my neat little black leather backpack (bought especially for this trip) screams 'sensible minimalist packer!' next to Rupert's enormous hard-shell suitcase.

'Christ,' I mutter as we struggle to lift it onto the train's luggage rack. 'What's in here? A dead horse?'

'Just a few footwear options,' he replies defensively, 'and thick sweaters and a fleece-lined jacket. That took up most of the room.' He catches my look as we find our seats. 'We *are* going about 250 miles north,' he reminds me.

'Yes, we are. But it's June, Rupert. You've packed as if we were going to Barentsburg for a winter break.'

'Barentsburg?' he repeats.

'A remote little town in Norway.'

'I didn't know your geography was so good!' As the train

rattles northwards, it transpires that he has also packed a full set of thermal undergarments and a new power pack for his phone. He has the air of someone who truly believes that he might never make it back to London alive. Still, it was generous of him to book us into first class, an entirely new experience for me. Every time someone comes along with a trolley, dispensing sandwiches and hot drinks, I accept them gratefully.

'You don't need to do that.' Rupert chuckles.

'Do what?' I ask.

'Have something every time they go past.'

I laugh because, obviously, he doesn't get it. 'It's that free bar thing. You know how everyone goes mental because they think it's going to run out?'

He frowns. 'Why would they think that?'

I shake my head, deciding not to go into it. Because Rupert wouldn't understand that, when faced with such abundance – for no money! – people can go a little crazy if they're not used to it. Like the child raised on the joyless breadstick/rice cake/carrot baton category of snack, suddenly unleashed on the neon-iced cupcakes at a party. Already, Zack has decreed that Poppy will ingest no sugar – ever. Not a single gram of it, like it's heroin.

The journey passes pleasantly, and I'm relieved that Rupert hasn't brought up the Dairylea incident again. *Fine,* I think. Being back at the bookshop has been surprisingly enjoyable and he has been more respectful and thoughtful since our 'break.' That, I think, is how we're viewing it. We were on a break, we needed to figure stuff out and here we are, back together again.

We arrive at Whitby and check into our hotel. Not a twin room, obviously, but separate rooms. Compared to the Love Heart Boudoir, the decor is restrained: soft grey walls, cream curtains and a vast bed, not merely king- or queen-size but... what? Emperor-size? There is also a vase of fresh white lilies, a bowl of fruit, a box of speciality teas, various biscuit options, several crisp and salted nut varieties and – thrillingly – a well-stocked mini-bar.

From the vast sash window I take pictures of the view: the choppy sea, the tumbling clouds, the higgledy-piggledy streets and dramatic silhouette of the abbey. There's so much history here – and I know who loves history. I want to turn and grab Shane's hand and squeeze it tight. I want to say, 'Isn't this amazing?' I want to share it all with him, or at least tell him that I'm back in Yorkshire, so soon after our trip. But what would I say? Instead, I unpack and iron my smart trousers and top for tomorrow, and my dress for tonight.

Rupert and I are meeting later for dinner in the hotel restaurant. His treat, he's assured me – 'but don't be going for the lobster thermidor!' I mean, as if. He plans to go through his speech with me in preparation for the all-day independent booksellers' conference tomorrow. He'll be one of several speakers and his talk will only last for forty minutes; I'm surprised by how nervous he seems. I am too – just a little – on his behalf. So, while he naps in his room, I pour myself a G&T from the mini-bar. And then, seated by the window with the glorious sea view, I dash off the message I've been desperate to write since we stepped off the train at Whitby station.

JOSIE

> Hi, just wanted to let you know I'm up north again. Whitby this time – a work thing (I'm back at the shop!). Hope you're good. I want to say I'm deeply sorry for how things ended and also thank you. Our trip was bonkers but also brilliant. I'll never forget it – especially our last night. Love, Josie xxx

With no hesitation, and no fiddling about with the wording, I send it. I wait for a reply, but there is nothing. To stop myself from constantly checking, I hide my phone in a drawer and run a deep, deliciously scented bath, and luxuriate in the bubbles for almost an hour. Later, still with no message from Shane, I trot down the wide, curved staircase towards the opulent dining room.

It's fine, I tell myself. At least I have my job back – and not even my job as it was. It's *better* now, and I'm a lucky woman to be staying here in this gorgeous hotel. As for Shane – I've tried and now it's time to forget him. There's nothing else I can do.

41

Despite several drinks with Rupert after dinner, I wake early, surprisedly clear-headed. He beams, waving, as I spot him occupying a window table at breakfast. 'Fabulous! Boarding-school eggs,' he enthuses when his full English arrives.

'Honestly, you like them like that?' I ask. For a posh hotel, the scrambled egg looks particularly rubberised.

'Oh, yes. Best part of the day.' He chuckles and sips his coffee, taking a bite out of the sausage. 'Texture of a horsehair mattress.' He grins, and I imagine his childhood home, a grand pile out in Berkshire, lumpen beds sprawled on by golden retrievers. For a moment, he looks wistful. I wonder if he's missing the big tin of Nescafé at the bookshop. 'Only because my mother was a top class egg-rubberiser,' he adds.

I laugh and spread honey from one of the miniature jars onto my toast. I decide not to mention how thrilling I find them – these tiny jars of honey and marmalade and jam. Our jovial conversation has petered out anyway, and having devoured the rest of his breakfast, Rupert has pushed his plate aside. 'I think

I'll pop back to my room and have a little lie-down before this thing today,' he announces.

I look at him in surprise. 'D'you feel okay? About doing your talk, I mean? You look a bit stressed...'

'Just a bit!' He grimaces. 'Public speaking? It's my worst nightmare.' He picks up his coffee and drains it, wiping his mouth on what I'd call a serviette and he would definitely call a napkin. 'Don't mind if I dash off, do you?'

'Er, no. Of course not,' I say, and off he goes. I'm grateful, actually, for a little time to dawdle over breakfast. Having been given a top-up of coffee, I'm planning on doing another circuit of the buffet, and remember how thrilled Cora was the one time I managed to take us abroad on holiday. The Spanish resort was a little down at heel but the breakfast buffet – 'a choosing breakfast', she called it – was magical. We'd heaped our plates, giggling over how much we'd taken, but still managing to guzzle it all.

However, when I go back up to the buffet my appetite has gone, and I think of Rupert in his room, revving himself up for the ordeal ahead. As I leave the restaurant I check my phone for the umpteenth time. Shane still hasn't replied – although my message has been read – and I take this to mean there'll be no more contact between us.

Charming, I think. But then my behaviour hasn't been exemplary either.

In the hotel foyer, a little concerned now, I call Rupert. 'Just thought I'd check everything's okay and if I can help with anything?'

'No, I'm fine, Josie. But thank you.'

I start to head up the thickly carpeted stairs. 'So you have all your notes and everything?'

'Virtually a thesis!' he exclaims.

'Can I pop up for a moment? Are you decent?'

He splutters. '*Of course* I'm decent.'

I find him pacing around his room and sweating visibly, his cheeks florid. He grabs a tiny bottle from the desk at the window and waves it at me. 'Rescue Remedy,' he announces.

'Does that work?' I ask.

'Hope so. This is a little embarrassing, Josie, but I should explain that I'm prone to panic attacks—'

'Oh, I had one too,' I cut in, 'when I was driving.'

'Really?' he exclaims, and I nod.

'It was pretty scary. A doctor told me it's your body's response to stress.' I don't add that simply talking to this new specialist at the surgery seemed to ease something in me. Perhaps I'd just needed to feel *heard*? I nearly cried as she explained – patiently – how a combination of progesterone tablets and oestrogen gel could help me. It seems I should never have been prescribed antidepressants at all.

'But Josie,' Rupert says, 'you're always so calm and in control!' Has he forgotten that I stormed out of the shop? 'I used to take beta blockers,' he adds, 'but my doctor said they were bad for my heart...'

'You have heart problems?' I exclaim.

He grins, teeth bared. 'Only in situations like this.'

I look at him, overcome by a surge of sympathy. I want to hug this man, panicking in his sea of notes, ink blots staining his fingers. It's often intrigued me, how he has this innate confidence whenever wealthy buyers saunter into the shop, whereas I often feel ill-prepared for life, as if dropped randomly into the wrong place – even with my own daughter.

'I'll do it,' I announce.

'What? You'll do *what*?' Rupert asks.

'I'll do your talk – your speech or whatever – if you'd like me to.'

He splutters and shakes his head. 'You can't do that—Can you?'

No, I can't, I think as I perch on an unyielding ornate armchair. At least, this kind of thing is *not* what I'm good at. Not at all. Some people, when they're raised by timid parents, go the opposite way. They're fiery and brave and won't let anything get in their way. With my mum and dad, their fearfulness seeped into me. The pulling out of every plug at night, bar the fridge. The refusal to go on holiday anywhere other than Mrs Blackfoot's guest house in Morecambe because 'it's what we know.'

My wonderful parents, I reflect a little while later, as I sit at the desk in Rupert's room, wading through his unintelligible notes for his speech. Lovely Mum and Dad, putting on their bravest faces as they'd waved me off to London with Dale Watson. It must have been awful for them. I'd been shocked when they'd announced, suddenly, that they were moving to the Northumbrian coast, to be near Mum's sister. Leaving the house they'd moved into just after it had been built in 1951! It seemed utterly out of character. But maybe they were actually braver than I was. After all, I'd left my home town in a hurry with no plans, no thoughts of how I'd survive, and barely any money. That wasn't brave. I was just running away – from Shane and Ravi, from everything, really. I didn't even know what I hoped to find.

I pore over Rupert's inky scribbles, relieved that he headed out to let me crack on with this alone. Checking my phone, I realise with a start that the conference kicks off in less than an hour. He only ever writes with a fountain pen from a little stationery store in Knightsbridge. However hard I try to decipher his blots and scribbles, it doesn't make any sense.

So I decide to start afresh. I glance through the tall bay window, aware that Rupert is out there somewhere, pacing around, possibly having a cigarette. For a moment I watch a woman strolling along across the lawn with a small, fluffy white dog. A gardener is clipping at shrubs. Nothing bad can happen here, I tell myself.

And then I focus on the matter in hand, using my notes app to write a speech. Realising that it wouldn't look good to be constantly checking my phone, I copy out my main points on a sheet of thick cream hotel notepaper.

I plan to talk about how a small business like ours – is it okay to say 'ours'? – is steeped in history and that's what people love, discovering our little tucked-away shop off Piccadilly. They come in, wide-eyed, as if they've discovered treasure which, in a way, they have. Or perhaps they're regulars. We have plenty of those. People who wander in for a browse and a chat, just for the joy of it. A tucked-away corner of London where they can enjoy a little respite from the bustle of the everyday. We specialise in art books because who doesn't love beautiful things? No one *needs* a precious book filled with sketches or etchings or the most amazing paintings ever made. But who doesn't love to see these things?

That's what I say as I stand on the stage, not in a band of three now, with Ravi as our frontperson, but completely on my own. A *solo performer.* In the huge conference room, with its glittering chandeliers, in front of hundreds of people, I talk about the passion we have for our bookstore and how every customer is special to us, whether they spend hundreds of pounds on a single book, or just want to wander around and inhale the atmosphere. How everyone is welcome.

'I've learned this from Rupert,' I say, catching his eye. He's sitting, bolt upright, at a table with some new friends he's made from a railway enthusiasts' bookshop in York. He raises his eyebrows and smiles. 'In our modern world,' I continue, my voice wobbling only slightly as it rings across the room, 'service and sales aren't enough. Yes, our online sales are the backbone of what we do. But that wouldn't happen if it weren't for our beautiful shop, tucked away in a little arcade, that people love to step into. We need the personal touch, and passion, and we need to *matter*.'

I stop and realise my hands are shaking. There's a tiny lull and the tinkle of crockery somewhere. And then the applause starts and I realise the whole room is clapping enthusiastically.

I press a hand to my mouth, hardly able to believe what I've just done; that I managed to pull this off. An image of Ravi, clutching the mic at one of our gigs, pops into my brain: how fearless she was. Perhaps a little of her bravery has finally rubbed off on me? Then I glance to my right, where one of the conference organisers mouths 'well done!', and I step down off the stage and stride across the room, weaving my way between tables.

Rupert stands up and waves. I zoom to his table and flop down with a gasp of relief, onto the chair next to him that he's saved for me.

42

I'm so unused to praise that I don't quite know what to do with it. 'You were great,' enthuses a small man, his sandy hair combed immaculately over the bald zone. 'That's what it's all about, isn't it? Passion?'

''Cause none of us are in it for the money,' a younger woman jokes.

Rupert pats my arm affectionately. 'You, Josie, saved my bacon today.'

I chuckle, about to say 'Oh, it was nothing' – but actually, it was a lot. As my heart rate gradually returns to something like normal, Rupert catches the attention of an elderly chap in a lilac shirt sitting across our circular table. 'Jonathan – it is Jonathan, isn't it?'

'That's right,' the man says.

Rupert glances at me with something like trepidation. 'Erm, Jonathan's experienced something similar to our processed cheese situation himself. With an order, I mean. Jonathan specialises in first-edition railway books...'

The man nods, fixing his gaze on me over the sea of coffee cups and water glasses and name cards. 'There have been a few of us,' he starts, 'and we've done a bit of detective work.'

I look at him, not getting it at all. 'Detective work about what?'

Jonathan smiles grimly. 'Well, it happened to me. Guy ordered a book online – a very special book. I know it's arrived, and I assume it's all fine, but then I get a complaint...'

'What kind of complaint?' I ask.

'Bit of salami stuck in it. Horrible and greasy, ruined the pages.'

'Just like ours!' I exclaim, turning to Rupert.

'So I refund him and ask him to return it,' Jonathan continues, 'and the email bounces back. He's gone. No way of contacting him. And then—' he taps his nose '—I dig around a bit, go on forums, and it seems this person has been doing this to a lot of booksellers...'

'And it's always the same,' the woman announces. 'A bit of food apparently stuck in the middle. A slice of ham, that's what our customer said – cheap, thinly sliced ham that had soaked right into the book...'

'Mine was a numbered limited edition,' Jonathan announces. 'It was fine when we sent it. Excellent condition. He'd faked it.'

'He – or she, we don't know – uses different aliases and orders from different booksellers,' the woman adds. 'But it's always cheese or meat—'

'Turning the book into a kind of sandwich?' suggests the red-headed man to my right.

'Exactly,' Jonathan says.

I look around the table, taking this in. The woman introduces herself as Magda and smiles warmly. 'I loved your speech,' she tells me.

'Thank you.' I sense my cheeks flushing. 'But... how does the person make money this way?'

'Because most of us are old school,' Jonathan explains. 'We give a refund before the book has been returned to us.'

'We operate on trust,' Magda says. 'With mine, I was so mortified that it had happened that I didn't even ask for the book to be returned. I refunded them and said they could keep it.'

I look at Rupert, wondering if he's planning to apologise for wrongly accusing me of book vandalism. Instead, he merely shrugs and says, 'So there we are. I didn't actually refund the customer, so no harm done!'

No harm done? I want to say. *What about you blaming me?* But instead, I chat with the booksellers and then settle into listening to the rest of the talks. When the day is over, I head up to my room for a little much-needed respite before dinner.

There I notice a missed call – from Pam, Ravi's mum. Strange, I think. But then it hits me that there's only one reason why she'd ring me. My chest tightens as I call back. 'I'm so sorry I missed you,' I say. 'I've been at a conference all day.'

'Oh, where are you?' she asks.

'Whitby.'

'Lovely! That was always one of my favourites when the kids were young. They loved all the scary stuff – the spooky abbey and all that. So, did you do the tour?'

'The Dracula tour?' Could this possibly be what she means?

'No, the band tour. The reunion tour...' She laughs her tinkly laugh.

'I'm sorry,' I say. 'My head's been in a whirl today. Yes, we did. I should have told you...'

'Don't worry. I'm just glad you did it.' *Not all of it,* but I decide not to mention that. 'I don't suppose there's any chance of seeing you, is there?' Pam asks. 'Before you head back south?'

'Oh, I'd love to but…' Mentally, I run through the obstacles. The distance involved, and how I'd get there. Yes, I'm in Yorkshire but my home town is hardly down the road.

'When are you going back to London?'

'Friday morning.' I'd persuaded Rupert to stay for the duration of the two-day conference, and to factor in a little sightseeing too. Just to show him that 'The North' isn't that scary after all.

* * *

'We can do that another time,' Rupert insists over breakfast next morning. And so I set off to my home town, having been offered a lift from Magda who, it transpires, runs a children's bookshop in Selby. From there I can hop on a bus. But when it comes to it, she insists on driving me all the way to the Kapoors'.

Magda parks a little way down the lane, and I get out and close the door. 'Thank you so much,' I say.

'Honestly, you're welcome. No trouble at all.' She smiles, and I wave as she pulls away.

My heart is hammering now as I approach the Kapoors' house. As if sensing that I'm near, Pam comes out to greet me. This time she's dressed casually in a lightweight mossy green sweater and trousers, and her long silvery hair is tied back in a ponytail. 'So good to see you,' she says, hugging me tightly. She takes my hand and leads me into the pale pink cottage.

In the kitchen, the kettle is clicked on immediately and a home-made cake is produced, and in among all of this she enthuses over the Polaroids as I set them out on the table. 'So lucky you had them with you!' she says.

'It is.' I've been carrying them everywhere with me, in the little zipped section of my bag, but I don't tell her that.

'Did you go to all the places?' she asks.

I hesitate, wondering how to put it. 'Not quite. We didn't make it to Huddersfield, but—'

'Oh, I'm sure that doesn't matter,' she says with a smile.

But it does, I reflect. *It really does.*

'Maybe you'll get there another time,' she adds.

'Yes, maybe. I hope so.' As she hands me a mug of tea, I look around the room. I had my first taste of fresh herbs in this very kitchen. They seemed to explode with flavour in my mouth. At home, our prehistoric herbs had gone grey in their jars and were reached for, tentatively, by Mum around once a year – as if she feared that a shake of the dusty old oregano might alter our minds irreparably.

I gaze at the framed photos of Pam, Kamal, Ravi and Dev on various trips and days out. A montage of faded prints in a clip frame depicts a family holiday in Spain. As a teenager, the Kapoors were the only family I knew who'd been abroad. It all seemed so magical. I couldn't imagine ever visiting another country.

As we're finishing our tea, Kamal appears and hugs me. 'We've been waiting for you!' he announces with a twinkle. I smile, not understanding, but follow obediently as he beckons me out to the front of the house, and across the neatly tended garden, past a blur of forget-me-nots. 'What is it, Kamal?' I ask.

'C'mon.' He grins and leads me round to the front of the garage. Pam is at my side, acting a little oddly. She's almost giddy, I realise – bubbling up like a child on her way to a party.

I glance at her quizzically, and then turn back to the garage. The door is open and I gaze in. This is it – the place where it all began. Shane's first drum kit is still here, and the faded burgundy velour armchairs we used to lounge around on. Posters of our musical heroes are still tacked to the walls. One of our tour T-shirts too. It's like a museum of us. But I am not taking in any of that, not really.

I stand wordlessly, watching as the tall figure lifts a box from a shelf. 'Shane?' Pam prompts him.

He turns and sees me and the smile breaks across his face. 'Josie,' he says.

Tears spring to my eyes. 'You're here!'

He places the box on the floor and strides towards me. 'Yeah,' he says, a little shyly. 'Just looking through some of our stuff. Old tapes, a few records – and I found these.' He hands me a sheaf of crumpled papers covered in scribblings. I squint to read the barely legible handwriting. It seems to be a mixture of Ravi's, Shane's and mine, and I manage to pick out snatches of song lyrics.

'I still don't understand,' I say, handing them back to him.

'I'll explain,' he murmurs. And somehow, as we step outside, Pam and Kamal fade away and it's just the two of us, making our way round to the back of the house, and down to the bench at the bottom of the garden. The very spot where we discussed the joys of service stations and modern bus travel just a few weeks ago. 'I came up to see Mum,' he tells me.

'Really?' I ask in surprise.

He nods. 'She's been in hospital. Pete got in touch to let me know.'

'Oh, no! Is she okay?'

We sit side by side, so close I can feel the warmth of him. 'She wasn't, but she's made an amazing recovery. Tough old girl.' He smiles. 'And she's binned Pete.'

'My God,' I exclaim. 'What made her do that?'

He shrugs. 'He wasn't there for her when it mattered. Wouldn't call an ambulance or drive her to hospital. Reckoned she was putting it on...'

'Putting on what?' I stare at him.

'Well, a heart attack, basically...'

I shake my head in wonderment, letting this sink in. 'So... how come you're here?'

He shifts position and his hand folds around mine. 'Mum really seems fine, but—' He breaks off. 'I needed a bit of a breather. I think she did too. So I called Pam to check if it would be okay to visit...'

I study his face. 'Pam knew I was coming,' I murmur.

He nods, grinning. 'Yes, she did.'

Did Shane know, I wonder? It doesn't matter now. 'It's so good to see you,' I say. 'And I'm sorry about what happened—'

'Hey, I'm sorry too.' He pauses, as if figuring out the best way to put it. 'It wasn't your fault. It was mine—'

'That's not true,' I insist.

He inhales slowly and smiles. 'Maybe it was both of us, and we just didn't know how to handle things, after all this time?'

'Yeah.' I nod. 'I think it was something like that...'

'So, d'you think we could finish the tour sometime?'

'What, and go to Huddersfield?' My heart soars.

'Sounds romantic, doesn't it?' He laughs.

I smile and don't even answer, because he knows what I want to say.

It does. It actually does. And then I look at him – *really* look at him, at the man I've always loved – and I kiss his beautiful mouth. His arms are around me and we are kissing, kissing, kissing, in the place where it all began.

When we stop, the sun slices through the clouds, turning the Kapoors' garden into a blaze of colour. 'I can't believe you're here,' I whisper, my head spinning.

His hands squeeze mine. 'Josie, I love you so much.'

'I love you too.'

He smiles and flushes slightly. 'I should tell you something else.'

'What?'

'Just that I always have, really.' He laughs. 'No, not *really*. Just that I always have.'

I smile and kiss him again, and when we stop he reaches into his pocket and pulls out a sealed white envelope. 'What's this?' I ask.

'No idea,' he says, handing it to me. 'Pam gave it to me.'

I study it, almost afraid to open it. *To Josie and Shane, Part 2,* reads Ravi's loopy handwriting on the front. 'What does she want us to do now?'

'A global tour?' he suggests with a grin.

'Oh, I'd be up for that!' As I open the envelope, I realise that, of course, Ravi wanted to bring me and Shane back together. I think I'd figured that out by the time we reached Grimsby. But it wasn't just that. She also wanted to push us, as she always had. She was the brave one – the one who made things happen around here. Our lives were – and *are* – anything but ordinary, and it's all thanks to her.

'It might sound crazy,' Shane says as I pull out her letter, 'but I feel that she's still here, all around us.'

'Me too,' I murmur as my gaze lands on the handwritten page. His arm winds around my shoulders, and I lean into him as we read it together.

Dear Josie and Shane,

Now you really must be wondering what all that was about. The tour, I mean. Making you go through all that again! You poor things. So why did I ask you to do it? To say sorry. To make it up to you. And to hopefully put things right.

I knew all along that the two of you were mad about each other. Not because I'm clever or particularly insightful, but because everyone knew. It was obvious. And I was hell-bent on not letting it happen because guess what? I loved him too. (Are you blushing now, Shane?)

I was madly in love with you, Shane Calvert. And I hated the fact. Hated that this thing was consuming me – this giant bloody crush that I could not shake off. A bit like the unsightly fucker I have growing inside me now, destroying the good cells. Of course, my crush wouldn't ultimately kill me. That's the difference. I should have stopped trying to control everything and everyone and just let you be.

That's why I sent you back on our crazy tour. To have your time back that I took from you. Yes, I made things happen for us, but at a cost.

For a few years, out in Australia, I had a boyfriend and he'd done the twelve-step programme. You know about that? Part of it is, you apologise to those you've hurt, and you try to make amends as best you can so you can be free.

And that's it, dearest Josie and Shane.

I am free now. I am happy. And I hope you are too.

Love, Ravi xxx

We sit there for a moment, the two of us, taking it all in. 'So, here we are,' I say finally, looking up at him.

'Yes,' he says softly. 'Back where it all began.'

I can't speak. My head has emptied itself of words, so I kiss him again. And this is where our future begins, as he takes my hand and we make our way back into Cherry Cottage, the place we have always called home.

* * *

MORE FROM FIONA GIBSON

ACKNOWLEDGEMENTS

Writing a book is a bit like a road trip. Fun of course – but bumpy in parts, and sometimes I don't quite know where I'm going! Luckily, I'm always in safe hands with my brilliant editor, Rachel Faulkner-Willcocks, at the wheel. Likewise with the brilliant Boldwood team: thank you Nia Beynon, Amanda Ridout, Wendy Neale, Claire Fenby, Ana Carter, Isabelle Flynn, Megan Townsend and Rachel Odendaal, to Gary Jukes for fantastic copyediting and to Christina de Caix-Curtis for a brilliantly hawk-eyed proofread. Thank you to my agents Caroline Sheldon and Safae El-Ouahabi. Dear Caroline, it's been wonderful working together for all these years. I can't thank you enough for your guidance, support and friendship, and will miss you hugely as my agent (but I know we'll stay in touch). Safae, I'm excited to be working with you and I'm sure it'll be wonderful. Thank you to my fabulous friends: Riggsy, Cathy, Liam, Susan, Ellie, Jackie, Maggie, Tania, Adele, Marie, Wendy V, Michelle and Sarra. To Elise and our ever-inspiring coaching group: Mif, Annie, Anne and Christobel. To Peter for the restorative Alnmouth break, and to Jen and Kath for a joyful week in Samos and a million other things. Where would I be without you? Finally, thank you to Jimmy for keeping 'life' going when I'm working crazy hours, to Sam, Dexter and Erin, and to my dad, Keith Gibson, who is still cracking on with his own amazing road trip at 91. All my love xx

ABOUT THE AUTHOR

Fiona Gibson writes bestselling and brilliantly funny novels about the craziness and messiness of family life.

Download your exclusive bonus content from Fiona Gibson here:

Visit Fiona's website: www.fionagibson.com

Follow Fiona on social media here:

- facebook.com/fionagibsonauthor
- instagram.com/fiona_gib
- bookbub.com/profile/fiona-gibson
- x.com/FionaGibson

ALSO BY FIONA GIBSON

The Women Who Needed a Break

The Woman Who Got Her Spark Back

The Woman Who Turned Her Life Around

The home of Boldwood's book club reads.

Find uplifting reads, sunny escapes, cosy romances, family dramas and more!

Sign up to the newsletter
https://bit.ly/theshelfcareclub

Made in the USA
Coppell, TX
19 February 2026

71964990R00157